What reviewers are saying about
***Tested by Fire,* Book One in the Baxter Series:**

"This first effort capably fulfills the series' promise to create 'an absorbing story with biblically satisfying solutions.'...The novel's sermons about God's limitless grace are nicely integrated with believable and sympathetic characters."—*Publishers Weekly*

"Herman depicts with clarity and insight the spiritual struggle of overcoming the past.... Those who enjoy suspense novels will appreciate this tale."—*CBA Marketplace*

"Kathy Herman's voice is almost poetic in her storytelling. The plot and suspense are well done."—*Romantic Times*

Day

of

Reckoning

THE BAXTER SERIES BOOK TWO

KATHY HERMAN

Multnomah®Publishers *Sisters, Oregon*

DAY OF RECKONING
published by Multnomah Publishers, Inc.
© 2002 by Kathy Herman

International Standard Book Number: 1-57673-896-5

Cover design by Chris Gilbert/UDG DesignWorks
Cover images by Index Stock
Cover image of girl by Brad Wilson/Photonica

Unless otherwise indicated, Scripture quotations are from:
The Holy Bible, New International Version © 1973, 1984 by International Bible Society, used by permission of Zondervan Publishing House

Multnomah is a trademark of Multnomah Publishers, Inc.,
and is registered in the U.S. Patent and Trademark Office.
The colophon is a trademark of Multnomah Publishers, Inc.

Printed in the United States of America

For information:
MULTNOMAH PUBLISHERS, INC.
POST OFFICE BOX 1720
SISTERS, OREGON 97759

Library of Congress Cataloging-in-Publication Data
Herman, Kathy.
   Day of reckoning / by Kathy Herman.
      p. cm. -- (The Baxter series ; Bk. 2)
   ISBN 1-57673-896-5 (pbk.)
   1. Textile industry--Fiction. 2. Fathers--Death--Fiction. 3. Layoff systems--Fiction.
4. Revenge--Fiction. I. Title.
   PS3608.E59 D39 2002
   813' .6--dc21   2001007593

04 05 06 07 08—10 9 8 7 6 5 4 3 2

To Him who is both the Giver and the Gift.

NOVELS BY KATHY HERMAN

Poor Mrs. Rigsby

THE BAXTER SERIES

Tested by Fire

Day of Reckoning

Vital Signs

High Stakes

A Fine Line

THE SEAPORT SERIES:

A Shred of Evidence (April 2005)

ACKNOWLEDGMENTS

I owe a special word of thanks to Belinda Lindley, whose life-changing response to the manuscript made me glad I had written it long before it found a cover.

To my friend Susan Mouser—thank you for all the times you've buttered my daily bread with your unique brand of encouragement.

To my prayer warriors, Pat Phillips, Judi Wieghat, Barbara Jones; the ladies in my Bible study groups at Bethel Bible Church; and my friends at LifeWay Christian Store in Tyler, Texas—thanks for your ongoing prayer support that sometimes feels almost tangible.

To my grandchildren, Nathan, Benjamin, Claire, and Selah— thanks for being welcome distractions who understand nothing about deadlines.

To my editor, Rod Morris—thanks for rubbing the polishing cloth of your experience all over the pages. You make me look better than I am.

To the entire team at Multnomah (and especially Sandy Muller for the extra measure of encouragement and effort on my behalf)— thank you for sharing my heart and for working so hard to get my books on the shelf.

And to my husband, Paul, my closest friend and the love of my life—thanks for all the times you've tiptoed, literally and figuratively, so I could keep writing without losing the momentum of the story. So much of your life has been unselfishly rerouted to accommodate mine. Not a single act of your kindness to me has gone unnoticed or unappreciated. You are an amazing example of His love. I can hardly believe you chose me!

And to the One who chose me before the foundation of the world—thank You for the privilege of serving You with my pen. I offer this book and pray it will leave a lasting impression on the hearts of Your people.

*See to it that no one misses the grace of God and
that no bitter root grows up to cause trouble and defile many.*

HEBREWS 12:15

PROLOGUE

The young man turned off his flashlight and slipped out the back door of the run-down, abandoned textile plant. He leaned against the rotting wood, his hands in his pockets, his breath turning to vapor in the February chill. He gazed up at the starry night and took mental inventory: His plan was ready, every detail factored in.

He had sworn from the beginning he'd never forgive G. R. Logan, not after what that ingrate did to his father and the others who worked here. G. R. barely got his hands on the reins of Logan Textile Industries before he shut down the Baxter plant, leaving 283 workers without jobs—just like that.

So what if his father had put in thirty years? So what if he had a wife, kids, and a mortgage, and was dependent on a pension? He was dispensable! Workers in Costa Rica could do the job for a fraction of the cost. All that mattered to G. R. was the almighty bottom line.

Well, it was time someone showed the rich and powerful Grant Randall Logan IV how it felt to be helplessly out of control, and to have what *he* valued most stolen from him.

The young man pulled his collar up around his ears and cut through the icy wind toward a gravel road that angled through the woods and onto the main highway. He returned to his rusty pickup, hidden in a thicket just beyond the woods, and climbed into the front seat. He surveyed the area to be sure he hadn't been seen. A grin spread across his face. People had no idea who they were dealing with.

As he pulled onto the main highway, the bitter cold seeped in through the rattling windows and nipped at his face and hands. His mind flashed back to the sound of weeping as he stood shivering at the cemetery, one arm around his mother, the other around his kid sister. Mr. Logan had never called...never even sent a note.

His fingers tightened around the steering wheel. "It's been five long years, *Mr.* Logan. Payback time!"

ONE

Taylor Logan worked studiously at the computer in her upstairs bedroom, finishing Friday's homework. The February wind howled woefully outside the ivy-clad stone walls of the Logan mansion.

Behind her, a white sleigh bed bore the spilled contents of her backpack. Papers were collated in neat stacks along the window seat of a tri-window alcove that graced the other outside wall. In the corner next to her bed, the teenager's school clothes were casually thrown over a powder-blue slouch chair, her shoes pushed underneath.

Her phone rang. She finished typing a sentence and picked it up.

"Hello."

"Taylor, it's Sherry. I thought you were gonna call."

"I was. My dad already asked if my homework was done. Thought I'd get it out of the way first. You know how paranoid he gets. Heaven forbid I should get an A-minus."

"Are you in your room?"

"Uh-huh. Can you hear Oliver purring? He's right here." Taylor fluffed the cat's white fur.

"He sounds happy. Speaking of happy…I talked to Rusty. He's really excited about the Valentine's Dance."

"Mitch, too. My dad's pretending to hate him, but I know it's an act. He doesn't want his little girl going out with just *anybody*. Has to be from some socially acceptable family. Kind of a pain, if you ask me."

"Well, you *are* quite a catch—from your long blond hair to your ballet toes." Sherry giggled. "I just thought of that."

"I can tell."

"Taylor, face it, you're practically perfect-looking. You've got two walk-in closets full of gorgeous clothes. You're poised, sophisticated—"

"Can we talk about something else?"

"I meant it as a compliment."

"I don't want to be different from anybody else at school."

"Well, forget that. You can't change who you are. Why would you want to? I mean, look at me: five feet tall, short hair, no curves. Wanna trade…? Taylor…? Come on, I only meant—"

"I know what you meant. But other kids might not want me around if I'm rich and pretty and pampered."

"But you are. And they do."

"I just don't want them to resent me for it. I'm an ordinary junior, as insecure as any of them."

"Yeah, I know. You nervous about going out with Mitch?"

"More for him than me. The only reason my dad's letting me is because Mitch's blood happens to be blue enough."

"I'll bet there's more to it than that," Sherry said. "All dads are protective, especially with girls."

"Mine treats me like this long-awaited princess because I'm the only girl born in five generations of Logans."

"And you're complaining? Sounds like fun to me."

"I guess. Look, it's almost seven. My parents'll be expecting me in the dining room. Talk to you later?"

"Yeah, I'll call you after my youth group gets back from the nursing home. 'Bye."

Taylor turned off her computer and walked to the full-length mirror on the back of a closet door, where she tucked a white silk blouse into her plaid wool skirt. While she slipped on her favorite flats, Oliver rushed over and rubbed the side of her leg, leaving a trail of white fur on her pantyhose. She scratched her old friend under the chin and grabbed the roller brush, removing all traces of the cat's loving gesture.

As the grandfather clock struck seven, Taylor hurried toward the winding staircase, to where the aroma of something delicious had already made its way.

Outside, under a dark veil of February night, a lone figure leaned against the wrought-iron fence, peeping through binoculars.

TWO

Assistant Manager Mark Steele had no sooner turned on the Open sign at Monty's Diner than Mort Clary walked through the front door. He hung his hat on the coat rack, picked up Saturday's edition of the *Baxter Daily News*, and dropped his quarter in the jar by the cash register.

"Mornin', all."

"Hey, Mort," said Rosie Harris. She poured a cup of coffee and set it on the counter. "Want your usual?"

"Yep."

She scribbled on her green pad, tore off the page, and stuck it on the clip. "Order!"

The door opened again. Reggie Mason came in, hung up his coat, and grabbed a newspaper. "Anyone got change for a dollar?"

"Take it out of the jar," Mark said.

"Anything juicy in this morning's paper?"

Mort grinned. "Yeah, Reg. Jimmy's Garage is rotatin' tires fer free if ya git yer oil changed."

"That'll put the zig in your zag." Rosie rolled her eyes.

"Says here it's been five years this month since Logan Textile

Industries closed up shop." Mort took a sip of coffee. "Lotsa folks're still sore 'bout that."

"Rosie worked at the plant," Reggie said.

"Sure did. Ten years. Had my job pulled out from under me. Been working here ever since."

"You were luckier than most. Some folks didn't get jobs for a long time."

"Who didn't get jobs?" George Gentry walked in the door with his wife Hattie.

"Folks who worked at the textile plant."

"Why are you talking about *that?*" Hattie said.

Reggie held up the front page. "It's been five years this month, that's all."

"Not worth rehashing," George said.

"Says you." Mort's eyebrows gathered. "But then, you ain't the one who wasn't workin', was ya, Georgie?"

"Where've *you* been?" George tapped Mort on the head with the newspaper. "People have moved on."

"Well, that's jus' swell, but if I hadn't retired the year before the layoffs, I'da been up a creek without a paddle."

"Well, you did, so it's moot."

"What's moot?" Liv Spooner walked in and sat at the counter.

Rosie sighed. "Don't ask."

"Some of us ain't over it yet." Mort spun around on the stool. "Ask Wayne. Weren't no picnic when his daddy got laid off."

Wayne Purdy stopped wiping one of the booths and looked up. "So it wasn't a picnic. Coulda been worse."

"Atta boy, Wayne. No point in digging up the past," Mark said.

Rosie wagged her finger at Mort. "You're a troublemaker. I liked you better when you talked about free tire rotation."

"Hey, I ain't the one who brung it up. It's here on the front page. Some folks won't mind rememberin' what a bum G. R. Logan is."

"It's a waste of time crying over what you can't fix."

"Well, thank you, *Dr. Laura.*" Mort whirled back around on the stool.

Rosie slid a plate of pancakes and bacon in front of him. "Take big bites, Mort. *Big* bites." She winked at Mark. "It's not polite to talk with your mouth full."

The Saturday all-you-can-eat special at Monty's Diner was chili and cornbread. By eleven, the place was already bustling with lunch traffic. Rosie Harris slid a bowl of chili and a basket of cornbread in front of Mort Clary, who was sitting at the counter.

"Why are you back for lunch?" she asked.

"Ain't no concern of yers. Don't fergit my milk."

"Sure thing, O bossy one."

"Mr. Clary knows a good thing when he sees it." Wayne Purdy winked at Rosie. "Best chili in Norris County, right?"

"Yep. Darn good eatin'."

Wayne turned around and almost bumped into a lady in a light blue uniform. "Oh—excuse me, Ms. Sullivan."

"How'd you know my name, young man?"

"You're the iced tea lady. Always take a slice of lime."

"How'd you remember that?"

"I thought it was kinda classy. How are things at the hospital?"

"Fine, thank you. A little hectic."

Wayne picked up the plastic tub and started toward the kitchen. Someone tapped him on the shoulder.

"Think I could clone you?" Mark Steele said.

"What do you mean?"

Mark lowered his voice. "Mort Clary twice in one day—and you don't let him get to you? Rosie's fit to be tied."

"Oh, Mort's not so bad. Kinda grows on you."

"Yeah, like the green fuzzy stuff."

Wayne grinned. "Pretend you're his mother. It helps."

Mark looked out across the diner. "Do you believe the crowd already? Not even close to noon."

"That's okay, boss. You only have to work a half-day."

"What do you mean, a half-day? I'm here for—"

"Twelve hours, I know. That's a half-day, isn't it?" Wayne grinned.

Mark punched him on the arm. "The cloning's off. I'm not sure I could handle more than one of you."

Sherry Kennsington rolled over and looked at the clock. She pulled a pillow over her face to block the bright sun.

"Sherry, wake up." Her older sister came in and flopped on the bed.

"Erica, go away. It's Saturday."

"Slagel's has shoes at 50 percent off."

Sherry pulled the pillow off her face. "Heels?"

"Everything! The sale started at 9:00."

"Nine o'clock? It's already 11:00! I know it's your day to have the car, but I *really* need to find shoes for the Valentine's Dance. Would you trade days with me? Pleeeease, Erica?"

"No."

"Then why'd you come in here and wake me up?"

"Because Taylor called and she's picking you up in thirty minutes." Erica smiled. "Let's see, the old Toyota…or a brand-new BMW…which would you rather ride to Slagel's in?"

Sherry jumped out of bed and opened the top drawer of her dresser. She reached inside an envelope, pulled out a stack of bills, and started to count. "I've got thirty-seven dollars. That should be enough."

"Don't tell Taylor you're robbing your piggy bank."

"She knows we don't have a bunch of money. It's no big deal."

"I know. She's really nice. I like her. Plus, that car is to die for."

"For your information, Taylor couldn't care less. She more interested in her grades."

"Not about the big date for the Valentine's Dance?"

Sherry smiled. "Well…that, too."

By 2:00, Monty's had quieted down. Mary Beth Kennsington sat with her husband in the first booth.

She leaned over and put her lips to his ear. "Joe, look who's here!"

He smiled and stood up. "Hey, lovebirds, would you like to join us or is this too *public?*"

Jed and Rhonda Wilson walked toward them holding hands. "We'd love to." They slid into the booth opposite the Kennsingtons.

"How was the Hawaiian honeymoon?" Joe said.

"Wonderful." Jed kissed Rhonda's hand. "Really great. Makes me wonder what took us so long to get with the program."

"Girl, you look radiant," Mary Beth said.

"Thanks. I keep pinching myself to make sure it isn't a dream. God is so good."

"Who'd have thought we'd have a wedding after being married for twenty-eight years?" Jed turned to Rhonda. "But you know, it seemed like this was the first time. We never really committed our-selves before. Such a waste."

Joe shook his head. "God doesn't waste *anything*, Jed. He can double up on the blessings now."

"I can't get over what the sun did to Rhonda's hair," Mary Beth said. "It's so blond."

Jed grinned. "Did you see the twinkle in those green eyes of hers? Reminds me of when we were in high school. You know…I think she's prettier now than she was then."

"*Sure* I am." Rhonda winked at the Kennsingtons. "That's because you're sitting close and don't have your bifocals on."

The four of them laughed.

"I'm glad you're back," Mary Beth said. "We have so much fun with you guys… Hey, Guy and Ellen just walked in."

"Watch this." Jed stood up and cleared his throat. "What do you get when you cross a respected attorney with the editor of the *Baxter Daily News?*"

Guy Jones shrugged. "A motion to suppress?"

"No, the best seat in the house!" Jed moved his arms like he was welcoming royalty. "Would you care to join us?"

"We'd love to," Ellen said. "I'd ask if you enjoyed Hawaii, but I'd have to be blind not to know the answer."

Wayne Purdy walked out of the back room and spotted Mark Steele near the cash register. "Boss, I'm heading out."

"Yeah, okay, Wayne. Enjoy your day off. See you Monday."

When Wayne opened the door to the diner, Taylor Logan and Sherry Kennsington came rushing in and nearly ran into him.

"Excuse me, ladies." He held the door and flashed a friendly smile.

"Thanks, Wayne," they said at the same time, and then raced for the booth where Sherry's parents were visiting with the Wilsons and the Joneses.

"Guess what?" Sherry said. "Taylor won first place and I won second at the county science fair. We get to enter our projects at the regional fair next weekend in Ellison!"

"How'd you find out?" Joe asked.

"We ran into Mrs. Powell at Slagel's. She got the winner's list by e-mail this morning."

"Congratulations!"

"You girls should be proud of yourselves."

"Hear, hear."

"Sounds like mud pie parfaits are in order," Mary Beth said.

All eyes turned to her.

"If you're full, we can split them."

"I wondered when you'd get around to dessert," Joe said. "You've shown unusual restraint."

Mary Beth put an arm around each of the girls. "Well, we have good cause to celebrate!"

THREE

Joe and Mary Beth Kennsington left Monty's Diner and strolled under the brightly colored awnings that stretched over the storefronts along the town square.

"I can't do this, Mary Beth. I feel like the Goodyear blimp. After three bowls of chili and all that cornbread, the mud pie parfait did me in."

She smiled and handed him two Tums. "I offered to eat your half."

They walked to their Jeep Grand Cherokee, parked at a meter in front of the courthouse. Joe held the door as Mary Beth slipped into the front seat.

He tried to get behind the wheel, but he had to move the seat first. "I'm never going to eat again."

Mary Beth laughed. "Loosen your belt before you suffocate."

He loosened his belt a couple of notches and took a slow, deep breath. "Ah, much better." He started the car and backed out of the parking space.

"Joe, wasn't it nice to see Rhonda and Jed looking so happy?"

"Like a couple of kids. Speaking of kids, I'm proud of the girls."

"Me, too. But I wish the setup for the regional fair was on a different day than the Valentine's Dance. They'll be pushed to get back in time. It'll spoil a little of the fun."

He smiled. "For *them?*"

"All right, I admit it. I'm as excited as they are. First dates, new dresses, high expectations. I remember what it's like to be sixteen."

"How interested is Sherry in Rusty Rawlings? I haven't heard her say much about him."

"Where have you been? Sherry's gone on and on about Rusty. It's obvious she's got a crush on him. You know, it's a bold step, taking the principal's daughter to the Valentine's Dance. He's probably nervous, like he's under glass."

"As well he should be," Joe said. "I'll be watching him like a hawk."

"Now, *Father,* your daughter's growing up. Give her a chance to act like it. We've taught her well."

"I know. Actually, Rusty seems like a fine kid. I've been impressed with him. Who's Taylor going with? That's the guy who ought to be nervous. I can't imagine having to walk up to the Logan mansion to meet *her* father. I think I'd pass."

"Well, Taylor's going with Mitchell Stafford. I think G. R. will approve."

"Isn't he Dr. Stafford's son?"

"Uh-huh. Taylor's nervous that Mitch is nervous. I have a sneaky feeling that Mitch thinks she just might be worth the stress. Anyway, he has the credentials G. R. will be looking for. He doesn't have anything to worry about."

Joe raised an eyebrow. "That's because you've never been a sixteen-year-old boy. Until you've walked that mile to the front door with sweaty palms, you can't know. Good grief, I'm glad I don't have to go through that anymore."

Mary Beth gave him a playful jab in the ribs. "Indeed you don't. You're stuck with me for life."

"Flirting with me, are you?" Joe pulled her next to him. "Wanna neck?"

"It's broad daylight."

"That's okay, it works the same."

"Joe Kennsington, you're incorrigible."

"And you're cute when your cheeks get red. I can still make you blush."

Joe settled for a kiss on the cheek as he turned the car onto Norris Street.

He turned into the driveway and turned off the motor. Twelve-year-old Jason bounded off the front porch and ran to the car. His fine, sandy hair had a crease where his baseball cap had been.

"What's for dinner, Mom? I'm starved."

"Jason, it's only four. I hadn't planned dinner until much later."

"But you didn't ask *my* stomach if it could wait that long."

"Well, Joe. It seems one of our blessings is on a different schedule. Can you handle dinner in an hour?"

"Not on your life. What can we feed this poor starving lad? Think, woman, think!"

"How about a large Papa Giovanni Pizza with everything?"

"Perfect." Joe got out of the car and gave Jason an affectionate pat on the back. "Son, in twenty-five minutes, you will have in your possession one of the food group wonders of the modern world. And it'll be *all* yours."

At 6:30, Taylor's white BMW pulled up in front of the Kennsingtons'.

"Your dad sure went on and on about you winning first place," Sherry said. "I'm glad we stopped by your house."

"I told you he's competitive. He expects me to win at everything."

Sherry started to open the car door and then stopped. "Do you think he'll let you drive to Ellison on Friday, or do we need to talk one of our moms into taking us?"

"I think Dad'll let me drive if I bat my baby blues and plead. But if that backfires, I'll let you know in plenty of time, and we can figure something else out. I don't think it's going to be an issue."

Sherry opened the car door and slid out. "Thanks for the ride. See you after church tomorrow."

"'Bye…call me…or send an e-mail."

The young man pulled his rickety truck off the winding country road and walked about a hundred yards. He stood for a long while, binoculars to his eyes, and surveyed the grounds of the Logan estate.

He saw headlights approaching and a white BMW pulling up to the front gate; when the wrought-iron arms swung open, the tail-lights disappeared into the four-car garage.

Couldn't her father even buy an American *car*? Not that it mattered. She wouldn't need it much longer.

FOUR

On Monday morning, Joe Kennsington prepared to out-line the rules for next Saturday's basketball game with a neighboring rival. A gentle knocking interrupted his thoughts.

"Joe?"

"Come in, Mrs. Willington."

"Here's the report you asked for. What are you smiling about?"

"Annual prank week," he said. "It's that time again."

"Well, I trust you're going to lay down the law at this morning's assembly."

"Mrs. Willington, you've been the principal's assistant for over thirty years. Has anything ever stopped the tradition?"

"Of course not." She smiled and sat down with her arms crossed. "There'll be violators. The question is, who, when, and where?"

Joe leaned back in his chair. "Last year's was especially creative, remember? Palmer's gym decorated from top to bottom, with yellow and white toilet paper around every seat."

"To mock their school colors. How could I forget?"

"Come on. It was a work of art."

"Well, Principal Harrison didn't think so," she said. "The show of adolescent tomfoolery elevated his blood pressure. Especially after the water balloon fight."

"I admit it was a mess. But our students cleaned it up."

"Took forever."

"I know, Mrs. Willington. It's best I put the kibosh on the competitive streak before it's unleashed again this year with renewed vigor." He chuckled. "But you have to respect the creative genius."

"Is that so?"

"Yes, that's so. I can't tell the kids, but I'm not going to sit here with you and pretend it wasn't funny. Admit it, Mrs. Willington. It was hilarious."

"Yes, it was. Tell anybody I said so and I'll deny it."

"Wimp."

She laughed. "Joe, this place was stuffy until you took over. Best two-and-a-half years in over three dozen."

"Thanks. That means a lot coming from you. You wield the power around here."

"Oh, I do not."

"Do too."

"Seriously…I've never seen students and parents warm up to a principal like they do to you. They're behind you 100 percent."

"They are, aren't they? I love this job." He looked at his watch. "Listen, I need to go if I'm going to hit the halls before the annual prank-deterrent assembly begins."

"Go for it. I prefer to stay out of the stampede."

"But that's the best part, Mrs. Willington—schmoozing with the students."

"Probably why I was never voted prom queen."

"Ah, but you *were* crowned the Queen of Hearts."

She blushed. "Says who?"

He pushed himself up from the desk. "And you carried red and white roses and had this cute little crown made of heart-shaped—"

"You've been into the school archives."

"And you, Mrs. Willington, were a *knockout.*"

Joe thought he saw the lines under her silver bangs disappear. He left his office and stepped into the hallway.

"Good morning, Mr. Kennsington."

"Hi, Jeremy. You're looking mighty sharp today."

Jeremy Haddon looked one way and then the other. "I'm going to ask Brenna Morgan to the Valentine's Dance."

"Well, good luck." Joe winked.

"Hey, Mr. Kennsington, how's it goin'?" said Tyrone Washington.

"Great, Tyrone. What're you up to?"

"Oh, sir, just behavin' like I'm suppos' to. I always maintain my high profile even in the off-season." He flashed a big smile, and there was a mischievous gleam in his eye.

"Well, see if you can keep our basketball team on the straight and narrow before Saturday night. Oscar down at Miller's Market said rolls of toilet paper are already disappearing from the shelves, and the thieves don't seem picky about whether it's one-ply or two."

"Really? Of course, bein' a football jock myself, I wouldn't know anything 'bout what the basketball team might be up to. But I'll see what I can do."

"Thanks, Tyrone. Students look up to you."

"Yes, sir. I'll keep that in mind."

Joe walked past Rusty Rawlings with a nod and a smile. No point in embarrassing his daughter, especially while he was wearing his principal's hat.

"Hey, Mr. Kennsington? Are you, like, gonna be at the Valentine's Dance?" asked Katlin Mosher, a sophomore with a fresh, angelic face.

"Sure. Just because I'm old doesn't mean I'm stale." He smiled. "I'll be there, Katlin, with my own valentine. Even us married folks can still be smitten with Cupid's arrow. How about you? Has some lucky young man won your heart?"

"Well, J. D. asked me to go. Like, what could I say?"

"I hope you said yes."

"I did. Oops, it's almost time for assembly. I better get moving."

Joe strolled down the hall and prayed for the students. He knew God had gifted him with the ability to keep the doors to their hearts open. And as long as he was able to reach them, he could influence them for good. He spotted a full head of auburn hair coming his direction.

"Hi, Erica," he whispered to his oldest daughter.

"Hi, Mr. Kennsington." She giggled and kept on going.

Mary Beth Kennsington sat in front of the fire in Rhonda Wilson's living room, enjoying hot chocolate and Toll House cookies.

"Mmm...these are good, Rhonda. Why do they always taste better at someone else's house?"

Rhonda passed the cookie plate to Mary Beth. "Take some more. I won't be able to stay out of whatever's left. My thighs will thank you!"

Mary Beth laughed and took two more. "Wasn't Bible study good today?"

"If I had known this stuff back when Jed and I struggled in our marriage, it could've saved us years of misery."

"Until you came to know the Lord, Rhonda, I doubt this level of forgiveness would've been possible."

"Probably not. We were too bitter. My getting pregnant was devastating enough for a couple of kids barely out of high school. But our parents rushing us into marriage about threw Jed over the edge. He did everything he could to shut Jennifer out. *And* me. I wonder what our lives would've been like without the resentment?"

"Well, you'll never know. But isn't it wonderful to feel free from all that now?"

"It really is, Mary Beth. The Lord changed the bad feelings into the kind of love I always wanted. The key was letting Him have it. Kind of miraculous when you stop to think about it."

Mary Beth saw Jennifer Wilson standing in the doorway and got up to give her a hug.

"I was hoping I'd see you," Mary Beth said. "Your mom said you were napping."

"I do a lot of that these days." She sighed. "Hope I'm not interrupting."

"Not at all. Your mom and I were just talking about the wonderful changes in her marriage."

Jennifer rolled her eyes and grinned. "I've never seen my parents so lovey-dovey. Dennis never treated me like that. Sure won't happen now." She put her hands on her middle. "I'm blowing up like a basketball and still have five months to go."

"You look lovely, Jen. Pregnancy brings out the glow."

"My mom's the one who's glowing."

"I noticed." Mary Beth looked at Rhonda and winked. "People tend to do that when God gets ahold of them."

"Jen, are you hungry?" Rhonda asked. "Can I fix you something?"

"I don't think so, Mom. My stomach's still queasy."

"If it's any consolation, it probably won't last much longer," Mary Beth said.

"I hope you're right, Mrs. Kennsington. If you'll excuse me, I'm going back to the dungeon."

After Jennifer left, Mary Beth sat down and turned to Rhonda.

"I wish she didn't have to go through the pregnancy single and make all the hard choices."

"I know. Good things are happening, though. You should see Jed, Mary Beth. He's accepted the fact that he's going to be a grandfather. And he's trying to give Jennifer the attention he withheld all those years. She's still resisting, but I think her baby's going to be the object of everyone's affection, and may be the way God chooses to heal our family. The one I'm still concerned about is Mark."

"Why's that?"

"The happier Jed and I are, the more resentful Mark seems. It's almost as if he doesn't want us to change."

"Things have been one way all his life," Mary Beth said. "He needs time to figure out the 'new you.'"

"You're probably right. I don't think he or Jen can get over their father and me going on a honeymoon."

"They're not the only ones. I have a feeling lots of folks never thought they'd see such a dramatic change in you and Jed… Rhonda, do you smell something burning?"

Rhonda's eyes widened and she turned her head toward the kitchen. "Oh no…my friendship bread! I didn't hear the timer. I'll be right back."

After Rhonda left for the kitchen, Mary Beth was hit with a strong sense that she needed to pray for protection. The feeling was unsettling and made no sense. *Lord, what are You trying to tell me?* Unsure how she should pray, Mary Beth began praying for Rhonda, for herself, and for her own family. She was aware of her heart racing.

"Well, that's the end of that loaf," Rhonda said. "Oh, sorry. I didn't mean to startle you… Mary Beth, is something wrong?"

"I don't know. All of a sudden, this heavy feeling came over me and I felt led to pray for protection."

"Has that happened before?"

"Not like this. It's probably nothing, but I think I'll go home and wait for the kids." Mary Beth started to get up, then sat back down and held out her hands. "Rhonda, would you pray with me before I leave?"

❦

A young man sat in his truck across the street from Baxter High School and watched Taylor Logan and Sherry Kennsington walk across the parking lot and get into the white BMW.

He grinned. "Better watch what you say, ladies. Never know who might be listening."

FIVE

On Tuesday morning, Mary Beth squeezed through the kitchen door with both arms full of groceries and slid the bags onto the countertop before picking up the ringing telephone.

"Hello," she said.

"Mary Beth? This is Marita Logan. You sound out of breath. I hope I'm not calling at a bad time."

"No, I just walked in from Miller's Market. What's on your mind, Marita?"

"Let me run something by you. Taylor's insisting the girls drive to Ellison in her car. How do you feel about that? I haven't let her drive outside Baxter without an adult."

"She seems responsible. I don't have a problem with it if you don't. Maybe they could take the old Ellison Highway. It doesn't have much traffic anymore. Might be safer for a first outing."

"I like that idea better. I'm having a hard time cutting her loose."

"I know what you mean. Listen, if you still have reservations,

I'd be glad to drive them myself. I'm half hoping for an excuse to go with them."

"Me, too. But it would spoil their adventure. The girls are so into this. The only thing more exciting right now is the *dance.*"

"I'll say! That's been the talk around here lately."

"It's Taylor's first date. She's ready, but I'm not sure her father and I are."

"This is Sherry's first date, too, but she's known Rusty a long time from youth group and school, and we've always heard good things about him. His parents are in our Sunday school class and seem like very nice people."

"Mitchell Stafford's father is chief of surgery," Marita said. "I'm sure he's a respectable young man."

"Joe and I plan to go over to Ellison early on Saturday. Would you and G. R. like to ride with us?"

"Let me check to see what our plans are. I'll get back to you. Well, if you don't have a problem with the girls driving over by themselves, it's all right with me. Taylor can take her cell phone. I'm sure they'll be fine."

On Thursday night, the Kennsingtons were gathered around the dinner table. Joe said the blessing, and immediately after the amen, he noticed grins on his daughters' faces.

"So, Dad," Erica said. "What'll you do if we have another toilet paper caper at Palmer this year?"

"Why do you look so hopeful? Do you know something I don't?"

"Not really. But what's the harm in a little festive decorating? It's fun, and both sides enjoy it."

"That's not the point. Principal Harrison asked that there not be pranks and mischief this year. As a student body, we should respect his wishes."

"Oh, Dad," Sherry said. "You know somebody's gonna do it."

"Well, there *will* be consequences. It's not right to hassle the other side when their principal has asked us not to."

"I heard there's gonna be a bonfire," Jason said. "Where they throw in dummies that look like the Palmer players. Cool!"

"Dad, the rivalry goes back a million years." Erica put a spoonful of mashed potatoes on her plate. "How can one grumpy principal put the brakes on everything? Somebody needs to give the man some prune juice."

"Erica, watch your mouth," Mary Beth said.

"Well, it's true. He's really cranky. Not like *you*, Dad. He's no fun at all."

Mary Beth took a bite of roast beef, but Joe could tell she was smiling.

"Sherry, what time do you and Taylor need to be in Ellison on Friday?" he asked.

"Setup starts at 3:30, so we'll leave around 2:00. That'll give us plenty of time to get there. We'll need about an hour to set up."

"That should put you back here between 5:30 and 6:00," Mary Beth said. "Not much time for the Valentine's Dance makeover."

"It's a squeeze, but we can do it."

"Sheesh, don't worry about Taylor," Erica said. "She could go in a brown paper bag and *still* look beautiful."

"Let's stay on the subject of the science fair for a minute." Joe looked at four pairs of eyes around the table. "Your mother and I are really proud of Sherry. All that work experimenting with plants paid off. I think she has a good chance of placing, maybe even winning. Wouldn't that be something?"

"She should've grown some kind of alien monster pods. That'd be *really* cool," Jason said.

Mary Beth smiled. "What your sister's accomplished *is* really cool."

"Dad, are you and Mom going to the dance?" Erica asked.

"Sure. All the faculty will be there."

"Yeah, but I bet you're the only one bringing a *valentine.*"

"I'll have the prettiest woman in the auditorium, bar none. But don't worry, Erica. We won't come near you and Jeff. I'll pretend I don't know you."

The doorbell rang, and Jason was on his feet and running toward the front door. He came back holding an envelope.

"It's for Sherry. But there was nobody out there."

"Jason, let me see it," Sherry said.

"I'll bet it's from *Rusty*. Something kissy-kissy."

He waved the envelope under her nose. She grabbed it and opened it.

"Who's it from? What's it say?" Erica asked.

"It's just a piece of paper with a typed message. A rhyme."

"Come on. Read it!"

"All right. It says, 'On the day of hearts, we'll finally meet. Then I'll lay my secrets at your feet. An admirer.' Wow! I've got a secret admirer." Sherry passed the note to her sister.

"I wonder who it is?" Erica said.

"Guess I'll find out tomorrow."

"Let me see it." Joe took the note from Erica's hand. "Sherry, I suspect there are a lot of guys who'd like to ask you out, but won't because dear old dad is the principal."

"Oh, Dad, anyone worth it won't chicken out. I'm curious if he'll show up at the dance. Yikes! I wonder what Rusty would think?" Her face turned red.

"This is so cool, Sherry. Wait till I tell everyone my sister has a secret admirer."

"No, don't tell anyone! Let me see who it is first. Erica, promise me, pleeeease?"

"Oh, all right. Party pooper."

"Speaking of party pooper, I need help with these dishes." Mary Beth was already stacking. "Come on, girls. Let's get this mess cleaned up. Jason, would you please take out the trash? I can't get another thing in there."

"I can't wait to tell Taylor!" Sherry said.

Mary Beth tugged lightly at her daughter's pixie haircut. "Cute as a button. Didn't I tell you?"

Across the street from the Kennsingtons', a young man crouched behind an evergreen hedge and peeped in the dining room window as the dinner dishes were being cleared from the table.

Had she gotten it? Binoculars held to his eyes, he moved his head slowly, until he spotted the note in Sherry's hand. A rush of adrenaline surged through him.

Suddenly aware of several dogs barking, he looked in all directions, then cut through the yard next door on the way back to his truck.

SIX

Mary Beth sat staring out her bedroom window as the sun peeked over the horizon and dissolved the hot pink swirls in the morning sky.

"Mary Beth…? Honey…?"

"Huh? Oh, Joe. Sorry, I was somewhere else."

"What's wrong? You've been quiet this morning."

"Sit with me for a minute." She patted the bed.

He sat down next to her. "What is it?"

"I'm not sure. I keep getting this weird feeling."

"About what?"

"I don't know. That's why I haven't said anything before now. I feel this sense of…danger—to the point where sometimes all I can do is pray. It happened again last night after we went to bed. It's a little scary."

"Why didn't you say something?"

"You were asleep. Besides, I'm not sure why it's happening or if it means anything at all. I've felt led to pray before, but never like this."

"Does it go away when you pray?"

"Eventually. But last night it took longer."

He put his hand on hers. "I wish I knew what to tell you. Maybe you should talk to Pastor Thomas. He usually offers good insight."

"I suppose so. If it happens again, I will."

Sherry and Taylor lifted the last box and laid it on top of the others in the trunk of the BMW.

"Think it'll close?" Sherry said.

"Only one way to find out." Taylor put both hands on the trunk lid and pulled it down hard. "Ta-da! Are we ready?"

"If there's still room in there for *us!* Okay, let's go tell my dad we're leaving."

The girls hurried into the school office and past Mrs. Willington to the principal's door.

"We're all set, Dad."

He looked at his watch. "It's 2:00 already? Did you get the car loaded?"

"We stuffed it all in," Sherry said. "We're in big trouble if we have to open the back doors or the trunk before we get there."

"Mr. Kennsington, thanks for excusing us so we can do this," Taylor said.

"You're taking the old Ellison Highway? That's the plan?"

"Yes, Dad. So stop worrying. We'll be fine."

"Of course you will. We'll see you at the dance."

"We should be there by 7:00," Sherry said. "If not, I'll call your cell phone or leave word on the answering machine at home. Okay, I guess we're ready."

"Wait. I'm going to take off my principal's hat for a minute." He got up and walked over to the door, and put one hand on Sherry's shoulder, the other on Taylor's. "I'd like to pray with you girls before you leave."

Sherry smiled at Taylor and shrugged. "Told you."

∽∘∾

Shortly after 2:00, Taylor's white BMW was rolling toward Ellison, the CD player going full blast.

The car started to sputter.

Taylor turned down the stereo and put her face in front of the gauges on the dash. "Why is it doing that?"

"Doing what?"

"Losing power. I've got my foot on the gas, but it's not doing anything."

"Maybe you're out of gas."

"No, I've got a full tank."

"What else could it be? It's practically new."

"I don't know, Sherry. It's never done this before."

The engine died. Taylor guided the car to the bottom of the hill and onto the shoulder. She tried several times to start the engine, but it wouldn't turn over.

"Now what?" Sherry said.

Taylor leaned her head back on the seat and sighed. "Tell me this isn't happening! Here's my big chance to do something on my own, and I can't get ten minutes from town before having to call *Mommy* and *Daddy* to come rescue me."

"I'll bet we can fix it." Sherry said. "Let's look under the hood. Maybe there's a wire or something we can put back on."

"Have you ever even looked under the hood of a car?"

"Well..."

"That's what I thought. We're both dumb when it comes to cars."

"I'm gonna have a look."

Sherry got out of the car and lifted the hood.

Taylor put her hands in the pockets of her suede coat. "It's freezing out here. Any ideas?"

Sherry shook her head from side to side. "Not a clue."

"If we can't get it started, forget the dance. We'll never get back in time. I hate this. It's not fair."

"Listen, someone's stopping," Sherry said.

Taylor looked around the side of the hood. A rusty old pickup pulled up behind the BMW.

"You girls having trouble?"

Boy, are we glad to see you!" Taylor said. "My car stopped running. We're on our way to Ellison to set up for the regional science fair. Can you help us get it started?"

"What seems to be the problem?" the young man asked, surveying the surroundings as the girls leaned under the hood.

Taylor shrugged. "I don't know. It died with no warning."

"Maybe it's catching," he said.

"What?" Taylor looked up. Her face paled. The man pushed the barrel of his gun against Taylor's temple as his eyes locked onto Sherry's.

"Don't even think about it! Move—both of you—in the truck!"

He held the gun to Taylor's head and grabbed Sherry by the arm. He herded the girls toward his truck and shoved them inside.

Taylor started to cry. "Why are you—"

"Shut up! Not another word!"

The man started the motor and quickly pulled the truck into the woods until he couldn't see the highway. He reached into his coat pocket and took out some pills and a bottle of water.

"Take these. *Now!*"

Mary Beth returned from the cleaners and took the clear plastic off her dress. Joe wouldn't mind her wearing the same one again. How special it would be, going to the dance with her husband, both their daughters, and their daughters' dates.

She pulled a shoebox out from the closet and rummaged through it until she found what she was looking for. She held up the photograph: tiny little Sherry on her first day of kindergarten, swallowed up in Erica's hand-me-downs. She blinked to clear her eyes and looked across the hall at the beautiful new dress hanging on the door to Sherry's room.

This was *her* night, her first date. And she would look lovely holding onto Rusty Rawling's arm.

"Take off your coats," the man said. "Now get in the back of the truck and lie facedown. Move!"

He bound their hands, then rolled them on their backs and taped their mouths. He slipped on a pair of leather gloves, and with a hunting knife he cut several locks of hair from each girl and put the locks into separate envelopes.

He cut the monogram from Taylor's cashmere sweater and a swatch from Sherry's blouse. He removed their shoes.

"On the day of hearts, we finally meet. I just laid my secrets at your feet." He laughed. "Got a secret admirer?"

Sherry's muffled fury amused him.

"Can't quite find the words? Don't worry, I'm getting it on *tape.*" He laughed again.

Taylor's eyes were wide with terror.

He zipped her into a mummy-style sleeping bag, pulled it over her head, and tightened the drawstring, leaving a small opening for ventilation.

"Nighty-night, you spoiled brat."

He repeated the process with Sherry, then pulled the tarp over the truck bed and secured it with bungee cords.

He hurried back to the highway on foot and stood among the trees, listening carefully for oncoming traffic. Hearing nothing, he rushed to the car and reattached the ground wire to the fuel pump, amazed that it had worked the way he hoped. *What are the odds?* He got behind the wheel, fastened something to the rearview mirror, and started to turn the key when he heard a car coming. He ducked until it passed, then started the engine and pulled Taylor's car into the woods.

He ran the short distance to his truck. He took off his gloves, lifted the tarp, and listened to the unmistakable sounds of deep sleep.

He looked at his watch—2:37. If he hurried, he wouldn't even need an alibi.

"Juanita, have you pressed Taylor's dress?" Marita asked.

"Si, Señora. Hanging in closet. Miss Taylor very pretty in pink."

Marita looked at her watch. "She should be home any minute. Has the boutonniere been delivered?"

"Si. Florist come already."

"All right, Juanita. Thank you."

Marita walked into Taylor's room and watched the sunset from the window seat. She felt a bittersweet tug at her heart. In two short years, this room would be empty and Taylor would be off to college.

Oliver paced back and forth and started to meow.

"Yes, I hear you. I'll let you out in a minute."

"What's the holdup, Marita?" Her husband's voice filled the room. "I want to see Taylor in her new dress. And meet this boy."

"She'll be home any minute, G. R. Can you believe our little girl is old enough to date?"

He walked over and picked up a white teddy bear from Taylor's vanity table and held it in his hands. "Remember this? I brought it back from London when she was little. Can't believe she still has it."

"Taylor's never parted with anything you picked out for her. She worships the ground you walk on."

"I know. And it'll take someone a whole lot sharper than Mitchell Stafford to steal her away from me."

The young man closed up at Abernathy's Hardware Store and slipped out the delivery door to the back alley. He loosened the bungee cords and looked under the tarp. Not a peep. He started the truck and pulled out of the alley.

He smirked. "Mr. Abernathy would croak!" In the past six months, he'd ripped off the two sleeping bags, an electric heater, fencing material, a gate, a padlock, a camping toilet, flashlights, art supplies, paint, and a vinyl tarp.

He drove a few blocks and stopped at a red light, and Hal Barker's squad car pulled up next to him. His heart pounded. He took a slow, deep breath and then rolled down the window.

"Hey, Sheriff. You working this evening?"

"No. I just dropped Wendy and Matt off at the skating rink. You done at Abernathy's?"

"Yes, sir. Just finished closing up."

"Got big plans this weekend?"

"Not really. I've got stuff to do at home."

"Me, too. Well, have a good one."

"You, too, Sheriff."

The young man rolled up the window and wiped the perspiration from his upper lip. When the light changed, he drove across town and out onto the main highway. He turned on CR 211 and drove three miles, then turned left and pulled to the end of a long gravel driveway and turned off the motor.

"We're home, girls."

"Mary Beth, it's 6:45. We need to leave. I know you wanted to be the first to see Sherry in her new dress, but the girls will be along shortly. I've got the camera. We'll get pictures."

"Joe, what could be keeping them?"

"Honey, they're fine. Stop worrying."

The phone rang.

"Hello, this is the Kennsingtons'."

"Mrs. Kennsington, this is Rusty. Has Sherry gotten back from Ellison yet?"

"She should be home any minute. Her father and I are on our way out the door, but I'll leave her a note to call you when she gets in. We'll see you two at the dance."

"Okay, Mrs. Kennsington. Sorry to bother you. I'm just excited, you know?"

"I understand, Rusty. It's a big night. See you later."

Mary Beth hung up. "I guess you heard."

The phone rang again.

"Hello, Sherry?"

"It's Marita. You sound as anxious as I feel. You haven't heard from them either?"

"No. But we all knew they'd be cutting it close."

"Taylor has a cell phone, Mary Beth. Why doesn't she call? I've called her a dozen times, but she doesn't pick up. I'm really worried."

"Marita, even if it took longer than they planned to set up, they had until 6:00. Assuming they stayed until closing and maybe grabbed a hamburger to go, that would put them back here within the next hour."

"But why doesn't Taylor call—or at least answer? All she has to do is pick up the phone."

Mary Beth's pulse raced. "I don't know, Marita, but let's not worry until we have to. Maybe the phone isn't working. They're probably having a ball and lost track of time."

Marita sighed. "Call me if you hear anything."

"I will. You have our cell phone number. Call us if you hear from them first."

∽∾∽

The young man carried one sleeping bag at a time and dumped each on the basement floor inside a ten-foot-square cage made of chain-link fencing.

He unzipped the bags, took the tape off the girls' mouths, and untied their hands. They were out cold. He put a plastic flashlight on the floor between them.

He closed the gate, secured the padlock, and glanced at his watch—nearly 7:00. He still had things to do, and not much time.

"Well, *Mr.* Logan, not too shabby for a kid who never got to finish high school."

SEVEN

The gymnasium at Baxter High had been transformed for the Valentine's Dance by the releasing of hundreds of helium balloons to the ceiling, their shimmering silver and red streamers dropping down to just inches above the tallest student.

The lights were low, the band played timeless love songs, and young couples danced cheek to cheek.

But Mary Beth shifted from one foot to the other and looked at her watch every few seconds.

"Joe, I'm scared. It's 7:20. Where *are* they?"

"Let me find out when they left the civic center."

"How?"

"I'll call Mike Weiss. He was in charge of the setup and ought to know something." He kissed his wife on the cheek. "Mary Beth, they're okay. You pray. I'll call."

As Joe hurried out of the gym, Rusty Rawlings and Mitch Stafford walked through the door, wearing black tuxedos and red bow ties. Rusty walked toward Mary Beth, his eyes downcast.

"Mrs. Kennsington, did we get stood up?"

"Absolutely not! Joe just went to call someone over in Ellison to see when the girls left. We'll know something soon."

"Thanks. Come on, Mitch, let's have some punch."

"Hello, Mike? Joe Kennsington over in Baxter."

"I haven't heard your voice in a long time."

"Listen, I'm sorry to bother you at home on a Friday night, but I'm wondering if you can tell me when my daughter Sherry and her friend Taylor Logan left the civic center this afternoon?"

"Hmm...if I remember right, Sherry's your little brunette?"

"That's the one. Any clue what time she cut out?"

"Truthfully, Joe, I don't remember seeing her, but it gets to be a zoo in there. Let me check the sign-in sheet. I'll be right back."

Joe tapped his fingers on the desk and looked at the darkness outside.

"You say she was here this afternoon?"

"That's right."

"Hmm...I don't show she ever signed in for the setup."

"Really? Could she have been there and just failed to sign in?"

"Actually, no. All students had to sign in for a pass, authorizing them to be in there. If she was setting up a science project, the security people would've required her to show it."

"Mike, what about Taylor Logan? Did she sign in?"

"Let's see here...Lobner, Lodder, Loftin...No, she didn't sign in either. Is there a problem?"

"Uh—listen—I can't talk now. I appreciate your checking for me."

"Joe, what's going on? Your voice is shaking."

There was a long pause. "Mike, the girls left for Ellison around two. They were going to set up and be back for the Valentine's Dance tonight. They haven't called and aren't answering the cell phone. This is completely out of character. Mary Beth and I are getting worried."

"Let me have the security team search the premises, Joe. I'll call you back. Where can you be reached?"

The cell phone rang in the gym, and Mary Beth grabbed it. "Hello, *Sherry?*"

"This is G. R. Logan! Do you have any idea where my daughter is?"

"Not yet. Joe's making a call to see what time the girls left Ellison."

"What's going on? Her date hasn't called either."

"Mitch is here at the dance with Sherry's date—waiting."

"Well, what are you and Joe going to do about this?"

"First of all, we're worried parents just like you, and I would appreciate your changing your tone. We'll get through this easier if we soften just a little."

"*Soften?* Woman, my baby girl is missing!"

The words sent chills up Mary Beth's spine. "Mine, too, but there's probably a good explanation for all of this."

"Well, what do you suggest we do? I can't just sit here while my daughter's unaccounted for."

"Joe's in his office calling the man who oversaw the setup this afternoon. We'll call you and Marita as soon as we know something. Let's work together and figure this out."

"All right. I'll be here by the phone. But I'm not waiting around much longer."

As Joe finished telling Mary Beth about his conversation with Mike Weiss, Erica came up and tapped him on the shoulder.

"What's the deal with Sherry and Taylor?" she said. "It's, like, *so* rude to stand up their dates like this. Those two better have a good excuse."

"Erica, why don't you let us worry about Sherry," Joe said. "That's why we're the parents…"

"And I'm the kid. I know." She walked back to the punchbowl where her date stood waiting.

Mary Beth looked at Joe, her eyes brimming with tears. "Do we tell her?"

"Let's wait," he said. "No point in spoiling what's left of her evening. We don't know anything."

Joe looked up and saw Rusty and Mitch walking toward him. He met them halfway to the punchbowl, hoping to spare Mary Beth from having to talk to them.

"Mr. Kennsington, Mitch and I are leaving," Rusty said. "Everybody here's a *couple*. It's depressing."

"I understand," Joe said. "I'm really sorry things got so mixed up tonight, but don't wander off too far. The girls might show up any minute."

He went back to where Mary Beth was standing, unable to ignore the panic in her eyes or the fear in his gut.

"Honey, take the car and go home. You tell Jason what's going on. I'll talk to Erica. I need to arrange for someone to lock up here, and then I'll walk home. I won't be ten minutes—"

The cell phone rang, and he grabbed it before it had time to ring a second time. "This is Joe Kennsington."

"Joe, it's Mike. Did your daughter show up?"

"No, not yet. Did you find out anything?"

"I had security comb every inch of the civic center, inside and out. The girls aren't there. Their booth spaces are empty. I'm sorry. Is there anything else I can do?"

Joe looked at Mary Beth and shook his head. Her countenance fell.

"If you're a praying man, we could use a little help."

"You've got it. Joe, let me know when they get home. I'll sleep a lot better."

"Me, too, Mike… Me, too."

∽ᴏᴏ∾

Mary Beth pulled the Grand Cherokee into the driveway and turned off the motor. She sat for a few minutes, looking up at the yellow-curtained window on the second story. The room was dark.

She opened the car door and stepped outside. What should she say to Jason? She felt herself trembling and pulled her coat tightly around her, though she knew it wasn't the cold causing her to shake.

She walked toward the lighted porch, and noticed something lying in front of the door. She hurried up the steps and bent down to take a look. An instant later, she recoiled in horror, her heart pounding.

"Ja...son...! Ja...son!" Mary Beth tried to call her son, but she could scarcely make a sound.

Marita watched as G. R. paced back and forth on the Oriental rug in his library, running his fingers along the leather spines of his nineteenth-century classics collection.

"I wish you would sit down," she said. "You're making me more nervous than I already am."

"I can't believe the superintendent in Ellison has no record the girls ever signed in. Why are we doing nothing while our daughter is missing?"

"We agreed to wait until 9:00. If the girls aren't back by then, we'll get with the Kennsingtons and call the police."

"Why waste any more time? I should be giving the orders, and—"

The phone rang. G. R. grabbed it.

"Hello!"

Marita heard the voice from where she sat. It was deep and distorted. "Check...your...mail...box." *Click.*

G. R. dropped the phone and rushed down the hallway, flung open the front door and ran out of the house.

Marita was on his heels. "G. R., wait for me!"

He sprinted down the long circle drive toward the wrought-iron gate.

Marita couldn't keep up with him. "Darn these shoes!"

She saw him key in the combination, and then the gate slowly opened. He squeezed through, and rushed toward the stone mailbox on the other side of the street.

He yanked open the lid, and she saw something fall on his foot. He kicked it away, and then stumbled backwards, losing his balance.

"Jason...! Jason...!" Mary Beth didn't recognize the sound of her own voice. She reached up and held her finger on the doorbell until she heard footsteps running inside the house. Jason opened the door.

"Mom? What's wrong? What are you doing down—"

"Mary Beth, are you all right?" Joe came bounding up the steps. "I was a couple of houses away and heard you calling for Jason. What happened?"

Mary Beth stared at the block of wood. Pinned to it with a butcher knife was a lock of brown hair, a swatch of clothing, and a blood-spattered note:

**On the day of hearts we finally met,
but you ain't seen nothin' yet!**

Marita laid her hand on her husband's back until he stopped dry heaving.

"G. R., what fell out of the mailbox?"

"Over there..." He pointed to something on the ground a few feet away. She felt him retch again.

Marita moved and stood over the object, her eyes attempting to focus in the light given off by the security beams.

"Oh, no…" She whimpered, slowly dropping to her knees. "No…no…no!"

On the ground lay Oliver, a knife plunged into his heart. The knife blade held a lock of curly blond hair, the monogram from Taylor's sweater, and a blood-splattered note:

Revenge is mine, Valentine!

At 9:15, billowy smoke filled the Baxter sky, while flames engulfed the only visible reminder of G. R. Logan's old textile operation. The young man watched from a high vantage point. From now on, *he* was calling the shots.

The textile plant would be gone in a few minutes. Good riddance! He had only called the fire department so they'd discover what he left at the entrance.

Wouldn't it be a shocker? The sign, which he'd made on plain white posterboard with black-stenciled lettering, was stuck to the guardhouse with a long knife dipped in Oliver's blood. He intended for its chilling words to haunt G. R. Logan the rest of his life:

An eye for an eye,
A lamb led to slaughter,
The price of revenge—
Your only daughter!

EIGHT

FBI Special Agent Jordan Ellis stood leaning against a vending machine, surveying the grim gathering at the Baxter Police Station. Chief Cameron had brought folding chairs into the officer's lounge to allow the Logans and Kennsingtons more privacy. Jordan loosened his collar and wondered if there was enough air in there to last the evening.

The families looked shell-shocked. He'd seen the blank look many times, but he never knew what to say. Nothing helped at this stage. He glanced at his watch. Give them a few more minutes.

He noticed the Kennsingtons' pastor had a calming effect. Jordan was glad Pastor Thomas decided to stay while the statements were given. The Kennsingtons seemed like a nice family. Too bad their daughter got caught in this. He wondered who had gone ballistic. Probably some redneck who'd worked for Logan.

He studied Taylor Logan's parents. The Missus sat with her arms folded and her lips pursed. Hardly said a word. Who could blame her? G. R. Logan was a real piece of work. Couldn't keep his mouth shut for more than a minute without telling the FBI how to do its job. And talk about edgy! Jordan could relate to hyper, but this guy was driving him nuts.

Jordan turned and whispered to Police Chief Cameron. "Who's the couple sitting by the Kennsingtons?"

"Jed and Rhonda Wilson. They're pretty tight with Mary Beth and Joe. They all go to the same church."

"Who's the lady reporter?" Jordan asked. "All we need is the press sticking their noses in this."

"She's not a reporter. Ellen Jones is the editor of the *Baxter Daily News.* A close personal friend of the Kennsingtons."

"Why don't we get started?" Jordan said. "The newspaper woman looks anxious to get on with it, and these families need to get home."

Aaron Cameron nodded and walked to the front of the room. "I've asked the sheriff to speak first since most of you don't know me that well yet. Hal…"

Sheriff Barker moved over next to Aaron and cleared his throat. "I want you to know I'm outraged by what happened tonight. Aaron asked me to speak first since I've known you a long time. When Chief Henley retired last month, he left some big shoes to step into, but let me assure you Aaron knows his stuff. He and I will be working with FBI Special Agent Jordan Ellis, who'll be in charge of this case. Aaron's department and mine are already moving under the FBI's direction. And mark my words: We won't stop until we get whoever's responsible."

"Thanks, Hal." Aaron took a step forward. "I have a fourteen-year-old daughter, and I'm appalled at the cruelty of the circumstances you find yourselves in. I promise to do everything humanly possible to assist the FBI in getting your girls home safely. Agent Ellis has a history of handling cases for the FBI in this region, so let me turn this over to him. Jordan…"

Jordan paused, reading the questioning faces in front of him. "This case will be handled as concurrent jurisdiction, which means that different branches of law enforcement will be working together as a team. I'll be in charge of the effort.

"We believe the girls are still alive. A ransom demand will probably be forthcoming, and the FBI has experience in what works and what doesn't. I need to insist that none of you engages in contact with the kidnapper on your own. We're the professionals. Let us do our job. We want your kids back alive. You need to trust us.

"Both families will have a surveillance team with sophisticated equipment to intercept any communication that comes through. Do not—I repeat, *do not*—attempt to make a deal on your own. No matter how tempting it may be, agreeing to the kidnapper's terms almost never gets the child back, always increases the danger, and is no guarantee the child won't be harmed. I don't say this to scare you, but it's imperative that we're all in agreement on the rules. We don't know if the kidnapper is acting alone, but we do know you can't trust whoever it is, and you need to understand that going in.

"The kidnapping appears to have been motivated by some unresolved issue with Mr. Logan, and we need to investigate the possibilities."

Mrs. Logan put her hands to her mouth and whimpered.

"Right or wrong, the kidnapper's perspective is everything," Jordan said. "I can't state that too strongly. We need to create a profile to help us narrow down the field of possible suspects. That's another reason why the FBI needs to listen to every communication, read every note, and know every detail of every contact. We need to know as much as possible about how this person thinks.

"And I'll be truthful with you, the waiting game is torture. You folks are going to need lots of support. We don't know who we're dealing with. And it *is* a matter of life and death. Every minute and every detail could be critical to the outcome. Does anyone have questions?"

There was a long, uncomfortable pause.

"Sir," Erica said, her voice barely audible, "what are the chances my sister...will really come home?"

"We'll do everything we know to do, young lady. Sometimes these things have a good outcome."

"Does that mean you aren't sure?"

"It means no one can speak with absolute certainty, but we'll do everything humanly possible to get your sister back."

"Well, couldn't we pray for what *isn't* humanly possible? God knows where Sherry and Taylor are. He can show us."

Jordan saw hope in the girl's eyes. How was he supposed to answer a question like that?

"Erica's right," Joe Kennsington said. "I'd like Pastor Thomas to lead us in prayer before we leave. My family is going to hold an all-night prayer vigil at our home, and anyone who'd like to come is welcome. Please don't feel obligated. We know you'll be praying wherever you are, but just know you're welcome. Our grief is not private, and neither is our relationship with the only One who knows where our girls are."

Jordan cleared his throat. "Are there any more questions?"

"I don't have a question," Ellen Jones said, "but I'd like to speak with you when we're finished here. I'd like to double-check my facts. Margie's holding the front page for tomorrow's edition."

Jordan forced a slight nod, thinking that was exactly what he *didn't* want. "Anything else?"

G. R. Logan sprang to his feet. His face was red. "I want to get something straight: If any of you are thinking this is *my* fault, think again! I can't help it if some nutcase has a grudge against me. I resent the implication, even in a note. I've done nothing to deserve this.

"And furthermore, I'm not praying. God hasn't done squat so far. Where was He when Taylor was abducted by this…this… maniac? Where is He now? Where is *she* now?" His voice cracked. "All my life I've gone to church, given tithes and donations, sent money to foreign missions. I've given generously to this community—and this is how God repays me? Well, count me out. I'll find

Taylor *without* God's help. Don't underestimate G. R. Logan. Come on, Marita, we're leaving."

He grabbed his wife's hand, pulled her up from the chair, and stomped to the door. Joe got up and whispered something to the Logans. G. R. paused, then pushed open the door and left the room.

Jordan shot Hal and Aaron a questioning look. *What was that all about?*

Sherry Kennsington lay in darkness so thick she couldn't see her hand in front of her face. She groped the area around her and felt the nylon sleeping bag and the cold, hard floor. Where was she? What did he want with them? The only thing she was sure of at the moment was a throbbing headache.

Her hand knocked something over, and she grabbed it. A flashlight? She picked it up and turned it on. Taylor was lying in a sleeping bag not three feet away. Were they in some kind of cage?

She saw nothing inside the enclosure except two sleeping bags, two bottles of water, and what appeared to be a camping toilet set up in the corner. She didn't have the strength to get up. She didn't even have the strength to whisper's Taylor's name.

Sherry lay there with her head and heart pounding. Was it a nightmare? Would she wake up in her own bed? She wasn't sure any of it was real. *Father, protect us.* She closed her eyes and drifted back to sleep.

Those in the Kennsingtons' living room stood quietly in a circle and held hands as the prayer vigil continued into the wee hours of Saturday morning.

Joe was aware of every tick of the mantel clock, magnified in the stillness between prayers. He tried to harness his thoughts, refusing to think about what might be happening to Sherry.

"Father, I feel so helpless," Joe said. "I have a responsibility to protect my daughter, but right now, I can't. That's such a hard reality for me. Please help me to trust You. I know she's not been out of Your sight for a moment, but it's so hard not knowing if she's all right. There's no way to know what's happening to—" His voice failed.

Pastor Thomas continued the prayer. "Lord, You've promised that no one can snatch those who are Yours from Your hand. Sherry's Your child, Father. Be with her. Give her the grace she needs to get through this trial.

"We pray also for Taylor. Lord, we don't know if she knows You, but we're certain that You know *her*. Father, bring her through this and use it to bring this child to Your throne of grace.

"And Lord, please be with Marita and G. R. as they seem to be facing this terrible ordeal without You. Soften their hearts to Your love and Your sovereignty. Please give us all courage and hope and peace as You send angels to watch over these girls. In Jesus' name we pray, amen."

Joe had lost count of how many times they had repeated themselves in prayer. He looked at Mary Beth and wondered which was heavier, her eyelids or her heart. Jason was sacked out on the couch. Erica looked as if she could keel over at any moment.

He felt a hand on his shoulder. "Joe, we should leave, and let your family get some sleep," Pastor Thomas said. "You have to be exhausted. Jed opened the church earlier, and Rhonda got volunteers to take shifts and pray through the night. We'll keep the vigil going. Right now, you need to sleep."

"Thanks, Pastor," Joe said. "I don't know what we'd do without our church family."

Taylor opened her eyes to the blackest black she'd ever seen. Her head throbbed. She remembered him zipping her into the sleeping bag in the bed of his truck, but where was she now? Where was Sherry? She rolled onto her side and felt around, surprised to find a flashlight. She turned it on and saw the other sleeping bag.

"Sherry…? Sherry…? Can you hear me? Wake up! Please wake up. I'm so scared!"

Taylor heard a swishing sound and then saw Sherry's face turn toward her. Her friend looked like a Raggedy Ann doll stuffed in a garbage bag.

"Oh…you're awake," Sherry said, her words forming a big yawn. "I woke up earlier, but you were still out. Where are we?"

"I don't know." Taylor moved the beam of light up and down the walls of chain-link. "It looks like a cage of some kind. It smells musty, like maybe we're in a basement. The floor is concrete. This place is creepy."

"Do you know what time it is? My watch is gone."

Taylor shined the flashlight on her own wrist. "Mine, too. I wonder how long we've been out?"

"Whatever was in those pills gave me a splitting headache." Sherry rubbed her temples. "Why is he doing this?"

"Listen…" Taylor whispered. "Do you hear footsteps?"

A creaky door slowly opened, and light appeared on a concrete wall in front of a stairwell.

Taylor latched onto Sherry's arm. "He's coming for us!" Her heart pounded wildly. She tried to stifle her crying.

The footsteps slowly descended the stairs and stopped. A bright beam of light made the turn and moved toward them at a slow, calculated pace.

Sherry put a finger to her lips. She took the flashlight and turned it off, then scrambled to get up, grabbing Taylor's hand and pulling her to her feet.

The girls cowered in the far corner as the light came closer and closer, finally reaching the chain-link prison. Taylor strained to see, but with the light in her eyes, she could make out only a shadow.

But then came a deep, throaty growl and two eyes staring at her from the other side of the gate.

NINE

Joe cradled Mary Beth in his arms. The house was quiet now, except for the screaming emptiness coming from Sherry's room. He prayed silently. Though the kidnapper remained nameless, Joe had no doubt from which camp this evil act originated.

"Mary Beth, are you awake?"

She nodded and nuzzled closer, wrapping her fingers around his forearm. "What do people do who don't have the Lord?"

"I can't imagine."

"What did you say to G. R.?" she asked. "He seemed to calm down."

"I reminded him that God loves Taylor even more than he does. He can't mean what he said. Guys like him are used to calling the shots, and he's feeling angry and scared and trapped. Taylor means the world to him."

"Like Sherry does to us. Joe, what will we do if...if something horrible happens to her?"

He gently stroked his wife's hair. "We have to trust God, Mary Beth. That's what we've told others for years. Now we have to walk our talk. I don't know what the outcome will be," he said softly, his voice raspy and emotional. "But I trust God to make something good out of it."

"If we survive…"

"We will, honey. I just wish we knew what He knows."

As soon as he said it, Joe was thinking he probably didn't.

Marita heard G. R. get out of bed and go upstairs to Taylor's room. She was glad he left. What could she say to him? It was no surprise to her that someone would want to get back at G. R. So many people got hurt in the plant closure…

"Grant won't allow you to do this," Marita had said. "It goes against everything he believes."

"I know how Dad feels," G. R. said. "But I've got the deciding vote, and I'm shutting it down. We can get the same job done in Costa Rica for a song. Why pay salaries and benefits we don't have to?"

"What about the workers who've been loyal to Grant all these years? Don't you owe them *something?*"

"Give me a break, Marita. They got what they earned. Times change."

"But some of them are close to retirement."

"So let Uncle Sam support them. It's not my responsibility…"

Many people in town still wouldn't speak to them. But had someone been hurt enough to steal the most valuable thing in G. R.'s life just to spite him? The thought made her shudder.

Marita felt warm tears drip down the sides of her face and into her ears. Losing Taylor was unthinkable. She turned over and punched her pillow. *This is all your fault, G. R.*

Taylor clamped her eyes shut and hung onto Sherry's arm, terrified of the creature with the glowing eyes and throaty growls. She glanced up at the shadowy figure standing next to it. Her heart hammered. She felt as if she were going to throw up. Was he going to put it in the cage with them?

"Well, girls, how do you like your new quarters? By the way, I dropped your parents a *note.*" He laughed. "I'm sure tomorrow morning's headlines will have everyone wondering whether or not you're alive.

"Just to show I'm not all bad, I brought you a pet to keep you company." He yanked on the animal's leash, and the growling intensified. "However, if you get close to the gate, or if you talk—or even whisper—Jack won't like it. Go ahead, ask me what I mean."

Taylor clutched Sherry's arm even harder. She didn't look at him.

He put his face directly in front of the gate. "I *said,* ask me what I mean!"

Taylor's pulse was off the charts, but she couldn't make her mouth say anything. She tried to stifle her crying, and then she felt Sherry's hand give hers a double squeeze.

"Wha—what do you mean?" Sherry said.

Jack lunged at the fence, growling and snarling with such ferocity that Taylor began to sob.

"See what I mean? Things will go much better if you do as I say. Jack *always* does." He flashed an evil grin. "He likes food and water twice a day, so I'll bring you something, too. I'm sure you've already discovered utilities are furnished—flashlight, toilet in the corner, and a space heater out here." The young man turned to Jack. "Sit!"

Like a robot, the animal obeyed.

"Don't cross me, ladies. Oh…did I mention Jack here is a pure-bred Doberman, and that his registered name is Jack the *Ripper?*"

TEN

Wayne Purdy watched huge snowflakes stick to the windows at Monty's Diner and melt into clear trickles that disappeared behind the blue cafe curtains. He glanced up at the clock. Why was the newspaper late?

"Wayne, would you clean up the spill in the kitchen?" Mark Steele rolled his eyes. "I knocked off a plate of pancakes trying to help Rosie."

"He means well." Rosie Harris winked at Wayne.

"Order up!" shouted Leo.

"That's my cue," she said. "See you guys around."

As Wayne cleaned up the spill, he heard the door to the diner open and a bundle of newspapers hit the floor.

"Sorry they're late. There was an accident on the bridge," said a male voice.

"No problem," Mark said. "We're just glad to get them."

Wayne dumped the mess into the trash, aware of the clanking of quarters dropping into the jar.

Rosie pick up three plates of strawberry blintzes and a ham-and-cheese omelette and headed for the corner booth. Wayne noticed Mark leaning on the counter, engrossed in the front page.

He tucked a newspaper under his arm, slipped into the store-room, and began to read.

BAXTER GIRLS BELIEVED KIDNAPPED

Two local high school girls were reported missing after they failed to sign in for setup at the regional science fair in Ellison yesterday afternoon.

Taylor Logan, 16, daughter of textile magnate Grant Randall Logan IV and his wife Marita Logan of Baxter, and Sherry Kennsington, 16, daughter of Baxter High School Principal Joseph Kennsington and his wife Mary Beth of Baxter, failed to return home for a much-anticipated Valentine's Dance at the high school.

Principal Kennsington told Police Chief Aaron Cameron that he last saw both girls in his office around 2 P.M. on Friday as they were leaving for the Ellison Civic Center to set up their winning science projects for entry in the regional science fair.

Superintendent Mike Weiss of the Ellison School District, who oversaw the regional science fair setup, said that neither Sherry nor Taylor signed in for a pass. No one on the premises recalled seeing either of the girls.

According to police, shortly before 9 P.M. someone left a message of an undisclosed nature on the premises of both the Kennsingtons and the Logans. At about the same time, the old Logan textile plant was discovered burning after an anonymous caller notified the fire department.

County Fire Marshal John Washburn suspects arson. For reasons known only to authorities on this case, no other details are being released at this time. An FBI investigation is underway, in cooperation with the Baxter Police Department and the Norris County Sheriff's Department.

Wayne wadded up the front page and threw it in the trash. That was it? That was how his long-awaited drama played out in the community? He took off his glasses and rubbed his temples, then grabbed his mop bucket and went out front.

Mark tossed the paper on the counter. "Hard to tell what's going on."

"Sounds like a pervert," Reggie Mason said. "Why else would anyone kidnap two girls?"

Wayne loosened his collar. *Revenge, Reg! You'd know that if Ellen Jones bothered to report the whole story.*

Mort Clary shrugged. "Prob'ly wantin' money. The way I hear it, them FBI fellas found some kind o' ransom demand spray-painted on the guardhouse near the burned-up textile plant."

"The paper didn't mention a ransom demand," Reggie said.

Rosie jabbed Mort with her elbow. "You made that up."

"Did not. I also heard them FBI fellas found some kinda message in a bottle floatin' in the Logans' swimmin' pool."

"What pool has water in February?" Wayne said, fighting the urge to call Mort an idiot. "Sounds like a dopey rumor."

Mort whirled around on the stool. "Some o' the high school kids was talkin' 'bout it last night. I heard 'em say the Kennsingtons found a skull and crossbones painted right on the front door! The whole neighborhood's freakin' out. Sounds like a real sicko at work. Whoever done it must be copyin' some dumb B movie."

Wayne turned his back and pushed the mop hard across the blue-and-white checkered tile.

"Hey, Wayne, you're gonna wear a hole in the floor," Mark said. "Slow down, tiger. You've got a lot of morning left."

"Just making sure the slush is cleaned up, boss. Don't want folks to slip."

"You know, I can understand someone kidnapping Logan's daughter for money," George Gentry said. "But why Sherry Kennsington? What's the connection?"

Reggie shrugged. "Beats me. The newspaper sure didn't give us anything."

"Maybe taking the daughters of two high-profile families would get the whole community's attention," Jim Hawkins said. "This person could be sounding a trumpet."

Wayne smirked. *How perceptive of you, Mr. Hawkins. I'm getting through to at least one of you. But if Ellen Jones won't report the facts, I'll just have to put on a higher profile performance.*

Ellen Jones sat at her desk, a copy of the *Baxter Daily News* spread out in front of her. The phone rang and she quickly picked it up.

"This is Ellen!" Her voice was short.

"I knew you'd be upset."

"Guy, I hate this! There's a fine line between leaving out the facts and lying."

"So you left out the gory details. You did what Jordan asked. Maybe he's right."

"This story insults the intelligence of this community. Leaving out facts will only serve to propagate rumors. How right can that be?"

"Look, Ellen, he has a point. By giving no attention to the bizarre, the kidnapper might feel forced into making contact with the parents. At least then the FBI would have something to go on."

"Or not. I've never seen such audacity. This kidnapper's not going to be forced into anything."

"Maybe not, but Jordan's in charge of the case."

"Well, he's not running this newspaper."

"Then why did you agree to withhold the details?"

She sighed. "I suppose out of respect for the families. The whole thing is macabre, and part of me hates for the families to have to see it in print…and, regardless of how I feel, it's only a hunch. We both know how far that'll get me."

"So, you bow to those who've done this before. Seems wise."

"But what if it works the other way?"

"What do you mean?"

"My holding back on the details could incite the kidnapper to force *us* to pay attention. What then? After what happened last night, it gives me cold chills. The writer of those notes is evil."

"What people don't know won't hurt them."

"So, you're saying ignorance makes them safer…"

"Ellen, I need to leave. I'm supposed to get my hair cut in ten minutes. If I'm late, I'll spend half my Saturday waiting. I hate that."

"You didn't answer my question, Guy."

"Double-check your punctuation, Madame Editor. I don't believe you used a question mark. I love you. Talk to you later."

Ellen hung up the phone and rested her elbows on the desk. She looked up at the oil painting of Reginald T. Baxter, the town's founder and first editor of the newspaper. He never compromised the truth. And it had worked here for a hundred years.

Ellen sat and stared at nothing. Did she have just cause to withhold the truth? The first amendment protected her right to print it. But what if the FBI was right?

ELEVEN

Jennifer Wilson opened the refrigerator and poured herself a glass of orange juice. She glanced over at her parents, sitting at the kitchen table. Was her mother crying?

"Oh…Jennifer." Rhonda dabbed her eyes. "I didn't hear you come in."

"I'm sorry. I didn't mean to interrupt—"

"Sherry Kennsington's been kidnapped," Jed said.

"Kidnapped! You're kidding!"

"Yesterday afternoon. Sherry left for the Ellison Civic Center with Taylor Logan. They never showed up."

"Couldn't they have run away, or taken off on some adventure? How do you know they were kidnapped?"

"We were with the Kennsingtons last night. The FBI's been called in. There were some threatening notes left. And a dead cat. Really sick stuff."

"This is unbelievable!" Jennifer lowered herself to the chair. "How are Mr. and Mrs. Kennsington handling it?"

Rhonda sighed. "They've left it in God's hands. But how do parents handle the fear of losing a child? I can't imagine anything more devastating. If I ever lost you…well, I can't imagine. You mean everything to me."

And nothing to Dad, she thought.

"You all right?" Jed asked.

Jennifer turned away, her lower lip quivering. When he put his arms around her, she stiffened.

"It's okay, honey. We're sad about Sherry, too."

Jennifer squirmed out of his arms but avoided looking at him. "It's more than that, Dad." She wiped her eyes with the sleeve of her bathrobe.

Jed handed her a Kleenex. "Wanna talk about it?"

"Not especially. I'm probably overly emotional because I'm pregnant…are you done with the newspaper?"

"Uh, yeah, sure. You done, babe?"

Rhonda nodded. "Poor Mary Beth and Joe."

Jennifer laid the newspaper out in front of her and began reading, aware of her mother rummaging through a kitchen drawer.

"Here it is. Jed, remember this?"

"Oh, yeah," he said. "Read it to me."

"In these hours, only faith holds the hopeful lamp, glimpsing glories of His face, able still to trace footprints across the water. Speak not lightly of faith, for but a single strand can span an empty shell of despair to the very heart of God."

Jennifer looked up. "Mom, is that from the Bible?"

"No, just something Mary Beth gave me. It meant a lot."

"You know, babe," Jed said, "we may have to be that single strand of faith for the Kennsingtons right now."

Jennifer listened in amazement. Whatever had changed her mother and father, she was beginning to want it for herself.

Joe stood at the kitchen window, the steam from his coffee fogging up the glass. The phone rang and he grabbed it.

"Hello," he said, his heart pounding.

"Joseph, it's Dad. Any news?"

"No. I'd have called."

"I know, son…I just needed to hear your voice again."

Joe blinked to clear his eyes. "Thanks. Sherry's empty room is tearing us up. The only thing holding us together is our faith."

"How's Mary Beth?"

"Quiet. The kids, too. It's hard, Dad. Really hard."

"Let us come up there, Joe. Your mother and I want to support you."

"You are. I think it's best if you and Mom stay there. Trust me, with her health she doesn't need this level of stress up close. Pray for Sherry. And try to stay sane. I'll let you know the minute I know anything."

"Have you called Mary Beth's folks? Do you need me to do some phoning for you?"

"Not at the moment, but I may take you up on it later when we know more."

"Okay, Joseph. Our arms are around you."

"I feel them…" His voice cracked. "Pray that Sherry does."

The grandfather clock struck 7:00 as dinner was served at the Logan mansion. Marita ate in silence, painfully aware of one empty chair.

She avoided eye contact with G. R, who sat facing her at the opposite end. Totally white-haired, he looked much older than his fifty-three years. The deep lines on his face seemed to her an appropriate symbol for the deep wounds he'd inflicted on everyone else. He was heady and arrogant. A bully. Not the dynamic, personable, handsome man she married. She hadn't entirely lost her feelings for G. R., but their relationship was more like steel than gold—manufactured, not genuine—and certainly not appreciating in value.

Randy looked tired after his hurried trip back from Costa Rica. Her son was a carbon copy of his father twenty-five years ago. Dark hair. Deep blue eyes. Persuasive smile. But unlike G. R., Randy was an able business politician, a stabilizing force in Logan Textile Industries. It was he who smoothed the rough edges hewn by his father's impetuous behavior. Randy was being groomed, and Marita was sure she would lose him to the business. Her deepest fear was that he would not be allowed to develop into anything other than the image of his father.

She glanced over at her father-in-law. Grant Logan was a brilliant, honest, and simple man, thoughtful and compassionate in both his personal and professional dealings. During the thirty years he ran the family business, he had earned respect and loyalty from those who worked for Logan Textile Industries. How she admired him!

Marita caught Helen's eye and looked away. Her mother-in-law was a quiet, gentle woman who was both supportive and wise. She knew when to speak out loud and when to speak with her heart. She had been a good partner for Grant, his quiet strength during the years he ran the company.

Marita felt her stomach tighten. Why couldn't she be more like Helen? But then, G. R. was nothing like Grant.

Marita saw herself in the mirror on the far wall. Under the chandelier and flickering candlelight, her hair looked fashionably styled, eyes perfectly outlined, lipstick neatly applied.

Even the pink silk dress she bought at Neiman Marcus covered her deadness like a flag draped over a casket. She wondered if it mattered anymore.

TWELVE

Ellen licked the chocolate off her fingers and threw another Hershey wrapper in the waste can. Did anyone understand her frustration? She glanced at the clock…7:20! Where had the day gone? She put some things in her briefcase and walked downstairs to the main door. She looked through the glass and was surprised to see the snow had melted and the pavement was dry.

When Ellen reached the parking lot, her heart started to pound. She stopped and looked in all directions, but saw no one. An eerie feeling made her skin crawl. She fumbled around in her purse. Where was the mace? Why hadn't she tested it? Her fingers found the tiny canister and she clutched it in her hand. She hurried to her white Riviera and started to get inside when she spotted an envelope under the wiper.

She snatched the envelope, got into the car, and locked the door. She sat for a moment and took slow, deliberate breaths. She opened the envelope with her thumbnail and pulled out a note. Two locks of hair fell into her lap—one soft blond curl and a straight brown one. Blood was spattered on the white paper. Her hands shook as she read:

Your job is to report the news.
Instead, you left out all my clues.
Just to prove I'm still a threat,
I'll show you something cold and wet.
In Heron Lake, near boat ramp five,
Something missing took a dive.
Get your facts straight, Mrs. Jones,
Or all you'll find next time are bones.
Report the facts, including props,
and I mean business—tell the cops!

Ellen double-checked to be sure the car was locked. Her eyes searched the dark night around her as she picked up her cell phone and dialed.

"Hello."

"Guy, it's me. I've got a situation. Uh—more than a situation, a mess. Well, it's worse than a mess. I need you. I'm really not sure what to do."

"Honey, talk louder, I can hardly hear you. Tell me where you are. I'll be right there. Are you hurt?"

"No. But I'm scared—*really* scared. I—I'm leaving my office now. Stay on the line and talk to me while I drive home."

"Ellen, your voice is shaking."

"I just need to feel your arms around me."

"Should I call the police?"

"No! Don't hang up! Please don't hang up!"

"Honey, I'm right here. I'm not going anywhere. Are you driving yet? Have you left the office?"

"Yes, I'm turning onto Second Street. I'll be home in just a couple of minutes." Ellen looked in her rearview mirror at the headlights behind her.

"You weren't assaulted, were you? I mean, you said you weren't hurt. Did—"

"No one physically harmed me. I'll tell you about it in two minutes. You can help me decide what I need to do. Just keep talking, Guy. Don't hang up."

Wayne went in the house, flipped on the light, and slammed the door. He walked through the living room and into the kitchen. Maybe Ellen Jones would print the whole story now. Maybe not. But he wasn't leaving anything to chance.

She had ruined everything! He had waited five years for this day and it was a dud—a zero! No one seemed up in arms about the kidnapping. Why should they be? The front-page story was a joke. He picked up an empty Coke can, crushed it, and threw it against the wall.

Wayne pulled out a drawer and dumped the contents on the floor. Where was the key to the shed? He got down on the floor and sifted through the mess until he found what he was looking for.

He got up and hurried toward the back door. He'd make *sure* they paid attention this time.

THIRTEEN

Jordan Ellis took a bite of pepperoni pizza just as his phone rang. He washed it down with Dr. Pepper and grabbed the receiver.

"Yeah, this is Jordan."

"This is Aaron Cameron. Ellen and Guy Jones are sitting with me in my office. Our perp hit again."

"When?"

"A few minutes ago. Ellen found one of those sick poems and two more locks of hair in an envelope under her windshield wiper."

"Did she see who left it?"

"No. But it's definitely intended as a threat. The kidnapper wants her to report every detail of the story."

"Tough."

"Jordan, that's not all. It says there's something underwater at boat ramp five."

"On Heron Lake?"

"Right. Says something *missing* took a dive. Heaven help us, I hope it's not what it sounds like."

Jordan sighed. "Did you say you were in your office?"

"Yeah. Want us to come to you?"

"Meet me at the lake. Call the game warden and the sheriff and have them meet us at boat ramp five. We'll need equipment and divers."

Heron Lake blended into the inky darkness, searchlights moving eerily beneath its surface, a helicopter circling overhead.

Ellen shivered as she stood with Guy, waiting to find out what was in the water.

FBI agents had taped off a sizable area at the top of boat ramp five, where it began its incline into the water. An ambulance sat ready. Equipment was available for pulling up whatever was down there. The flashing lights of law enforcement vehicles lit up the area where the access road had been blocked off.

The Kennsingtons and the Logans were wrapped in blankets, standing behind the yellow crime-scene tape. All eyes were on the lake.

"This is so creepy, Guy. Who would do this?"

"I know one thing: He terrorized the wrong woman tonight. He's not getting that close to you again. Not as long as I have anything to say about it."

Ellen turned and looked up at him. Guy stood like a fortress, his arms crossed, his hair whipped about by an icy wind blowing off the lake. She'd never seen him more resolute.

"I know you're upset about what happened—"

"It won't happen again," he said. "Don't worry. And no matter what they find down there, Ellen, it's not your fault."

She turned around and leaned her back against his chest, his arms wrapped tightly around her. "I should have listened to my instincts," she mumbled.

Chief Cameron walked over and stood next to them. "Rough night. Sorry you got drawn into this." He pulled his collar up around his ears.

"I can only imagine how scared those girls must be," Ellen said. *If they're still alive.*

"Look, the divers are coming up." Aaron took a step toward the lake.

Lights were swirling in the water around boat ramp five. One of the divers stood in shallow water, his mask pushed up on his forehead, his wet suit reflecting the flashing lights. Seconds later, four others divers surfaced.

"Well? What's down there?" Jordan asked.

"Sir, we found a late model BMW—white," said Mitch Crawford.

"And…?"

"And a car full of what appears to be science project materials. No sign of the girls."

"Okay, let's get this car up out of the water." Jordan motioned for the driver of the heavy equipment to move.

"Sir?" Mitch Crawford lowered his voice. "There's something really odd hanging from the rearview mirror—an unmatched pair of girls' shoes. I thought you ought to know. The parents will probably notice."

"Okay, Mitch. Thanks for the warning."

Jordan stood with his arms folded, his fingers rubbing his chin.

Hal Barker came and stood next to him. "I heard."

There was a long pause.

"We've got a real sick entertainer on our hands, Sheriff. Doesn't fit the profile we put together."

"What now?"

"I've dealt with only one other perpetrator like this. Let's hope it taught me something."

Jack sat in front of the gate, his ears at attention. He began whimpering.

Sherry glanced at Taylor, whose eyes were wide with terror. She turned off the flashlight and waited as the dreaded footsteps slowly descended the stairs. It seemed like an eternity until the bright beam of light rounded the corner and shone directly in her eyes.

"Are we awake?" Wayne patted Jack and scratched his ears. "I'm talking to you, ladies...*answer me!*"

Sherry dug her fingers into Taylor's arm and took a deep breath. "Yes, we're awake."

Jack lunged at the front of the cage, snarling and baring his teeth.

Wayne grinned. "Jack, *sit.*"

The Doberman instantly obeyed.

"There now, that's better. I see the three of you understand the house rules."

Wayne unlocked the padlock and opened the gate. The girls tripped over themselves, scrambling to the back, while he dropped two sacks and two bottles of water on the floor.

"I'm taking Jack out for a quick *bite*. You two will be dining in." He closed the gate, secured the padlock, and then led Jack into the darkness and up the stairs.

Sherry waited until the door closed and she heard footsteps on the creaky floor above them. She turned on the flashlight. "I've looked this place over, and I don't think there's any way for us to get out."

"Do you think Wayne's going to hurt us?" Taylor asked. "I can't bear the thought of him touching me. What if—"

"Don't start thinking that way. It's like he's getting some weird thrill out of scaring us. Why do you suppose he kidnapped us?"

"Probably for ransom," Taylor said.

"Suppose I just came with the package?"

"I don't know, Sherry. I'm terrified he's going to hurt us. Probably the only reason he hasn't is he knows my father will pay him anything he wants as long as I'm alive."

"Well, I know one thing for sure: My family's praying, and we have to trust God."

"I want to, but what if He doesn't get us out of here? What if—"

Sherry put her hand to Taylor's mouth. "No 'what if's' allowed. Wayne doesn't own me—God does. And He's already paid a ransom for my life. Somehow this'll all work out. Try not to think the worst. I've been praying a lot, and it's helped. Maybe you should, too."

"But I don't know how to pray all day long. I keep saying the same things over and over."

"That's okay. It's gotta be better than thinking about our circumstances. By the way, the hand gestures we've been using make sense, don't you think?"

Taylor nodded. "Better than having Jack throw himself on the cage like a wild beast. I hate him. He's horrible."

"Well, God's in control, not Jack the jerky Doberman."

"You think God will get us out of here?" Taylor asked.

"He's here with us. I know that."

"But aren't you scared? I'm so afraid..." Taylor started to cry.

Sherry put her arm around her friend, her heart pounding, her eyes clamped shut. "Lord, I believe You're here with us. Please help us feel Your presence."

Ellen sat in the family room, her body yielded to the comfort of a leather chair, her feet on the ottoman. She sipped hot tea and stared at the crackling fire.

"Are you finally thawing out?" Guy asked.

"What's the latest?"

"Taylor's car has been pulled from the lake and put into evidence. You'll never guess what they found inside."

"What?"

"A small listening device. Probably how the kidnapper knew the girls were driving to Ellison."

Ellen shook her head. "How'd the parents react?"

"Not as bad as when they saw the girls' shoes hanging on the rearview mirror." Guy stood behind the chair and rubbed her shoulders.

"I felt so sorry for Mary Beth and Marita...having to identify the shoes. No mother should have to do that."

"Jordan thinks the girls are still alive," he said.

"I know."

"You don't?"

"I'm afraid to think too hard about it." She sighed. "I guess the parents realize *I'm* in this now?"

"Jordan told them what happened tonight. They're really sorry."

Ellen got up and stood in front of the fire. "I've made a decision. I refuse to be silenced *or* manipulated."

"What do you mean?"

"I'm going to do what I should've done in the first place—report the story. Not because of the poem, but because it's who I am. I can't let Jordan or the kidnapper tell me what to do."

"I don't think that's such—"

"Have you got a better idea? If I report the news the way I always do, the kidnapper will be satisfied, the community will be informed, and I'll be able to look myself in the mirror."

"Even if you antagonize the FBI? Ellen, you're tired. Why don't you get a good night's—"

"Don't patronize me. I'm not going to change my mind."

"Why don't you wait until tomorrow, see if you still feel the same?"

She shook her head. "I want all the facts on tomorrow's front page."

"You don't have time."

"Honestly, Guy, give me a little credit. I called Margie hours ago and had her hold the front page. All we had to do was include what happened tonight. The factual story was already written. We just didn't print it."

～○～

Wayne turned onto the gravel driveway, pulled the truck to the end, and killed the motor. He leaned forward and rested on the steering wheel.

"Yes!" He pumped his fist.

He waltzed in the front door and into the kitchen. He tossed his keys on the countertop, reached into the fridge, and popped open a can of Coke. A grin spread across his face. He began to laugh, and he laughed louder and louder until he was doubled over with euphoria.

FOURTEEN

Before the sun was up Sunday morning, Wayne walked in the back door of Monty's and nearly bumped into Mark Steele.

"Here I am, in record time," Wayne said.

"You're a lifesaver. Thanks for coming in on your day off."

"No problem," Wayne said. "Glad I'm not the one with the flu." There was a loud thud at the front door. "I'll get the newspapers."

"Yeah, thanks." Mark tossed him the keys. "Go ahead and open up."

As soon as Wayne turned on the open sign, Mort Clary walked in and hung his coat and hat on the rack.

"Mornin', Wayne."

"Hey, Mr. Clary."

Mort took a newspaper off the stack, then put his money in the jar and sat at the counter.

Wayne picked up a newspaper, his eyes fixed on the front page. He heard the door open several times, but was only vaguely aware of his surroundings.

REVENGE PLOT UNFOLDS IN KIDNAPPING
OF LOGAN AND KENNSINGTON

Local authorities and the FBI have now confirmed that macabre messages left by the kidnapper of Taylor Logan and Sherry Kennsington blatantly point to a revenge plot against local textile magnate G. R. Logan.

The 53-year-old president and CEO of Logan Textile Industries said that he was unaware of any personal grudge against him or his company.

Neither the Logans nor the Kennsingtons have received a ransom demand or any personal contact by the kidnapper. However, a bizarre chain of events, which started Friday evening, has made the motive evident…

Wayne scanned the front page, which gave every detail known so far and included a picture of Taylor Logan's car being pulled from Heron Lake. His little side trip had paid off. He was suddenly aware of voices and noticed the early crowd gathered at the counter.

"This is an outrage!" Rosie Harris shook her head.

"Who could be *that* ticked off?" Reggie Mason said.

"No suspects so far." Mark read over Reggie's shoulder. "Wanna bet it's someone who worked for him?"

"That's my guess," Wayne said, moving closer to the counter. "But if the person doesn't have a criminal record, even DNA evidence wouldn't be of much use."

George Gentry looked over his shoulder. "So unless they catch the person, the FBI will never know who masterminded the whole thing."

"Probably not."

"Poor Taylor," Rosie said. "That 'lamb led to slaughter' line gives me cold chills."

"I feel sorry for the Kennsington girl." Leo wiped his hands on his apron. "Sounds like she got caught in the middle of this."

"I'll bet them girls show up dead," Mort said. "This sicko ain't gonna stop with a buncha hot-air threats."

Liv Spooner sighed. "I wonder if the kidnapper's already killed them and is just playing mind games? Hanging their shoes from the rearview mirror…talk about cruel."

"I don't know how the Logans and Kennsingtons can deal with any of this," Hattie Gentry said. "And the way G. R. doted on Taylor…well, he has to be devastated."

Wayne nodded. "Poor guy."

"You know what scares me?" Mark said. "It could be someone we know."

Streaks of golden pink burned the pale blue horizon as the Joneses emerged from the house for their morning jog.

"It feels great to be outside," Ellen said.

"I wish you'd change your mind."

"I refuse to let the kidnapper make a prisoner out of me, Guy. And I don't need you to keep me safely locked up at home. I'm not changing my routine. It's a gorgeous, crisp day." She took in a breath of air and blew the vapor at him, then smiled and took off running.

Ellen wasn't about to admit she would never have gone out alone this morning. She was watchful of their surroundings as they jogged under a canopy of bare branches down the block of restored Victorian homes. A few neighbors waved. The Miltons' yellow lab ran alongside. Nothing out of the ordinary.

When they had jogged to the city limits, Ellen stopped and leaned forward to catch her breath, her hands on her knees. "Guy, what's that orange thing on the water tower? I can't make it out."

"Looks like the high school kids put up a big banner. There ought to be a way to make access more difficult. A kid could get killed up there."

"Come on. I'll race you to the highway," she said, starting to run.

Ellen realized he wasn't behind her, and looked over her shoulder, surprised to see he had fallen back. She stopped and watched as his pace became slower and slower until he finally stopped, staring up at the water tower.

"Is this some kind of sick joke?" he said. "Who would...?"

Ellen hurried back to where he was standing and looked up, her eyes squinting. *What?* I don't have my contacts in."

Her husband's face was ashen. "Heaven help us..."

"Guy, you're scaring me! What is it? What's up there?"

Ellen sat on a tree stump near the water tower, her body trembling, her stomach queasy.

"We need to call Jordan Ellis right away," Guy said, "before the Logans or the Kennsingtons see this."

Ellen saw a dozen cars parked on the shoulder of the highway. People were already out of their cars, gawking and pointing.

"I'm not comfortable with Jordan Ellis," she said. "Call Aaron."

"All right. I programmed his number in my cell phone last night."

When Guy reached for his cell phone, Ellen was surprised to see his snub-nose .38 tucked into the waistband of his sweats.

"Aaron, this is Guy Jones. Looks like our kidnapper created his own headlines... No, you need to see this for yourself... Get in your car and meet me and Ellen at the water tower."

Joe Kennsington traced the pattern on the vinyl tablecloth over and over with his index finger.

"Dad, why do we have to go to church?" Erica said.

"You already know the answer."

"But what good will it do? I don't feel like praying. And I don't wanna see anyone."

"This isn't the time to stop praying. And we need strength and support from our church family to deal with this."

"Your father's right," Mary Beth said.

Erica pushed herself up from the table, then walked heavy-footed out of the kitchen and flopped down on the living room couch.

Jason sat staring at the newspaper.

"What is it, son?" Joe asked.

"Nothin'."

"Say it. It might help."

"I wish they wouldn't've found the car."

"It might contain clues that could help us find your sister."

Jason's lower lip quivered, his eyes filled with tears. "The shoes…"

Mary Beth put her hand to her mouth and rushed out of the kitchen.

Joe sat with his arms around Jason, wondering if it was possible to be strong for all of them. The doorbell rang.

"Son, I need to get that. Are you all right?"

Jason nodded.

Joe walked to the front door and realized Mary Beth was beside him.

"Oh…Pastor," he said. "What brings you out so early?"

"Has anyone from law enforcement called you this morning?"

"No. Why?"

"May I come in?"

Joe opened the door and the three of them stood in the entry-way. Pastor Thomas laid one hand on Joe's shoulder and the other on Mary Beth's. The look in his eyes sent Joe's pulse racing.

"I don't want you hearing it from someone else, though how can I tell you…?" His voice cracked. "Something is…hanging from the water tower. But prepare yourselves, it's…well, it's not good."

Joe's heart sank. "Has something happened to Sherry?"

Pastor Thomas's lip quivered. The answer seemed to be stuck in his throat.

The phone rang at the Wilsons'. Jennifer let it ring three times and then picked it up, wondering why no one else did.

"Hello."

"Jennifer, this is Pastor Thomas. May I speak with your dad, please?"

"I think he's out getting the paper. Would you hold for a minute?"

Jennifer got up and stuck her head out the front door. "Dad, the phone's for you. It's Pastor Thomas."

"Okay, Jen. Thanks…"

"What are you staring at?" She stepped out on the porch.

"Cars stopped along the highway. Must be a wreck or something. Did you say Pastor Thomas was on the phone?"

"Uh-huh." Jennifer handed him the cordless.

He took the phone and stepped inside. "Hello, Pastor…the water tower…? Yeah, I was just out getting the paper and noticed some cars stopped…are you serious…? Good grief! Where are Joe and Mary Beth…? This is awful…of course, we'll pray…should we come over there?"

"What is it, Dad?" Jennifer whispered.

Her father's eyes brimmed with tears. He shook his head.

"Okay, Pastor…no, I'll tell her…we'll see you at church… thanks for the call."

Jed hung up the phone and sat for a moment. He wiped his eyes.

"Dad, what is it? What's happened?" She had never seen her father so shaken.

"Jen, let's get your mother in here. We need to pray."

⌐∞⌐

Marita picked at her breakfast and then pushed away the plate. "G. R., I think we should go to church this morning."

"Oh...and why's that?"

"We need prayer support. We can't do this alone."

"If God's in control, what difference does it make what we pray? He's already decided what's going to happen. I haven't noticed He's helped one iota."

"G. R., please—"

"I'm not going to church. Go if you want."

"But—"

"Juanita!" he shouted. "I'm finished. You can clear these dishes."

"Shut me off, G. R., I'm used to it. But you can't shut God off like you do everyone who doesn't agree with you. Believe it or not, He's more powerful than you are. And you need Him!"

"No, I don't." He got up and squeezed past her.

A second later, the phone rang and G. R. picked it up.

Hello...yes, she's sitting right here...can't you just tell us what it is...? All right, I'll buzz you in." G. R. hung up the phone.

Marita's heart pounded. "What is it?"

"Jordan Ellis is sitting at the front gate. There's been a new development."

Ellen stood at a distance, holding Guy's hand, feeling as if she were a prop in someone else's nightmare.

A crowd had gathered near the water tower that marked the southern boundary of the Baxter city limits. People were crying, clinging to their children. Many seemed dazed, others outraged. Chief Cameron and Sheriff Barker's officers were keeping the crowd back while FBI agents sealed off the area with yellow crime-scene tape.

Ellen turned her eyes upward and squinted. Hanging from the

railing that encircled the tank atop the tower was a huge orange banner, flapping in the breeze.

She couldn't make out the words. But after Guy read them to her, they were forever burned into her memory.

Hear ye, Hear ye, open your ears.
It's far too soon to dry your tears.
Cruelty is the perfect way
To make G. R. Logan pay.
I'm never setting Sherry free.
She's seen my face—how can it be?
But Taylor I'll destroy for spite,
A sacrifice to make things right!

Wayne was sweeping under a booth when Mark Steele came in and sat down.

"Can you believe the way this place cleared out when Reggie told everyone about the sign on the water tower?"

"Why don't you go over there, Mark? I don't mind staying."

"No, that's okay. I don't need to see it. I got the picture."

"Yeah, I hear you," Wayne said.

"How can a person hate enough to resort to something that extreme?"

Wayne shrugged. "Maybe what seems extreme to everyone else feels like justice to someone who got the shaft."

"Hard to figure. Have you ever hated anyone, Wayne?"

"Depends on what you mean by hate."

"I don't know—wanted to see someone hurt because they ticked you off."

Wayne grinned. "Mort. But I didn't mean it."

Mark punched him on the arm. "You're bad."

"Hey, what can I say?"

FIFTEEN

S herry lay covered in darkness, the sound of Jack's breathing an ever-present reminder of her helplessness.

Somewhere outside the cage, the sound of water dripping was magnified as the hours passed. Drip...drip...drip... Sherry listened until she thought she would scream, her feet fidgeting inside the sleeping bag.

She picked up the flashlight and shined it on Taylor, but her friend didn't wake up. Sherry swirled the light, writing imaginary words across the darkness until the beam of light found Jack's glowing, eerie eyes. The Doberman responded with a deep, throaty growl.

What was that stuck in the gate? A rolled-up newspaper!

Sherry slowly rose to her feet, and then inched forward until Jack began to snarl. She sighed and turned off the flashlight, deciding to leave the newspaper there until Taylor woke up.

Sherry lay back down. Emotion rose deep within her, tightening her throat, causing her to ache. How long had it been since she had hugged her father good-bye and left the high school for

Ellison? Would she ever go home again? She was again aware of the drip...drip...drip...

She heard a swishing sound inside the other sleeping bag and quickly sat up. She snapped her fingers; and when she had Taylor's attention, she pointed the flashlight directly at the newspaper and posed a questioning look. Taylor nodded, then put her hands over her ears and closed her eyes.

Sherry darted to the gate and snatched the paper. Jack lunged at her, throwing his body on the cage with such ferocity that Sherry turned off the flashlight and huddled next to Taylor, her heart racing.

Minutes later, Jack quieted down and sat in front of the gate, then lay down and heaved a heavy sigh. Sherry slowly slid the rubber band off the newspaper. And when Jack didn't react, she turned on the flashlight.

Taylor looked at her and mouthed the words, "I hate him."

Sherry pushed the two sleeping bags together, and spread out Sunday's edition of the *Baxter Daily News*. She held the flashlight and started to read the news account of their kidnapping.

It was far worse than she imagined. What must her parents be thinking...the notes...the knives...the blood...the cat...the locks of hair...and swatches of clothing? It was all so horrible!

Taylor gasped. Sherry moved closer and read the lines Taylor was pointing to. "An eye for an eye, a lamb led to slaughter, the price of revenge, your only daughter."

Taylor fell into her arms, trying to muffle her sobs. Jack sat at attention and began to snarl and bare his teeth. Sherry wanted to throw something at him, beat on him—anything to make him go away! She wanted to go home! She wanted to get Taylor out of that dark, awful place.

Sherry held onto Taylor until they became chilled and started shaking, and then each crawled back into her sleeping bag.

Taylor lay in the dark, letting the horrible words sink in. She hated Wayne Purdy for what he was doing, not only to them, but also to her father. Why was he going to kill her? What had her father ever done to *him?*

"A lamb led to slaughter"…she blinked away the image. Tears poured down the sides of her face and into her ears, soaking her hair and forming puddles on the nylon fabric beneath her head.

She pictured her parents' faces. Did they know how much she loved them?

Sherry did what she'd seen her parents do: She prayed with all her heart. She put her life in God's hands. Eventually, a peace settled over her—a kind of peace that made no sense—and she stopped being afraid.

Hours passed. Taylor lay immobilized with dread. With no way out and no one to protect her, what hope did she have?

All of a sudden, from out of the black void, came Sherry's clear soprano voice. Taylor braced herself…but Jack didn't flinch.

Blessed assurance, Jesus is mine!
O what a foretaste of glory divine!
Heir of salvation, purchase of God,
Born of His Spirit, washed in His blood.
This is my story, this is my song,
Praising my Savior, all the day long;
This is my story, this is my song,
Praising my Savior, all the day long.

Taylor picked up the flashlight and shone it on Sherry, who knelt on the sleeping bag, her eyes closed and her hands folded.

> *Perfect submission, perfect delight,*
> *Visions of rapture now burst on my sight;*
> *Angels descending bring from above,*
> *Echoes of mercy, whispers of love.*

Taylor felt a stirring in her soul. Her heart beat wildly. The heaviness lifted…and to her astonishment, the basement was no longer dark! No light had been turned on. It just wasn't dark. Filled with wonder, she opened her mouth and began singing the chorus with Sherry:

> *This is my story, this is my song,*
> *Praising my Savior, all the day long;*
> *This is my story, this is my song,*
> *Praising my Savior, all the day long.*

Sherry's brown eyes flew open when Taylor joined in the singing. The girls looked at each another in amazement, reaching up to heaven in perfect harmony, while the docile Doberman fell asleep at the gate.

SIXTEEN

Jennifer Wilson helped her mother clear the lunch dishes from the dining room table and began loading the dishwasher.

"Jen, I can do this," Rhonda said. "Why don't you get off your feet?"

"I'm all right, Mom. It's the least I can do."

Jed walked into the kitchen. "I talked Joe and Mary Beth into staying for a while," he said softly. "I don't think they should be alone right now."

"Want me to make coffee?" Jennifer asked.

"That'd be great, honey. Thanks."

Jennifer heard her mother's sniffling and wasn't surprised when Jed took Rhonda in his arms.

"Shhh...God's still on the throne, babe. We need to be strong."

"I know. But what do we say to them?"

"It's tough," he said, his voice cracking. "I never thought I'd see the day when Bart Thomas was too torn up to give a sermon, but it was great the way Charlie Kirby took over. I guess that's the way the body of believers is supposed to work."

"I don't know if we're equipped to help Mary Beth and Joe through this."

"Yes, we are, Rhonda. Who knows them any better than we do? Or cares about them more?"

"But we haven't been Christians very long. What can we possibly say to them that they don't already know?"

"Probably nothing. Maybe they just need to be reminded of what they taught *us.*"

Jennifer turned on the coffeemaker and turned around. "For what it's worth, you're both pretty amazing. You might not think so, but I think you're helping."

The girls' singing went on for quite some time, and then seemed to wind down naturally. Darkness once again enveloped the basement.

Sherry turned on the flashlight and pointed it at Jack. She took a deep breath and squeezed Taylor's hand harder than she meant to. "This is a test," she said.

Jack once again lunged snarling at the gate.

Sherry didn't move. After he quieted down, she sat cross-legged on her sleeping bag, Taylor next to her. Sherry took her index finger and slowly formed the letter A on the cement floor, followed by W, E, S, O, M, and E.

Could she explain what had happened? Or comprehend this joy that made no sense? The sound of her stomach growling brought a smile. For once, her heart was fuller than her stomach was empty.

She looked at Taylor, reliving those moments when the mysterious light seemed to absorb the darkness as they sang. But fear had already chased the wonder from Taylor's face, and Sherry knew that not worrying about Wayne's threat would be an ongoing struggle.

༔

Marita sat and stared out the window of the library as G. R. paced. He'd been ranting for thirty minutes.

"Whoever's doing this is going to get his! He'll never get away with it! He's going to pay!"

"G. R., stop it!" Marita stood up. "I'm not interested in the kidnapper paying. I want our daughter back alive. And unless you can do something about that, I don't want to hear anymore!"

"Then leave, and take your whining with you!"

Marita left the room, and her heart sank when she heard him lock the door. She walked into the kitchen where Randy sat, his elbows on the table, his chin resting on his hands. She sat down next to him.

Neither said anything for a few minutes.

"Hard telling who Dad made angry enough to do this," Randy said. "Poor Taylor. I feel so helpless, Mom. I wish I could do something. *Anything.*"

"Think positively," she said.

"What good will *that* do?"

"It can't hurt."

"Mom, it's going to take a lot more than positive thinking to get Taylor home."

"Then pray, Randy. We can't do this by ourselves."

Marita choked back the tears. She had never felt so alone in her life.

Joe Kennsington woke to the sound of the phone ringing and remembered he was still at Jed and Rhonda's.

"Excuse me, Joe?" Jed said softly. "Chief Cameron is on the phone." He handed Joe the cordless phone.

Joe cleared the cobwebs from his head and cleared his throat. "Hello, this is Joe."

"This is Aaron Cameron. I'm sitting in my squad car outside your house. I hate to add to your burden, but the place is covered up with media."

"Already?"

"Looks like KJNX didn't waste any time, but they aren't the only ones. There are stations here I've never heard of. It's so congested, it's hard to get down the street."

"That bad?"

"I'm afraid so."

Joe rubbed his eyes and looked over at Mary Beth. "One thing my family doesn't need right now."

"Never holds back the media, Joe. They have some strange notion we have this 'right to know' anything and everything. It's a big pain, I can tell you that."

"What do you suggest?"

"How about if I come get you when you're ready and escort you home?"

The phone rang at the Joneses. Ellen picked it up at the same time Guy picked up the extension.

"Hello," they said in unison.

"It's Aaron Cameron. Are you both on the line?"

"Guy, are you still there?" Ellen asked.

"Of course I'm here. I'm *supposed* to be screening your calls." He sounded irritated.

"Look outside your front window," Aaron said. "Tell me what you see."

Ellen peeked through the plantation shutters. "I don't see anything unusual."

"Me either," Guy said.

"Good. I was hoping you wouldn't. I just had my officers escort the Kennsingtons into their house. The place is swarming with media. Looks like a carnival over there. Same at the Logans'."

"Shouldn't come as a surprise after this morning," Guy said. "This is huge. Every news team will want part of the action. It's beyond me how someone could pull a stunt like that without being seen."

"Well, our attention was diverted," Aaron said. "We were busy pulling a white BMW out of Heron Lake. But don't worry. This town's crawling with FBI and media. The kidnapper's free publicity days are over... Ellen, how are you holding up?"

"Oh, I—"

"Are you kidding?" Guy said. "She and Margie have been e-mailing and faxing information back and forth all day. I won't let her leave or she'd be right there in the thick of things."

"We have the presses running at capacity," Ellen said. "Tomorrow's issue will be a sellout. I should be down there, not sitting here like a prisoner."

"I don't want her out of my sight, Aaron. I don't want this guy getting near her again."

"He's liable to try," Aaron said. "The headlines may be the only way this creep can steal the spotlight now that the town is crawling with law enforcement. Which brings me to the main reason for my phone call. Jordan wants round-the-clock protection for Ellen. I agree with him and won't take no for an answer."

"I'm all for it," Guy said. "But good luck selling it to the lady on the extension. Now that there's a media blitz, I guarantee you she'll try to stay a step ahead of it."

"*Hello?*" Ellen said. "Would you two stop talking like I'm not on the line?"

"Ellen, you need protection," Aaron said. "I would suggest it even if Jordan hadn't."

"What would be involved?" she asked.

"Jordan would assign you a couple of FBI agents. But the only way it's going to be effective is if you agree to cooperate completely."

"I run a newspaper. I refuse to hide."

"You don't have to hide, just stand under the FBI's umbrella… Did I hear a yes?"

She sighed. "All right. But only if I can keep working."

"Great," Aaron said. "I'll tell Jordan. And both of you…keep your eyes and ears open."

Wayne sat in his pickup, observing the scene at the water tower. How many cars and trucks and vans were in the area? This was better than he ever imagined.

He got out of his truck, walked to where the crowd had gathered, and wandered around, listening.

"Hey, Wayne, wait up!" Mark Steele worked his way through the crowd and walked over next to him. "I guess curiosity finally got to you."

"Kind of hard to drive by all this without taking a look. Quite a spectacle, eh?"

"Did you see the orange banner before they took it down? That thing was huge."

"Yeah, I saw it."

"I think it's a bluff," Mark said.

"What makes you say that?"

"Who announces it to the whole world *before* they kill someone? Usually it's after the fact these people take credit for it."

"Like you have experience with *these people?*" Wayne laughed and punched Mark on the arm. "You sound like Mort."

"Thanks, Wayne. I could've gone the rest of my life without that crack."

"Oh, lighten up. You know I'm kidding. What've you heard?"

Mark shrugged. "The FBI won't say anything. But the cops think there'll be clues when the evidence is analyzed—according to what George Gentry told Reggie Mason, anyway."

"Wonder when that'll be?"

"Hard to say. I know one thing—I sure wouldn't want to be in G. R. Logan's shoes. It must be tough, knowing someone's threatening to kill his daughter and someone else's out of spite. Just look at the media down here! They'll be talking about this all over the country. What's your spin?"

"Seems pretty clear," Wayne said. "Someone's going to get even with Logan by killing his daughter. The only mystery is, *who?*"

"The FBI'll figure it out." Mark looked out into the crowd. "But probably not in time."

SEVENTEEN

Velma and Rebecca Purdy were driving back from the Ellison Mall when they heard a radio news flash about the water tower incident. They hurried home and turned on a live broadcast from KJNX-TV.

Velma shook her head. "I'm not surprised someone would have it in for G. R., but who would go to this extreme?"

Rebecca didn't take her eyes off the TV.

"Can you believe all the media around the Logans' estate?" Velma said. "I wouldn't have recognized the place."

"Mom, look! There's the sign that was hanging on the water tower."

Velma moved closer. KJNX ran a film clip shot earlier in the day, giving her a chance to read the words on the orange banner. She blinked to clear her eyes, then got up and turned off the TV. "We've seen enough."

"Poor Sherry and Taylor!" Rebecca said. "I wonder if Wayne knows what's going on." She grabbed the phone and dialed her big brother's number and waited. "I wish Wayne would get an answering machine." Rebecca hung up the phone and redialed. "Come on, Wayne. Pick up…"

"Honey, he's probably at the water tower with everyone else in town."

"You know, I don't have school tomorrow because of President's Day. Could I drive to Baxter? I know my way around. I could just hang out at Monty's until Wayne gets off, then hang out with him before he goes to work at Abernathy's. I'd really like to see him."

Velma raised her eyebrows. "And maybe see for yourself what's going on over there?"

Rebecca eyes brimmed with tears. "Mom, I went to school with Sherry Kennsington…"

"That's why I don't want you getting caught up in this."

"But I can't pretend it isn't happening."

"You have such a tender heart, Rebecca. And you have no experience with this kind of thing. It can be really upsetting to kids your age."

"Mom, I'm sixteen. I'm not a baby."

"I know. But you're *my* baby."

"Well, I haven't been there since Christmas break, and Wayne hasn't seen me drive yet. Please?"

Velma looked into her daughter's pleading eyes. "Rebecca, you've only had your license for two weeks."

"You said I'm a responsible driver."

"Yes, but highway driving is different than town driving."

"All I have to do is stay on the highway and not turn till I get there. I know the way, Mom. Please…"

Velma didn't say anything.

"So can I go?"

Velma wet her thumb and wiped away the mascara streaks under Rebecca's eyes. "Honey, when you're in Baxter, everything's going to seem real."

"Mom, it *is* real."

Velma sighed. "I suppose I could ride to work with Charlotte… I'm not all that comfortable with this, Rebecca."

"I'll be fine."

"Promise me you'll be careful, and call when you get there and again before you leave. I want you home before dark."

"I promise." Rebecca hugged her mother. "Wayne doesn't know I got my driver's license. He'll be surprised."

Velma's eyes rested on a family portrait hanging on the wall above the TV. She'd had it taken just before Roger lost his job. Such happy smiles...

While the photographer had been busy adjusting the lenses, Velma whispered in Roger's ear. "Look at your socks."

Her husband pulled up the pant legs to his only suit, staring at one black sock and one red one. "How'd I do that?"

"Daddy's going trendy, Daddy's going trendy," Rebecca chanted.

Wayne looked at Roger and shook his head. "Dad, the only thing redder than that sock is your face."

All four of them broke into laughter. The photographer captured the moment, and when the proofs came back, Velma bought the deluxe package.

Wayne was a senior then. He loved tinkering with computers and electronics of all sorts.

Rebecca was eleven, somewhere between tomboy and ballerina. Quite the chatterbox.

Those two kids were more than she'd ever bargained for.

"Velma," Dr. Ross had said. "I asked your husband in here because I have something important to tell you...you're pregnant!"

"I'm *what?*"

A toothy grin widened between the doctor's bushy mustache and beard. He put one hand on her shoulder and shook Roger's hand with the other.

"But *you* said—"

"Forget what *I* said. I'm just a lowly doctor, humbled again by the Great Physician."

Velma turned to Roger, who threw his arms around her.

Six months later Wayne was born—and seven years later, Rebecca. Wayne was protective of his little sister. The baby couldn't squawk without Wayne letting Velma know.

"Mom, Rebecca's crying."

"She's all right, Wayne. I put her down for a nap."

"But how can she sleep if she's crying?"

"She'll fall asleep. Just give her a couple of minutes."

When things got quiet, Velma went in to check on Rebecca, surprised to see Wayne sitting in the rocker, humming a lullaby, Rebecca curled up on his shoulder.

"She just needed a hug, Mom. She's asleep now…"

Velma smiled. Wayne still had a way with Rebecca.

She got up and cleared the Sunday paper off the couch, and glanced again at the portrait on the wall. The older Wayne got, the more he looked like Roger—stocky frame, receding hairline, dark eyes.

Those eyes…where had the sparkle gone? A part of Wayne had died with his father, and Velma feared he would never amount to anything.

Wayne hurried in the front door, dropped the newspaper on the couch, and picked up the picture of his father.

"I did it, Dad! You should've seen their faces! After what I hung on the water tower, everyone knows G. R. Logan's gonna pay. It was beautiful. You'd be proud of me!" Wayne felt a twinge as he looked at his father's face. "I want him to be as miserable as we were…"

Wayne had come home from school and had heard his mother crying. He stood outside his parents' bedroom, eavesdropping.

"Roger, you've got thirty years' experience. That has to count for something. Don't give up. Someone will hire you."

"To do what, Velma? The textile business is all I know. I'm too old to start over. I see the look in their eyes every time I put in an application… I don't want their pity. I just want a job."

His father's despair seeped into Wayne's soul. He wanted it to be all right. But it wasn't.

When the utilities were turned off, his mother went looking for work even though she had no skills to fall back on. When she couldn't find anything, the stress was too much for his father.

"Mom, something's wrong with Dad!" Wayne shouted. "He won't wake up!"

His mother rushed to the recliner, and knelt beside it. She picked up Roger's hand and held it to her cheek. "Roger…talk to me…say something…Roger!" She felt for a pulse. But even before Wayne dialed 911, Roger was gone.

The doctors said he died of an aneurysm. Wayne blamed Mr. Logan. After that, life got even harder.

"Mom…I took a job. *Full* time."

"No, you can't quit school, Wayne. I won't let you."

"Just until we get on our feet. You can go to cosmetology school."

She turned his face toward her. "You need to finish high school, Wayne. Then go on to college. You have a chance to be somebody."

"Dad would want me to help for now. What kind of a son would I be if I expected you to do it all? I don't want the stress to kill you, too."

His mother passed the state exam and was licensed in cosmetology, but her new career never got off the ground, and there was never enough money. Wayne continued working to help out. When his great-aunt passed away, his mom inherited a nice home in Ellison—a sizeable town with lots of beauty salons.

"It's a good job, Wayne. I'll finally be able to support us."

"That's great, Mom. I'm happy for you." Wayne sat at the kitchen table, staring at his hands.

"What is it, son?"

"Nothing."

His mother sat beside him, and put her hand on his. "You're not coming with us, are you?"

The silence seemed to last forever.

"Mom, I'll help you and Beck as long as you need me to. But I can't leave Baxter. This is the one place I feel close to Dad."

Her eyes brimmed with tears.

"You're certainly old enough to be on your own. I'm not wild about selling the house anyway. It wouldn't bring much, but your happiness means more to me than the money…"

Wayne blinked to clear his eyes. He put down the picture of his father and flopped on the couch. He stared at the ceiling, aching for what *had been*.

The move to Ellison was a good one for his mom and sister. Wayne made regular visits. And Beck stayed in Baxter with him during Christmas and spring breaks, and off and on during the summers.

But his mother had never come back. How could she just wipe out the past? He promised himself he never would. Never!

EIGHTEEN

Monday morning's stack of the *Daily News* had sold out even before Rosie poured the first round of coffee. Wayne held up the jar of quarters and smiled at Mark Steele, then went over and stood beside him.

"The news is hot this morning," Wayne said.

Mort Clary sat at the end of the counter, absorbed in the front page.

"He's hardly said a word," Mark said. "I've never seen Mort serious. Don't tell me there's a heart in there somewhere?"

George Gentry leaned in his direction. "I wouldn't go that far."

"I hear ya whisperin' over there," Mort said. "Can't a fella be in a quiet mood without ever'body makin' a federal case outta it?"

"Of course, you can." Hattie Gentry lowered her voice. "Behave yourself, George. Everyone's fragile."

"So how come you're in a quiet mood?" George leaned his elbows on the counter and looked down the row at Mort.

Mort's face and neck turned red. "Whaddya think? This here stuff on the front page!"

"Yeah, it has us all a little speechless." George took Hattie's hand in his. "Can't help but wonder about those girls."

Mort sighed. "I was rememberin' back when Taylor was born. I was workin' for her granddaddy back then. Never saw such celebratin' in all my life. Them Logans like ta never let up."

George nodded. "She was the first girl in several generations."

"I didn't know nothin' about that, Georgie. But I remember the first time G. R. brung that little doll down to the plant and showed her off. First time I ever knew the man cared about somebody besides hisself."

Probably the last time, Wayne thought.

"I remember that. I was there!" Rosie said. "One of those Kodak moments. He worshiped that little girl."

Mort nodded. "Acted like a different fella. Now I ain't sayin' G. R. wasn't a stinker, downright ruthless when he closed the plant. But killin' the guy's daughter… Well, he ain't bad enough to deserve *that.*"

"What's gotten into you?" Mark said. "Just last week you were neggin' G. R. Logan, saying he was a real bum."

"I stir up lotsa stuff. Don't mean nothin'. But this ain't no laughin' matter."

The phone rang at the Kennsingtons'. Joe hurried to pick it up.

"Hello."

"It's Jordan. Sorry to bother you so early."

"No problem. Time is relative these days."

"Did you see the morning paper?"

"I haven't read it yet. It was hard enough seeing a picture of the water tower on the front page."

"Yeah, I'm sure. My agents tell me the media onslaught at your place is at the crisis point. How are you and Mary Beth holding up?"

"We're praying. It's completely out of our hands."

"Well, one thing that *is* in our hands is providing protection for your family. Frankly, I'm glad there're no classes today, and I suggest you keep the kids out of school and stay home until this is over."

There was a long pause. "Jordan, please don't take this wrong, but we're not going to hide out. I think whoever has Sherry and Taylor already knows what we're doing. We've decided to go about our lives the best we can."

"I'd rather you wouldn't."

"I know. Listen...we appreciate the FBI's protection. But my family belongs to God. I don't know if you understand how deep that goes, but nothing can touch us that doesn't first touch His nail-scarred hands. He has a plan. And ultimately, He's in control. Obviously, we need to be sensible. But we don't have to walk around terrified to move.

"We had a family meeting, and we're all in agreement on this. After today, the kids and I are going back to school. I think it'll help the community to see us out there. They're hurting, too."

"You amaze me," Jordan said. "Where do you people get the strength to hang on?"

Joe put his arm around Mary Beth, who'd been beside him listening to the conversation.

"Oddly enough, Jordan, the strength doesn't come by hanging on, but by *letting go.*"

Jordan tapped his fingers on the desk. "Come on...pick up."

"This is Agent McCullum."

"It's Jordan. How are things over there?"

"Solemn as Columbine—with one glaring exception."

"Logan's still in a snit?"

"That would be a *yes.*"

"Adam, guys like Logan go nuts being held hostage by an unseen enemy they can't fight. I relate to that."

"Then maybe you can reason with him."

"Just hold things together," Jordan said. "I've got a team working around the clock, contacting everyone who got cut in the plant closure. Family members, too. It's going to take some time to contact each individual, assuming we can find them all.

"We're also checking out the management team at Logan Textile Industries and rival companies, trying to sift out enemies. Whoever this is has been in the area for at least two or three days. We're checking motels and bed-and-breakfasts throughout the county. We're also questioning out-of-towners staying with local residents. At this point, Adam, everyone's a suspect."

"You think it's someone who lives here?"

"Maybe. We'll have a better feel for it when we hear what the profilers have to say… What's it look like outside?"

"Oh, the media's already got its heels dug in. Can hardly see the road in either direction once you're outside the front gate. Same ol' madness."

"Okay, McCullum. Try to stay off Logan's toes. I'll check back later."

Jordan Ellis sat with his feet on his desk, his hands clasped behind his head. There was a knock on the door, and he assumed a more professional posture.

"Come in."

Sheriff Hal Barker and Chief Aaron Cameron entered the room and shook hands with him.

"Glad you could make it," Jordan said. "Just pull up a chair. There's coffee over there if you want it."

"None for me," Aaron said. "I'll be content to sit without a phone in my ear."

Hal poured himself a cup and sat down. "Looks like you're the one who needs a shot of caffeine, Jordan. Rough morning?"

"They'll all be rough, Sheriff, till we get those girls back alive."

"Think we will?" Aaron asked.

"I *always* think we will." Jordan got up and walked around, his hands in his pockets. "I asked you to come over here so I can give you our profilers' perspective on the kidnapper."

"Let's hear it," Hal said.

Jordan unfolded a piece of paper and started reading. "This type of individual is male, probably working alone. Harbors a longtime grudge against someone more powerful, who took something away from him, resulting in his feeling insignificant and out of control.

"His close attention to detail is part of a carefully choreographed drama, which is moving toward a day of reckoning. But first he'll maintain possession of the thing most valuable to the target of his revenge, until his flaunting of it ceases to have the desired effect."

"Meaning what?" Hal asked.

"In a nutshell, messing with Logan's mind is more satisfying to him than killing the girls, which means we may still have a window."

Marita watched G. R. pace like a caged animal until she thought she would scream.

"Will you sit down! You're wearing a hole in the rug!" she said.

"Who do they think they are, telling me what I can or can't say?"

"Dad, the FBI advised us not to talk to the media." Randy put another log on the fire. "Don't take it personal."

"I'll tell you what I take personal: the FBI sitting on their duffs. Why are these people hanging around my house instead of out finding my daughter?"

"*Our* daughter," Marita said. "And there are agents all over the area doing what they're trained to do. Jordan Ellis has experience in this, G. R. We don't. It's important we let him lead. It's our best chance to get Taylor back."

Randy closed the fireplace screen and stood up. "Mom's right. The FBI wants to get Taylor back almost as much as we do. They're the good guys, remember?"

"Good for *what?* Do you see Taylor anywhere? We're wasting time. Trust me, your old man knows how to get results. Throw out a reward and you'll be amazed at the people who'll suddenly know something. There's absolutely nothing people won't do for money."

You should know, Marita thought.

"Dad, if the guy wanted money, he would demand a ransom."

"So he doesn't care about money. Someone out there does, and might be willing to tell what they know for a reward. What've we got to lose? Beats wearing a hole in the carpet while some no-name from my past plays games with Taylor's life." G. R.'s lower lip quivered. He sat down. After fidgeting for a minute, he jumped up and headed toward the front door.

Marita sighed. "What are you doing, G. R.? The media is stacked up from here to town. You can't go anywhere."

"I don't need to go anywhere." He opened the coat closet and grabbed his leather jacket. "Come on, Randy, it's time the Logans took the bull by the horns."

"G. R., tell me you're not doing what I think you're doing!" Marita said.

She gave Randy a please-try-to-stop-him look as her son slipped on his London Fog and followed his father out the front door.

Marita peeked through the beveled glass and saw them walking briskly down one side of the circle drive toward the front gate. She grabbed her coat and hurried after them.

"G. R. don't do this," she pleaded.

"Why not? The media's camped outside my gate as far as the eye can see. If the FBI can't get results, I *will.*"

"Randy, reason with him."

"Dad, we've been advised against doing this."

"Both of you listen. I'm a businessman and this is a free country. Somewhere out there in the midst of the tired, the poor, and the huddled masses yearning to breathe free, there's a snitch waiting for a cash incentive to tell what he knows. I'm about to make it worth his time."

Marita heard footsteps pounding the ground and saw Agent McCullum run past her until he was at G. R.'s side.

"Mr. Logan, where are you going?" he asked.

"Where does it look like I'm going?"

Agent McCullum dropped back and was immediately on his cell phone.

Marita continued walking behind G. R. and Randy, looking beyond them to the swarm of reporters standing outside the front gate.

When they reached the gate, they were hit with a barrage of flashing cameras and a flood of questions. G. R. keyed in the combination, waited until the gate opened, then raised his hand, signaling reporters to quiet down.

"I have something to say."

Mikes were shoved in his face, and TV cameras started to roll.

Marita's pulse raced. *Please don't do this, G. R.!*

Randy stepped in front of his father, his back to the mikes, and spoke quietly. "Dad, why not let me handle this? You said yourself it's what I do best. You don't come across well under pressure."

"Son, I'm going to say what's on my mind. Don't fight me."

"Dad, this feels wrong. Let's think it through."

"This maniac is running my life. Do you know how that makes *me* feel? Now step aside."

Randy stepped aside. He dabbed the perspiration from his upper lip and looked despairingly at Marita.

G. R. spoke without hesitation. "I'll pay fifty thousand dollars to any person who gives information leading to the arrest of the low-life scum who has my daughter. Nobody, and I mean *nobody*, takes on G. R. Logan without a fight. I won't stop until—"

Agent McCullum walked in front of G. R., keeping his back to the cameras. Marita strained to hear what he said.

"Mr. Logan, the call you've been waiting for is holding at the house. Let's go." McCullum turned around. "This press conference is over."

G. R. turned and rushed toward the house, Agent McCullum at his side.

FBI agents also escorted Marita and Randy up the circle drive, and as they approached the house, she heard shouting inside. They reached the front door and entered the foyer, where Agent McCullum and G. R. were having a confrontation.

"How dare you trick me," shouted G. R. "I'll have your job!"

Marita looked quizzically at one of the agents.

"There was no phone call, ma'am."

"Mr. Logan, you were doing more harm than good," McCullum said. "I realize you're emotional right now, but outbursts like that play right into the kidnapper's hands. You have to trust us if you're to stand any chance of getting your daughter back alive."

"You haven't made one move to get her back," G. R. shouted. "Yet you have the gall to come into my home and *censor* me?"

Marita wanted to put a cork in his mouth.

"All we asked you to do, sir, is avoid talking to the media."

"How can I do that when some maniac is running my life, making me look completely powerless in front of the entire country—"

"With all due respect, Mr. Logan, our concern is for the safety of your *daughter.*"

"And mine isn't? Is that what you're implying?"

"Look, I'm sure you care very much for your daughter, but this isn't the time to go public. Anything you say—"

"Well, *I* have something to say." Helen Logan's voice resounded with such authority that all eyes turned to where she stood in the doorway of the library. She struggled across the threshold, lugging something two-thirds her size.

Helen gave her son a piercing look Marita would never forget.

The matriarch of the Logan dynasty gripped the sides of a framed oil portrait of Taylor. She raised it as high as her strength would allow, her feeble arms trembling under its weight. Her usually soft voice was strong and commanding.

"G. R., which is more important: saving your precious daughter or saving your precious ego?"

Marita stood with the others, paralyzed by a profound silence far more intimidating than the earlier shouting.

G. R. merely hung his head and charged up the winding staircase.

NINETEEN

Ellen Jones sat at her desk, holding a hand mirror in front of her face, while Margie put a stack of articles on her desk.

"Ellen, what *are* you doing?" Margie asked.

"Practicing my smile. It's getting harder to manage one."

"Oh, will you stop your pouting. It's not the end of the world that you've got FBI agents watching out for you. Besides, that Jeff Barnett is adorable."

The phone rang.

"Might want to put a smile in your *voice*," Margie said, backing out the door.

"Hello, this is Ellen."

"This is Mayor Kirby. How are you doing after the events of the weekend?"

"Let's just say about the only division of law enforcement not riding herd on me is the coast guard."

"Well, things *are* escalating."

"That's an understatement."

"The out-of-town media driving you nuts?"

Ellen looked out her window. "They're driving everyone nuts. It's chaos."

"I've decided to speak out before this thing gets any crazier," Charlie said. "Get out there and make a statement directly to the community. People are outraged. I've got seven kids of my own, and I can't imagine what these two families are going through..." His voice cracked. "It's a horror story. Every parent's worst fear."

"When and where?" she asked.

There was a long pause.

"Charlie?"

"Okay, Ellen. Herein lies the rub: Your *favorite* TV station has agreed to cover it live this afternoon on the town square. Lots of folks are off for Presidents' Day, so the timing seems right. I know how you loathe the electronic media, but this is one time when I need the news out there instantly. KJNX will carry it live and then run it again tonight. That way, even if only a handful of people show up, everyone will have the opportunity to view it."

"What about the other networks?" she said.

"My hope is that they're so wrapped up elsewhere, we can pull this off with little media fanfare."

"Charlie, why are you calling me?"

"I want you there. Granted, you can't get it in print as quickly, but you always get it *right.*"

"This wouldn't be your way of appeasing me since you're about to sell out to those electronic gods from KJNX?"

"Ellen, you know me better than that. Cut me a little slack. This is one time I need to use them. Besides, how can they misrepresent me if all I do is give my statement? I don't plan to answer any questions. I know they lie like a rug."

Ellen smiled. "Good answer. What time?"

"They'll be ready to roll at 2:30."

∽∘∾

Ellen instructed FBI Special Agent Jeff Barnett to turn into the student parking lot of Baxter High School and park near the sidewalk.

"Okay, Mrs. Jones. Now what?"

"I'm going to walk around to the front of the building and see what's going on."

"I'd advise you to reconsider," Barnett said.

"There's a story here. I can't ignore it." Ellen pulled the handle on the door just as Agent Sam Zimmer opened it for her.

"No problem," Zimmer said. "Barnett and I will be a few yards behind you. You won't know we're there."

Ellen got out of the car. She bunched a scarf up around her neck and began walking into the wind toward the front of the high school.

She looked out across the front lawn, where scores of teenagers wandered under a covering of bare trees. Some exchanged hugs. Others stood crying. Another group held hands in a prayer circle around the flagpole.

Wide yellow ribbons were tied around the trunks of two huge oak trees on either side of the front steps. Though their loose ends were flapping in the wind, she could make out the name "Sherry" on one and "Taylor" on the other.

A mound of flowers, cards, and candles had been placed beneath both trees, whose outstretched branches had welcomed every student who ever walked up the front steps of Baxter High School.

Her eye was drawn to the outdoor Christmas angels someone had arranged beneath the trees. She wondered if angels really existed. Did *God*? Ellen didn't think so, yet she wanted to believe someone was watching over Sherry and Taylor.

She closed her eyes and drank in the hope of these students— every last drop she could hold.

Ellen felt a hand on her shoulder. She opened her eyes and looked into the drawn face of Father Donaghan.

"Tragic," he said softly, shaking his head from side to side.

They stood in silence, absorbing the gravity of the situation.

"Thank God you're all right, Ellen. I've been praying for you."

"You're kind, Father. I'm sure you're praying even harder for the girls."

He squeezed her hand, and then walked slowly toward the flagpole.

Ellen was aware of Barnett and Zimmer standing behind her.

"Relax," she said. "He's the priest from St. Anthony's."

"So we gathered." Barnett looked around in all directions. "Are you about ready to get out of the open?"

"I need a few more minutes."

Ellen strolled a short distance down the sidewalk, then turned and faced the school. Her ivy-covered alma mater presented a nostalgic backdrop to this tragic scene. A flood of memories rushed over her. The basic insecurities that churn deep in the hearts of teenagers hadn't changed much in thirty-plus years. But the world around them was vastly different.

Kids were forced to look at the dark side of life almost before they had a chance to play in the sunshine. Was there no place left where parents could shelter their children from violence? If this evil could happen in Baxter, it could happen anywhere.

Ellen's heart was full of things to say, but no feature story could be written while the fate of the girls was unknown. For now, she would simply report the news.

She blinked to clear her eyes, then looked over at Agents Barnett and Zimmer and gave a slight nod. The three of them walked back to the van in silence.

The phone was ringing at the Kennsingtons'.

"Not again!" Mary Beth groaned. "Joe, I don't want to talk to anyone."

Hello, you've reached the Kennsingtons'. We can't come to the phone right now. Please leave a—"Hello, this is Joe."

"Oh, you're home…it's Aaron Cameron. Don't worry. I'm not calling with bad news."

"That's a relief."

"Have you or Mary Beth been by the high school this morning?"

"No. It's a holiday."

"I know. But you ought to see the kids down there. They've created quite a show of support. You might want take a look before it gets saturated with media. It's a pretty moving sight. When I left, there was a prayer circle forming around the flagpole. Jordan's agents can take you down in the van, so no one has to know you're there. You decide. I just thought you should know."

"Thanks. I'll see if Mary Beth wants to go along."

"Might be a little emotional, Joe. It's quite an outpouring."

"Whatever the students have done, I'm sure it came from the heart. It'll bless us, even if it hurts."

"I admire your courage."

"You've got to be kidding," Joe said. "If I stopped to think about what's happening, I'd fall apart."

"You sound calm."

"Only because I let go and decided to trust the Lord. Feels like I'm dangling in midair with Him holding my wrists. At least I know He's got me."

Marita Logan sat in the window seat in Taylor's room. For a split second she thought she felt Oliver rub up against her, and reached down to pet him.

"Mrs. Logan?" An FBI agent stood in the doorway. "No cause for alarm. The telephone's for you. It's the police chief. Do you want to take it in here?"

"This is Taylor's private line. I'll take it in the library."

She hurried down the winding staircase and into the library. She sat down and picked up the phone.

"Hello," she said, sounding out of breath.

"Mrs. Logan, it's Aaron Cameron. I apologize if I'm bothering you, but I understand your husband isn't taking phone calls."

"He's under a lot of stress. He already lost it once this morn..." Marita's voiced cracked with emotion. "I'm sorry...we're all about to break."

"I can only imagine what you must be going through. I called to tell you there's an impressive show of support going on at the high school. There's a whole crowd of kids down there, praying and standing with you. Parents, too."

"That's so good to hear," she said. "We're isolated over here."

"If you'd like to see it, Agent McCullum can sneak you in and out without anyone knowing. But once the media gets wind of it, you won't be able to get close to the high school."

"I may go. G. R. won't, I'm sure. He's upset with the public school system. He's convinced that if Taylor had enrolled at Jane Lindsay Reynolds, this never would have happened. It's easier than taking some of the blame himself."

"Blame? No one had a clue this was coming. It's nobody's fault."

"Oh, come on, it's not like G. R. can just wash his hands of..." Marita paused. Maybe she should bite her tongue.

"Mrs. Logan?"

"Look, Chief, my husband isn't responsible for what happened to Taylor, but I'll lay you odds he's responsible for whatever happened to the kidnapper."

"Mrs. Logan, I don't see—"

"He steps on people. Rolls right over them, and keeps going. Did he really think it would never catch up with him? And now it's about to destroy what we both love most!"

"It's not a good time to analyze, Mrs. Logan. Nothing makes sense right now."

"You're too kind. I realize it would be unprofessional of you to agree with me. But I think any person who keeps stepping on someone else until the bitterness is oozing out of him is just asking to get some of it back."

"It all boils down to choice. Every person chooses his own response to whatever comes his way. Being a victim is no excuse to victimize. Maybe that's the cop in me, but that's what I think."

"Well, I think you don't know G. R. very well."

Aaron sighed. "Look, I called to let you know what's happening at the high school. If I can be of help, feel free to call me. My wife and I have your family in our prayers."

"Thank you. You know G. R. isn't speaking to God. Until now, that's probably the *only* person he isn't speaking to."

Jordan Ellis dialed the number of the FBI lab and asked for John Richards. He tapped his fingers on the arm of his chair. Why was everyone moving in slow motion?

"Agent Ellis...what a surprise," John said.

"Have you gone over the samples?"

"Most of them. The locks of hair, the shoes, and the clothing swatches definitely belong to the girls. We know the blood is feline. The angle of the knife blade in the cat, the block of wood, and the sign on the guardhouse suggest we're dealing with a right-hander but there's not much here, Jordan. The knives were clean. The notes were clean—even printed on plain white bond, with standard black ink from an inkjet printer. The posterboard and permanent marker used on the sign found at the plant can be bought at any office supply store. Even the stencil shapes used on the lettering are a dime a dozen. Nothing incriminating on any of it. A trail with no tale."

"Real funny, John. I'm in stitches."

"Actually, we did find something that could be significant—

strands of black hair in the note to that newspaper woman, on the cat, and dried in the ink on the posterboard. Maybe our perp is thinning."

Jordan sighed. "It'd be nice if this Yule Brenner-to-be had a criminal record so we could get a DNA match and maybe know who we're looking for."

"I'm working on the banner samples. You'll be the first to know if we get something."

Jordan hung up the phone and leaned back in his chair, his feet on his desk. He'd handled a lot of cases for a guy forty-one. The outcome was often lousy, the details sometimes grisly, and the perps usually worthless. Plus, the victims' families didn't always cooperate.

Still…there was something he liked about cracking the mind of a criminal—something about outsmarting the wise guys and taking back control from someone who'd misused it.

He looked out the window of the temporary FBI headquarters on the second floor of the county courthouse. Between the trees, he could see the water tower in the distance on the edge of town.

Somewhere out there, the perp was enjoying the show. Jordan wanted to fast-forward this horror flick and stomp on the tape. He hated guys who hurt kids. He hated bitterness and revenge and how it destroyed victims. He'd seen it so many times—the victims now victimizing. It was such a vicious cycle.

He studied the photographs of Sherry and Taylor, gazing for a long time into their innocent eyes, then blinked away gruesome images from previous cases.

Jordan got up and paced in front of the window, his hands in his pockets. *God, I haven't talked to You for a while. If You're listening, it's okay with me if You run this show.*

He figured if Joe Kennsington could let go and feel stronger, maybe it wouldn't hurt him to try it.

TWENTY

Rebecca Purdy walked into Monty's Diner and sat at the end of the counter.

Mark Steele waltzed over with a big smile on his face. "Rebecca! I didn't know you were in town."

She put a finger to her lips. "It's a surprise. Where's Wayne?"

"In the storeroom, unpacking boxes. Stay put. I'll go get him."

"Okay, but don't tell him I'm here."

Rosie Harris came over and gave her a hug. "I thought that was you. Cute coat, kiddo. You look good in red."

"Thanks, it was my Christmas present from Wayne."

"Wish I had more time to talk," Rosie said. "Can you believe how busy it is? I think you got the last seat in the house." Rosie worked her way down the counter, pouring coffee refills.

Rebecca smiled at the man sitting next to her, then picked up the menu and pretended to read it. When she heard the sound of Mark's voice, she turned and looked up.

"There at the end of the counter, Wayne…a lady's here to see you."

Rebecca sat straight-faced, waiting for her brother's reaction.

"Beck? How'd *you* get here?"

"I drove." She held up the keys, a grin spanning her face.

"You got your license?"

"You don't seem glad."

"Oh, no. I'm—I'm—thrilled. Just surprised, that's all."

"Shocked is more like it." Mark laughed. "You should see your face."

"Mom let me drive over since there's no school today," Rebecca said. "I tried calling, but never got an answer."

"When'd you call?"

"Yesterday afternoon—about ten times. Where were you?"

"At the water tower, with half the people in town. Didn't you and Mom hear about what's going on?"

"Yes, and it's horrible. I stopped at the water tower on the way into town. Gave me goosebumps."

"Yeah, you and everybody else, "Mark said.

"So, why are you here, Beck? You know I have to work."

"Stop looking so serious," she said. "I came to take you for a drive before you go to Abernathy's. How come it's so busy?"

"All those media people have to eat somewhere."

Mark nodded. "Yep. And we're positioned at the top of the food chain. I need to get back to work. Nice seeing you, *hot rod.*"

Rebecca giggled. "Same here."

"Beck, stick around till my shift's over," Wayne said. "I'll buy your lunch while you wait."

"Okay, yum! I'll have a cheeseburger, onion rings, and a Coke."

"You *have* to try Leo's cherry pie. It's even better than Mom's." Wayne scribbled the order and put it on the clip. "Okay, I've gotta get back to work." He started to walk away, and then turned around. "So, you're gonna hang around here, not at the house, right?"

"Uh-huh. I just came to show off." She rattled the keys.

He smiled. "So don't leave without me."

⌒∞⌒

Wayne kept an eye on Rebecca. She had eaten lunch, read the newspaper, and thumbed through several fashion catalogs that Rosie dug out. Then she'd had a second helping of cherry pie. At the moment she sat at the counter, using a straw to push ice around in her Coke glass. He glanced up at the clock. *Another fifteen minutes.*

The door to the diner opened, and Sheriff Barker walked in and sat at the counter next to Rebecca.

"Well, if it isn't little Miss Purdy." He gave her long blond hair a playful tug. "Where'd the pigtails go?"

"Oh, please...I'm sixteen."

"*Sixteen?* That means I'm older than I thought!"

"I've got my driver's license now. I drove here by myself."

"Well, that's a milestone. Come to see Wayne?"

"Uh-huh. I'm gonna take him for a ride after he gets off."

"You and your mom following the kidnapping story?"

Rebecca nodded. "I went to school with Sherry Kennsington. We're the same age. It's awful."

"Yeah, it is."

"My mom almost wouldn't let me come today. Thought it'd make me too sad."

"Did it?" Hal asked.

"Kind of. And scared."

Wayne picked up his plastic tub and began busing dishes, making sure he stayed within earshot.

"Gobs of people were mad at Mr. Logan after the plant closed," Rebecca said. "My mom and dad sure were. But who could do something this horrible? Taylor and Sherry didn't even hurt anybody. It's not fair."

Didn't Mom ever tell you life isn't fair? Wayne piled the dishes into the plastic tub and moved to the next booth.

"It's not even rational," Hal said. "Bitterness on this scale will keep eating the guy up, no matter how it ends. It'll never be over."

Well, Sheriff, aren't you the know-it-all? Wayne glanced up and saw Rebecca looking his way. He forced a smile.

"Are you gonna be ready to leave at 2:00?" She pointed to her watch.

"Oh, sure. I'm almost done."

"You two have big plans?" Hal asked.

"I'm taking my brother for a spin."

Wayne grimaced. "Help! I'm going to die. Someone save me."

"No, you're not. I'm a good driver. Ask Mom."

"Easy for her to say. I'm the one who has to get in the car with you!"

"Well, try to stay out of the media's way," Hal said. "Even us seasoned drivers are doing that."

"Oh, Wa-ayne…" Rebecca dangled the keys, her eyes full of mischief. "I'll be outside warming up the car."

"Well, it's been nice knowing you, Sheriff." He winked at Hal. "Let me clock out, Beck. I'll be right with you."

Wayne walked through the door to the back room, leaned against the wall, and exhaled. He loosened his collar, then took off his glasses and massaged his temples. *Stay cool. She'll be out of the way in another hour.*

Ellen stood facing the courthouse, avoiding eye contact with Monica McRae, anchorwoman for KJNX.

"So what's your beef with KJNX?" Agent Barnett asked.

"It's a long story."

"We're all ears," Zimmer said.

"Eyes, too, I hope. There are more people here than I thought there would be."

"How old is the courthouse?"

"A century old," she said. "Isn't it magnificent?"

"Well, Mrs. Jones, is that actually *warmth* I hear in your voice?" Barnett stood with his arms folded, the corners of his mouth turned up.

Ellen felt the color flood her face. She stood back and admired the Baxter icon with its reddish stone walls and white rounded pillars, and the grounds around it, which made up City Park. "I love this town. It has charm."

"Not to mention a maniac on the loose," Barnett added.

Her eyes looked across the red-brick street and wandered down a row of quaint shops set off by colorful awnings that overhung the sidewalk.

"Is that Monty's Diner way down there?" Zimmer asked. "Isn't that where we got take-out the other night?"

"Yeah," Barnett said. "But Jordan says we need to *dine in* and get a load of the locals. Some really colorful types." He nudged Zimmer with his elbow.

"While you two city slickers amuse yourselves, I'm going to find a place to sit."

She walked across the brown lawn of City Park to several rows of white folding chairs in front of the courthouse. She found an empty chair on the end.

Mayor Charlie Kirby, wearing a dark suit and red tie, slid out of Aaron Cameron's squad car and was escorted to the podium. He had two tiny yellow ribbons pinned to his lapel.

Ellen turned on her recorder while the mayor got situated and the news crew from KJNX got into place. Charlie bowed his head for a few moments. A hush fell over the gathering. He began to speak.

"My dear friends, it is with heavy hearts that we gather today in City Park. Every citizen of Baxter feels at home on these grounds.

This is where we come together to play, to push baby carriages, to walk dogs, to enjoy reading, or to catch up on each other's news. It's part of our community neighborhood. It's always been a safe and happy haven for all.

"Now two of our children are missing—Taylor Logan and Sherry Kennsington. We have waited and watched and prayed for their safe return. God has surely heard our prayers, and we must trust Him to answer.

"I came here to talk about what's been going through my mind, and perhaps through yours, too. I kept asking myself, What kind of monster would take a personal grudge this far—hurt innocent kids to get back at someone else? What kind of bitterness is capable of producing such unconscionable behavior? But then came a stark realization: There's only *one* kind of bitterness. It starts as a tiny seed. And how big it grows is entirely an individual choice.

"The Bible instructs us in the book of Hebrews, chapter 12, verse 15: 'See to it that no one misses the grace of God and that no bitter root grows up to cause trouble and defile many.'

"Regardless of your religious beliefs, I think we can all agree that painful, unresolved issues in our lives leave us wide open to all sorts of interpersonal problems.

"Bitterness is a double-edged sword, as destructive to those wielding it as it is to the people they hurt. And it doesn't just stop...it must *be* stopped. Like so many other things, it requires a conscious choice.

"We are a close community. There is a family spirit in Baxter unlike any place I have ever been. But even we could not avoid reaping what was sown here.

"These innocent girls were taken from their parents out of spite because a grudge grew out of control in someone's heart. My challenge to the community, as we continue to watch and wait and pray, is to examine *ourselves*.

"Are we harboring anything against a neighbor? A spouse? A family member? An employer? If so, will *we* choose to forgive—whether it's fair or not? Will we let go of it so we don't become part of the problem?

"And if we are hurting someone else, will we choose to stop, before our insensitive behavior sows seeds of bitterness?

"Two young daughters, two families, a whole community, and the entire nation are enmeshed in this sad, horrible drama as a result of one basic evil: *bitterness.*

"My friends, the challenge facing us today is to rid ourselves, individually and collectively, of unresolved anger. Whoever kidnapped these girls had a choice. We all do.

"Life involves hard things. How we respond to those difficult things will make the difference in what we become. And what we become is what we bring to this community.

"Baxter is one of a kind. It's always been a peaceful place to live and raise a family. Surely none of us were aware that this destructive force was growing in our midst until it was acted out.

"Please, for your sake, for your children's sake, and for the sake of our wonderful town, don't be part of the problem. Forgiving and letting go of anger, as difficult as it is, will be far easier than facing the consequences.

"Let us cleanse ourselves of this so we never again have to see a neighbor face this kind of devastation.

"And to the Kennsingtons and the Logans...we stand with you and will not rest until this nightmare has ended. God help us all."

As Charlie left the podium, the entire gathering rose to its feet in applause.

Ellen stood at the window, mesmerized by snowflakes that seemed almost suspended in air. What would it feel like to be so free? Margie's voice startled her.

"Ellen, Mayor Kirby's on the phone."

"Thanks, Margie." Ellen sat down and picked up the receiver. "Hello, Charlie."

"Well? What did you think?"

"That was some address. I wasn't expecting anything quite so…"

"To the point?"

"More like a bull's-eye," Ellen said. "You know I'm not religious, but you gave me some food for thought."

"I'll take that as a compliment. Goodness, my adrenaline's pumping like I'm back in seminary. Ever since this thing started, I've wanted to tell the community what's on my heart. I couldn't hold it in."

"I keep wondering why you're not pastoring."

"You mean I'm not?" Charlie laughed. "I don't have a pulpit, and I leave out the hallelujahs, but I take every chance I get to share God's Word."

"Well, it was a persuasive address."

"Thanks. The true test is whether or not people respond to the challenge."

"Charlie…what's going to happen if these girls show up dead?"

He sighed. "It'll break us, Ellen. The very thought makes me shudder. But you know what scares me almost as much? Realizing the number of people still angry with G. R. Logan. Aaron said even Logan's wife went off. Doesn't sound like she has much respect for him, either."

"Have you seen the way he treats her?" Ellen said. "I can imagine how bad it was with employees."

"The problem may be deeper than we realize."

"What do you mean?"

"Look, Ellen, I don't know anyone who isn't outraged that this kidnapper could hurt a child. Make no mistake about that. But I saw how people here suffered when the plant closed. I've listened to their grievances. I've seen families torn apart, lifestyles dramatically altered, hardships endured long after it closed. Trust me, there are those who relate, albeit unconsciously, to the guy's grudge. Though they don't want the girls to get hurt, on some level they're deriving personal satisfaction from seeing G. R. Logan turned into a victim."

"Charlie, they can't do anything about how they *feel*."

There was a long pause.

"As long as they believe that, Ellen, it's never going to change."

TWENTY-ONE

Y ou've got your driving down pat, Beck. I'm impressed. I haven't been scared once."

"So I'm doing okay?"

"Better than okay. Great."

"Thanks. I practiced a whole lot." She glanced at her watch. "Uh-oh, it's already twenty till. Guess I better drive you back so you can get to Abernathy's."

"Just pull over and make a U-turn."

Rebecca slowed the car and pulled onto the shoulder. She looked both ways, then made a U-turn and headed back to Baxter.

"Beck, you're going straight home, aren't you?"

"Uh-huh. Mom wants me back before dark. I need to call her before I leave, though."

"Let's stop at the pay phone at the Texaco on First."

"It's long distance…"

"I've got all the quarters you need. Let Mom know you're on your way—and then roll on down the highway."

"I'm glad tonight is Bible study. I can't wait to tell my friends I got to drive to Baxter by myself."

"You and Mom still involved at that church?"

"Wayne, don't start...I like church. You oughta try it."

"I don't believe in God. All that faith stuff's a crutch, Beck. One of these days you'll wise up."

"Or *you* will."

"Look, if it works for you and Mom, fine. Just don't try to turn it around like I'm the one who's lost. Which reminds me, don't miss your turnoff."

Rebecca pulled into the parking space next to Wayne's truck.

"It's gonna feel weird driving home instead of having you drive me."

"Tell me about it."

She paused. "Seems like I'm forgetting something."

"Just a hug." He put his arms around her. "I'm glad you came. I always enjoy spending time with you."

She kissed his cheek. "Thanks for lunch. And the quarters." Wayne got out of the car and opened the door to his truck.

Rebecca rolled down the window. "Maybe Mom'll let me do this again soon. It was fun."

"Yeah, it was. You're a good driver, Beck. I'm really proud of you."

Rebecca backed out of the parking space, her heart warmed by Wayne's approval. She drove down Holmes and around the square, then stopped for a red light at First. Her eyes followed a teenage boy who got out of a car and walked into Music Mania. *That's what I forgot! I knew there was something.*

Wayne parked in the alley behind Abernathy's Hardware Store and walked in the delivery door.

"Right on time." Lou Abernathy tossed him a piece of butterscotch. "Ready to go to work?"

"Rarin' to go, sir."

"You look mighty chipper."

"Just spent an hour with my kid sister. She got her driver's license and drove the car over to surprise me. Did real well."

"She that old already? Mercy!"

Wayne raised his eyebrows. "Now if I can just survive the boyfriends…"

"You two are close, aren't you?"

"Yeah, it's always been that way, more so since Dad died."

"Well, I'll say one thing: The girl couldn't ask for a better father figure. You're much like your dad, Wayne."

"Thanks, Mr. Abernathy. That means a lot, coming from you. Well, where to?"

"The paint department. A contractor called a while ago needing several custom formulas for a rush job."

Rebecca turned onto CR 211 and set the cruise control at 55 mph. A few minutes later, she pulled to the end of the long gravel driveway and shut off the motor. She sat for a moment, her eyes fixed on the house she grew up in. Good thing her mom hadn't seen it this way—paint peeling, gutters rusted and overflowing with leaves.

Rebecca remembered helping her dad and Wayne paint the house gray and the shutters white. She could almost smell the turpentine as she sat there.

Where was Jack? He always popped up in the front window when he heard a car. Maybe Wayne chained him out back.

Rebecca got out of the car, savoring the smell of wood burning in someone's fireplace.

She put her hand in the flower box and felt around until she found the key, then unlocked the door and pushed it with her shoulder several times until it opened.

"Jack? Here, boy…" She whistled. "Jack, where are you?"

The old piano caught her eye, and she sat on the bench and slowly ran her fingers over the keys, remembering when she used to sit on her dad's lap and watch his hands make beautiful sounds. Why hadn't she ever learned to play? Rebecca extended her two index fingers and played a couple of rounds of "Chopsticks." Unexpected emotion clouded her eyes.

She stood up and walked into the kitchen.

"Yuck!" The linoleum was dingy and sticky. Dirty dishes were piled in the sink. The trash can was overflowing and smelled sour.

Why weren't Jack's dishes on the floor? Rebecca unlocked the back door and stuck her head outside. Where was he?

She walked down the hall to her old bedroom, pulled out a CD from the top drawer of the dresser, then hurried down the hall past Wayne's room.

Wait a minute!

She backed up and stood in the doorway. What was all that on the wall above Wayne's computer?

She went over to take a closer look and was surprised to see a dozen newspaper clippings about G. R. Logan closing the plant and sending jobs to Costa Rica. Her dad's obituary and the "In Memoriam" leaflet from the funeral home were tacked next to pay stubs from jobs Wayne had worked. And what was this? A newspaper clipping listing the names of his high school graduation class—with a big black X through it. Why did Wayne want this stuff?

Rebecca started to feel guilty for snooping in her brother's room. She turned to leave, when she spotted a huge display on the wall by the door.

"What the…?" She went over and stood in front of it.

Arranged in a circle were photographs, telephoto shots, of Taylor Logan and Sherry Kennsington. Thumbtacked to the wall outside the circle were dozens of newspaper clippings about the kidnapping, taken from the *Baxter Daily News*, the *Ellison Gazette*, and the *Myerson Tribune*.

Rebecca's eyes froze on the center of the circle. From a long knife stuck in the wall dangled a bungee cord with two mismatched girls' shoes.

Rebecca sped toward Ellison. There had to be an explanation. He couldn't have made those awful threats—no way. It wasn't true…couldn't be true…she wouldn't let it be true.

Wayne had given her piggyback rides and taught her to ride a bike. He was the one who always came to her make-believe tea parties and pretended to enjoy her first awful batch of cookies.

He didn't laugh when she had a crush on her fourth-grade teacher. Wayne helped her with her homework, read to her, took her to the library.

He let her stay with him during school breaks. He rented movies, took her shopping, gave her spending money. Wayne was proud of her. He loved her. He could never hurt anyone.

Rebecca heard a siren and glanced in her rearview mirror. Her heart sank. A police car was behind her, lights flashing.

She took her foot off the accelerator and coasted, prepared to pull over. The police car whizzed by her so fast that a surge of wind shook the car.

"Rebecca…? Honey, are you awake?"

Rebecca lay there with her eyes closed.

"Honey…?" Her mother turned on the light.

"Oh…Mom…I must've fallen asleep." Rebecca sat up and rubbed her eyes.

"When did you get home? I've been really worried. You didn't answer the phone."

"Sorry. I don't feel good. My stomach's upset."

"Hmm…you don't seem to have a fever," Velma said, the back of her hand on Rebecca's forehead. "I guess you won't be going to Bible study tonight. Would you like some chicken noodle soup?"

"I just wanna sleep."

"You sounded so excited when you called. I can't imagine what could've hit you that quickly."

Rebecca couldn't have imagined it either. If only she hadn't gone to Baxter.

TWENTY-TWO

The girls were awakened by the sound of footsteps coming down the stairs. Jack whimpered, his stubby tail wagging, his ears at attention.

Sherry jumped up and pulled Taylor to the back of the cage just as the bright light rounded the corner and moved toward them.

"Jack! How's man's best friend?" Wayne stroked and patted the Doberman's sleek black coat. Jack began yapping, running in circles, and jumping in the air.

"I see my other pets aren't as wild about me. Look at them hunkered back there, not at all interested in a three-dog night." He laughed. "Stand up!" Wayne unlocked the gate and went inside.

Sherry felt Taylor trembling. She thought her own heart would pound out of her chest.

"The house was unlocked when I got home." He moved closer until his face was less than an arm's length away. "Somebody was here. I wanna know *who!*"

Sherry looked over at Jack and clutched Taylor tightly.

"You nervous with the gate open?" Wayne snickered and turned to Jack. "Silence!" He turned back around. "Now, tell me what you know…or would you rather I have Jack pull it out of you?"

Taylor began to cry.

"One time we heard footsteps," Sherry said. "And a piano, I think." She looked at Jack. He gave a low, rolling growl.

"Jack, silence!" Wayne said. "Go on, what else?"

"Uh, it sounded like someone running and then a door slammed. Jack was all excited, so we thought it was you; but when you didn't come down, we figured you left." Sherry felt herself shaking.

"When? What time?" he asked. Jack began to snarl. This time Wayne ignored him and glared at Sherry. "Well?"

"W-w-we don't know what time. It happened a long time after you brought us something to eat last time."

Wayne moved closer and got right in their faces. Sherry's heart pounded so loudly she thought he could hear it.

"If I find out you lied to me, I'll feed you to Jack." He stepped back and dropped two lunch sacks on the floor. "Enjoy today's special. Oh—you'll wanna read *this*." He tossed Sherry a rolled-up newspaper. "What can I say? I have a way with words." He laughed, and was still laughing when he left the cage and locked the gate. "Better read it while you can."

When Wayne went up the stairs, Sherry laid out the front page of Monday's paper, and she and Taylor read the words from the banner that had hung on the water tower.

The girls fell into each other's arms and cried until they were wet with tears and began to shiver. Each crawled into her sleeping bag.

Velma heard the phone ring. She tucked the covers around Rebecca and went into the living room to answer.

"Hello?"

"Hi, Mom. It's Wayne. Just calling to make sure Rebecca got home okay."

"She did. She's sick, though. I can't imagine what happened between 3:00 and now to knock the wind out of her. She was in bed when I got home… Wayne? Are you there?"

"Yeah. Did she say what was wrong?"

"Just that her stomach hurt."

"You think it's the flu?"

"It's probably some kind of bug. I suspect she'll be better tomorrow."

While Sherry and Taylor slept on the basement floor, light encircled them and wings overshadowed them. The Word was whispered into the dark silence.

Sherry sat up, her heart racing. Was someone there? She turned on the flashlight and spotted Jack lying in front of the gate. She lay down again, her eyes wide open. What was this peace that seemed to have its arms around her? She yielded gladly to its amazing strength.

Sherry felt Monday's newspaper in a heap next to her. She accepted that she was going to die and would soon be with her Savior. But how could she keep her mind on Him and not dwell on how death would come? Lying there hour after hour made it almost impossible to think about anything else.

During the moments when she was able to surrender her fear, she worried that Taylor was going to die without having accepted Jesus.

Sherry wanted to talk to her about it, but Jack was always there. She sighed. Why hadn't she talked to Taylor a long time ago instead of thinking she'd do it "one of these days"?

She wondered what made Wayne hate G. R. Logan enough to decide to kill Taylor and her. How did that kind of hate happen? How could anyone get so far off track?

She thought about the notes and the knives and Oliver and the words at the plant and on the water tower. How could he think any of that was funny? Her anger burned until she could hardly hold it in, and she almost blurted out, *I hate him!*

The words raged in her head, and she felt ashamed. Soon she would die and meet Jesus face-to-face. How could she look into His eyes feeling like this?

Sherry lay there a long time. *Lord, forgive me. I know I shouldn't hate him. I don't wanna hate him.* Tears stung her eyes.

She remembered something Pastor Thomas had said: Seeking shelter in the shadow of the Almighty didn't always mean hiding behind Him or beneath His wings; sometimes it meant walking close enough to stay in His shadow.

Sherry stared blindly into the blackness that encased her. What if she saw this darkness as God's shadow and chose to stay next to Him? Would it change the way she felt? *Lord, I need to know You're here with me. I can't do this by myself. I don't wanna feel dark on the inside.*

Her heart started to pound, and pound harder. She lay perfectly still, holding her breath. A few verses of Psalm 63 ran through her mind…and then poured out in a beautiful melody unlike any she'd heard before. Sherry sang with her whole being, energized by the truth of the words.

> *On my bed I remember you;*
> *I think of you through the watches of the night.*
> *Because you are my help,*
> *I sing in the shadow of your wings.*

Taylor awakened to the sound of Sherry's singing. She took in every word, memorizing what she heard, until she felt her despair melting. God had not abandoned them! She began to weep.

She wiped her eyes with her sleeve and sat up, surrounded by light, and looked at the face of Sherry Kennsington. Taylor had always admired her friend's stubborn strength, but for the first time she longed to understand its source.

Jordan Ellis paced the floor early Tuesday morning. He picked up his cell phone and dialed.

"FBI lab."

"This is Ellis. Who's this?"

"John Richards, who else?"

"Didn't sound like you. You're there early."

"Early? Try *late*, Jordan. I've been here all night, trying to pull this evidence together."

"Got anything?"

"Fingerprints on the banner that don't match anything on file. Could be his. Or whoever sold the guy the nylon tarp. Hard telling where he got it. Could've mail-ordered it or bought it at a sporting goods store.

"We found multiple strands of black hair dried in the black paint used on the banner. They match the others. We can place him with the dead cat, with the blond hair in the note to the editor lady, and now at the water tower. It's the same guy."

"But?"

John sighed. "But we don't have a DNA match. Nothing on file. Sorry."

"No big surprise," Jordan said. "This is no career criminal. This guy worked for G. R. Logan. I can smell it. We're working around the clock, putting together lists and contacting former employees and business associates, trying to sift out enemies. We'll contact everyone on the lists, and we'll put each of them under a microscope."

"And I thought *my* job was hard. At least evidence can't lie. Getting the truth out of people's a whole nother ballgame."

"Yeah, and you'll notice we're not batting a thousand."

"So he's thrown a few curves. It's not over yet."

"Let's try to keep it from going into extra innings, John."

"That's why I'm still here."

"Yeah, I know. Thanks. Burning the midnight oil's a killer, but I really appreciate the effort."

"By the way," John said. "What do you think about this Mayor Kirby? What he had to say wasn't exactly politically correct."

"I can tell you one thing, his finger was pointed right at me. I've known G. R. Logan only since Friday, and *already* I hate him." Jordan chuckled.

"In one ear and out the other."

"It wasn't completely wasted on me. I decided to hate Logan just until this case is solved. Seriously, John, if people took his advice, this world would be a better place. Then again, I'd be out of a job."

"Nah, Jordan, you're like a bad penny. You'd show up somewhere else."

"Think so, eh? Listen, I need to go. I'm due in a meeting with the team that'll be at the high school when classes resume today. Could be a mess over there. Let me know if you find anything else."

"Yeah, I will."

The basement was filled with light when Sherry's singing came to an end. The girls looked at each other, wide-eyed.

"Sherry, the words to that song—it's like they were written for me! How did you know that's what I needed?"

"I didn't! I'd been praying about how to handle things better. Then some Bible verses came to me, and I had this melody in my mind. The song just came out!"

"You didn't know what you were going to sing?"

"No. I didn't think about it at all. It was so cool." Sherry looked at Jack, and then at Taylor. "No Jack attack either. Just look at him. He's sound asleep."

"I love all this light! How does that happen?"

"Listen," Sherry said. "I have to ask you something I should've asked you a long time ago."

"What?"

"Do you know where you're gonna be...if we...don't get out of here alive? I'm sorry to be so blunt, but it's important."

"I guess I'll be in heaven... I hope so, anyway."

"You're not sure?"

"How can we be sure until we get there? Why are you talking about this? It's creepy."

"Taylor, have you ever, like, been to the foot of the cross? I mean have you ever realized that Jesus died for *you,* that He didn't just take the whole youth group as a package deal? Because it doesn't work that way. Each of us has to choose Him as our Savior and accept His forgiveness for the things we've done wrong. Have you ever done that?" Sherry noticed that the light in the basement was starting to fade.

There was a long pause. Taylor lifted her eyebrows. "Are you asking me if I'm saved?"

"Yes! That's exactly what I'm asking."

"I guess so. I'm not sure what I'm supposed to be saved from. But since I go to church and try to do what's right, I just assumed I was."

"There shouldn't be any doubt, since it's a deliberate decision to let Jesus have your heart. Have you ever done that?"

Taylor shook her head. "Maybe I would if I understood."

"It's not hard. Just realize you're a sinner and confess to God the things you've done wrong. Then ask Jesus to forgive you and come into your heart. Pretty simple, really. You learn as you go. The really cool thing is after a while you won't even wanna do things that are wrong, and He'll help you change so that, more and more, you act like Him, and—"

"Is that what's happened to you, Sherry? Because you act more like Him than anyone I know."

Sherry felt her face get hot. "I'd like to act like Jesus, but most of the time I don't."

"I think you do."

"Well, if I do, it's because He's living in me. That's what I meant by changing us from the inside—"

Jack lunged at them with such ferocity that Sherry jumped back. She clutched Taylor's arm, her heart hammering, her eyes closed. "Ask God to show you. He will."

Joe Kennsington sat in his office, his arms resting on the desk. He was lost in a photograph taken on field day last May...

"Dad, over here!" Sherry's giggling echoed across the football field.

Joe threw a long pass right into his daughter's waiting hands. She took off down the field, evading students and teachers who tried to snatch the flag from her waistband. Sherry ran all the way for the winning touchdown, and two varsity football players placed her on their shoulders and paraded her around the field...

"Joe?" Mrs. Willington leaned on the open door. "May I come in?"

"Uh, sure. I didn't see you standing there."

She walked over and wrapped her arms around him. "I'm not going to ask how you are." Her gray eyes penetrated his defenses.

"You always know." He looked down. "I meant to call. I knew you'd be worried."

"I was, but I didn't expect a call... Are you ready to talk to the students this morning?"

"It's not going to be an easy message."

"I know. I know you better than my own son. I can almost read your mind."

"So what am I going to tell them?"

"I'd say you're going to challenge them. Probably to do something that goes against reason." Mrs. Willington's eyes filled with tears; her lower lip quivered. Joe had never seen her look so fragile.

"Tell them what's on your heart, Joe. But if you ask what I think you're going to...I'm not sure I can—"

There was a knock at the door. Joe looked up and saw Charlie Kirby, Pastor Thomas, and Jed Wilson.

"I hope we're not interrupting," Pastor Thomas said. "We promised we'd come at 7:00 to pray before the assembly."

"No, come in. Mrs. Willington was just...encouraging me to say what's on my heart. And since I value her opinion, I need to get prayed up before going out there."

The bell rang at 7:55, summoning students to the weekly assembly. FBI agents positioned themselves as inconspicuously as possible while students streamed into the auditorium.

Joe Kennsington walked up the steps to the stage, his knees wobbly, and stood for a moment off to the side. He wasn't sure how he would get through this, but he knew he would.

Joe looked out at a sea of faces and spotted Erica sitting in the third row, her friends gathered around her. He made eye contact. Her pretty face looked drained, but she acknowledged him with a slight nod.

When the 8:00 bell rang, Principal Kennsington stepped in front of the mike. He took a sip of water.

"I'm glad we're meeting this morning because I have some things I'd really like to say. You know about the terrible events that happened over the weekend. My family and I have appreciated the support from citizens in this community." His eyes moved from student to student. "But *nothing* has meant any more to me than what you put under those yellow ribbons outside, because I know the sentiments came from deep inside..." Joe paused and took a slow, deep breath.

"This student body is an extended family for me. The unique experience of having my two daughters here has made it even more so. Today is…very difficult. Having Sherry taken from us…has been a pain unlike—" Joe stopped and swallowed the emotion, wondering if he was going to lose it—"unlike any that I could ever have imagined. But looking into your faces this morning, I know this has been difficult for you, too.

"I don't know what's going to happen. My family has put the situation in God's capable hands. But I do know this: When bad things happen to good people, the Lord is not absent. He just sees a bigger plan. I believe that. I've tried to live my life that way, but I've never been tested to my limit until now. No matter what the outcome, my faith and trust in God will not fail. I know He loves Sherry and Taylor more than anyone else could. He has a plan, a purpose, in all of this.

"Students, there's one thing I ask of you: Don't let this make you cynical. Pray for whoever's responsible! It's difficult to hate someone you pray for.

"We can't turn back the clock and bring Sherry and Taylor home. That's up to God. But each of us can choose, right here and now, not to let unforgiveness wreck our lives. Will you join with me and leave your anger at the door when you walk out of here?

"For Taylor, for Sherry…" Joe's lower lip quivered, his hands shook. "For *all* of us…be strong. Real strength comes through forgiveness, never through anger."

The students rose and applauded, their feet stomping the bleachers. Mrs. Willington nodded with approval, a tear trickling down her cheek.

Joe felt himself trembling. Every part of him wanted to embrace the anger, but the Lord who resided in his heart had taught him differently.

TWENTY-THREE

Wayne bent down, slit open a box, pulled out jumbo-sized plastic jars of ketchup, mustard, and pickles, and stacked them on the shelves in the storage room.

"How's it coming?" Mark Steele put a hand on his shoulder.

"One more box."

"You're missing all the fun," Mark said. "Mort's on a roll, butting heads with George and Hattie over what the mayor said. As usual, his mouth's way ahead of his brain. So how was your ride with *Hot Rod?*"

"Great. Beck surprised me how good a driver she is."

"You're awfully quiet this morning. Seem kinda subdued."

"Now that's a big word." He forced a smile. "Busy's more like it."

"If you don't wanna miss Mort in full form, hurry up with that box."

"Okay, I'll be right out."

Wayne clenched his jaw. Could the morning drag any more slowly? He'd hardly slept last night, wrestling with what to do. It had to have been Beck who was in the house, or he'd have been arrested by now. But why'd she go out there? How much did she see? He looked at his watch and sighed. She wouldn't be home from school before he started his shift at Abernathy's.

Wayne picked up the last box and dropped it on the floor. He'd planned too long and played too well to lose now. Not even Beck was going to get in his way.

And what was with Charlie Kirby's statement? Wayne didn't want forgiveness. He wanted outrage! He took the box cutter and stabbed the cardboard, then slit the tape across the top of the box and yanked open the flaps.

Things were getting too risky. Maybe it was time to get rid of the girls.

Rebecca Purdy heard footsteps moving toward her bedroom.

"Honey, I'm leaving for work now," Velma said. "Take it easy today. See if you can shake this bug."

"Okay, Mom."

The front door closed and Rebecca heard her mother drive off. She lay for a long time, counting the tiles on the ceiling. She watched a spider inch its way down the molding and then disappear.

How could she confront Wayne about what she had seen? Her eyes filled with tears, and she hugged her pillow.

It was probably all a misunderstanding. Her brother didn't even have a temper.

Ellen Jones sat at her desk, warming her hands with a cup of coffee and studying the icicles outside her window. She caught a glimpse of someone standing in the doorway.

"A penny for your thoughts," Margie said.

Ellen half smiled. "That should about cover the value."

"Why so pensive?"

Ellen folded the newspaper and looked at Margie. "Truth be told? Charlie's address. I've never really considered what bitterness does. Charlie thinks we should examine ourselves to see if we're part of the problem."

"Ellen, you don't have a bitter bone in your body."

"What about the long-standing wall between my dad and me—the one we mutually constructed when I pursued journalism against his wishes?"

"Your dad's against women in any workplace. If he had his way, we'd all stay barefoot and pregnant, standing by our men, never using our brains."

Ellen traced the rim of her cup with her index finger. "Thirty years and the wall's still there. But *he* won't be much longer."

"This is really bothering you."

"You know, he's never said one positive thing about my marriage, or that Guy and I raised Owen and Brandon to be the fine young men they are."

"Because you didn't do it *his* way?"

Ellen nodded. "Probably. Dad held fast that I should 'give up all that foolishness at the newspaper' and stay home."

"Guy never put a lid on all that talent, Ellen. And you've been a wonderful wife and mother."

"You know what hurts the most, Margie? Even after the accolades I received for my feature stories during the McConnell investigation, Dad never said a word. Not *one* word." Ellen's eyes burned with tears. "Why is his approval even important to me?"

"He's your father."

"I know. Charlie's words made me uncomfortable, but I don't see how letting go of my right to be angry at my dad would do one thing to improve the community—or me, for that matter. The wall is the only thing protecting me from my father's cutting remarks."

"So the wall stays."

Ellen sighed. "For now, at least. I need to think about it."

❧

Jennifer Wilson sat reading the mayor's statement on the front page of Tuesday's newspaper. Why should she get rid of all the anger she felt for her dad and Dennis and every other male on the planet? They were all alike! Men had always disappointed her, rejected her. She had a right to be mad.

Jennifer laid the newspaper at the end of the kitchen table and pushed her chair back.

"Good morning," Jed said.

"Oh…Dad."

"Why so grim?"

"Just tired, that's all."

"Want me to make you breakfast?"

"No, I'll get it later."

"I wouldn't mind," he said. "It'd give me a chance to pamper you a little. How about some granola and strawberries for you and that growing grandchild of mine?"

"Dad, I'm not hungry."

"I thought the nausea was gone."

"I can take care of myself, all right?"

"Sorry, honey, I didn't mean to upset you. I just thought you might like—"

Rhonda walked into the kitchen, her eyes half open. "Lead me to the coffee."

Jed gave her a hug, then turned her around and pointed her toward the coffee, giving her a gentle push.

"So, Jen, what's the latest on the kidnapping?" Jed asked.

"The mayor wants everyone to get rid of unresolved anger." Jennifer rolled her eyes. "That's his answer to all our problems."

"Not a bad starting point."

"It's not that easy," Jennifer said. "Besides, who can let go of stuff just like that?"

"Probably no one, without a struggle," Rhonda said. "But once we make the choice, God can work wonders. Look at your dad and me."

Jennifer bit her lip.

"That's how things changed for us," Jed said. "We unloaded all the baggage and gave it to God. What a difference."

"For *you*, maybe. That's not necessarily the answer for everyone." Jennifer got up and walked to the sink. She poured herself a glass of water.

"If there's a better answer, I've yet to hear it," Jed said. "Too bad it took me twenty-eight years to figure it out."

"No kidding," she mumbled.

Rhonda looked at Jed and shrugged. "What's this about, Jen?"

"What's *what* about?"

"Something's bugging you."

There was an uncomfortable pause.

"What is it, honey?" Jed said. "You can tell us."

"I don't know. I just don't like someone who thinks they have it all together telling everyone else what *they* need to do."

"Charlie doesn't pretend to have it all together," Rhonda said. "He's struggling to come to grips with the kidnapping, just like the rest of us."

"I'm not talking about Charlie..."

Jed pulled out a chair. "Jen, come sit down. Don't you think it's time we talked?"

She stood at the sink, staring at her father.

"Jen?"

She hung her head. "I can't. I'm just not ready."

Margie walked into Ellen's office, her arms full of mail.

"Here you go, lady. All this is yours." Margie laid a huge bundle of mail on Ellen's desk. "Is there anything else you need before I go to lunch? I'm going home and walk that stubborn old poodle of mine. Poor thing. Can't hardly get her out the door anymore."

"No, I'm fine. I'll work on the mail," Ellen said.

"I'll be back before you dig through it all. If you get lonesome, talk to that cute agent-what's-his-name out there." Margie winked.

Ellen smiled. "I thought you were leaving…"

"I'm gone."

After Margie left, Ellen made three stacks: things to do immediately, things to do later, and things to do someday if she found the time. Her eye was drawn to an envelope marked "Personal and Confidential." She carefully slit it open with her letter opener and removed the letter. She began to unfold it when two locks of hair fell out—one blond, the other brown. Ellen's heart pounded wildly. She read the words:

> **I admit I felt a sense of power**
> **When my words hung on the water tower,**
> **And I'll strike again if I'm ignored,**
> **Or if things get quiet and I feel bored.**
> **You remember what they say:**
> **Idle hands make devil's play.**
> **You never know what I might do,**
> **Or when I plan to waste the two.**
> **I'm out of sight, not out of mind,**
> **Lest G. R. think that I'm benign.**
> **Report my news, details and such.**
> **And rest assured, I'll be in touch!**

"Jeeeeeeff!"

Agent Barnett flung open the door and rushed into her office, his gun already out of the holster. "What's wrong?"

"I got another of his disgusting rhymes." Ellen sat frozen, her throat tight, her breathing shallow.

Agent Barnett put his gun back in the holster and walked around to her side of the desk. He slipped on surgical gloves. "May I take a look?"

Ellen nodded and pushed her chair back.

Agent Barnett picked up the note and read it.

"Look at the postmark," Ellen said. "Saturday. The only pickup on Saturday is at 3:00 P.M. That means he mailed it *before* he left me the first one on Saturday night."

Jeff Barnett took his cell phone from his pocket and dialed.

"Sir, our perp is back. He sent another rhyming note to Ellen Jones with two more locks of the girls' hair... Sure, let me read it..."

Ellen listened as Agent Barnett read the rhyme and relayed what she told him about the postmark. It made her skin crawl, hearing the words read out loud.

Barnett put his cell phone back in his pocket and turned to her.

"I need to bag the evidence." He put the envelope, the note, and the locks of hair into clear bags, then sealed and labeled them. "The boss thinks it would be wise for you to work at home today. Might feel a lot safer."

Ellen twirled her pencil like a baton. "No."

"No?"

"I'm not caving in to this guy. I'll do whatever I have to do until we find the girls, but I'll *not* be a victim. I refuse to live in fear. Now if you'll excuse me, Agent Barnett, I have work to do."

Jordan Ellis dialed Ellen's direct line, his fingers tapping the desk.

"Hello."

"This is Jordan Ellis. I don't want you playing into the perp's hands. We can't allow him to manipulate you."

"I don't plan to be manipulated," she said flatly. "I'll report the news. Period. So he doesn't want to be ignored...I wouldn't have ignored him anyway."

"You're not thinking of printing this?"

"Let him live with the illusion he's calling the shots. If he perceives he's in control and that I'm his only link to getting his story told, he'll continue to contact me. And since I have FBI protection, I feel better about letting him speak out than wondering what he's up to."

"It's not a good idea."

"The guy's a showman, Jordan. He thrives on attention. The more coverage I give him, the more time you have to find the girls."

"It's possible he's already killed them."

"My instincts tell me he hasn't," she said. "He's still flaunting the fact that he's in possession of G. R.'s daughter. That fits his profile. He's enjoying the control."

"Listen, do *you* want to be controlled, Ellen? Because that's what's happening here."

"No, it's not. I'm not giving him an inch. Let him think he's manipulating. He might make a mistake that will break this case wide open."

"I don't know..."

"Look, Jordan, I know you're concerned for my safety. So am I! What've we got to lose at this point? He intends to kill them. If he hasn't, we might have some time. If he has...well, I'm going with the hope that he hasn't."

Jordan changed the phone to his other ear. "Ellen, this isn't the time to get stubborn. Do you realize how touchy this is? There's no guarantee that anything you do will keep him from harming those girls. If you make him mad and something happens to them, you're gonna get a heap of guilt you don't deserve. Can you handle that?"

"I know I can't handle what's happening to the Kennsingtons, the Logans, and everyone else who cares about those kids. I think I'm more scared when he's quiet. As long as he's communicating, there's a chance the girls are alive."

"Do you realize what you're getting yourself into? Don't you want to discuss it with your husband first?"

"Guy may not like it, but he'd be surprised if I did anything else."

"I don't like the way this feels." Jordan sighed. "But truthfully, we *could* be asking for it if we walk out in the middle of this perp's performance."

"That's how I'm looking at it. And with FBI spread all over town, the newspaper might be the only stage he has left."

"I'm uneasy about involving you personally."

"Well, that's two of us. But like it or not, he's already involved me."

"Ellen, let's have a meeting with your staff so we all understand and agree on the rules. I don't want this guy getting close to any of them. I'm going to beef up security."

"Okay. I'll get something set up for this afternoon."

"Yeah. Fine. Let me know when." Jordan hung up the phone. He got up from his desk and paced, then stopped at the window, his eyes looking out beyond City Park to the water tower. *Where are you hiding those girls, you miserable...?*

Jordan leaned against his desk, unwrapped a stick of gum, and put it in his mouth. He crushed the wrapper in his fist and squeezed until his knuckles turned white. If he didn't catch this guy soon, there could be three dead bodies instead of two.

TWENTY-FOUR

On Tuesday afternoon, Rebecca Purdy awoke to the sound of the doorbell. She got up and looked out her bedroom window. Two men in dark suits stood on the front porch. They rang the bell again and waited, and then knocked a few times. She hid behind the curtain and watched as they left something in the door.

When the men pulled away, Rebecca went to investigate. She slid open the chain lock and cracked the door. Two business cards fell on the porch. She reached down and picked them up. *Special Agent Henry Black...Special Agent Carl Matthews...FBI!*

Had Wayne been arrested? Was she in trouble for withholding what she knew? She decided to hide the business cards in the drawer of her nightstand. But how long would it be before they came back? If her mother found out, it would break her heart!

She went into the bathroom and sat on the side of the tub, her head in her hands, a sheen of cold sweat on her face. Feeling dizzy, she lay down on the tile floor, aware only of the room getting fuzzier and fuzzier.

⌒⌒

Wayne's rusty old truck barreled down CR 211. He looked at his watch. He still had forty-five minutes before he had to be at Abernathy's.

He turned into the gravel drive, pulled to the end, and shut off the motor. He banged his palms on the steering wheel. Why did Beck have to stick her nose in this?

Wayne flung open the door to the truck and hurried to the front door. He unlocked it and headed for the basement.

Rebecca came to, her clothes soaked with sweat. She pulled herself up off the floor and slowly walked to her room, keeping a hand on the wall for balance. She lay down on the bed and hugged her pillow.

God, please help me. What should I do?

A fear unlike any she had ever known gripped her. What if telling what she saw caused Wayne to stop loving her?

Rebecca felt a flood of sorrow wash over her. Wasn't there another way? She buried her face in her pillow and sobbed.

Sherry lay in her sleeping bag, thinking about the song and the wonderful light. God felt so near. She was starting to wonder what heaven would be like when Jack sat up and whimpered.

She heard footsteps moving quickly across the floor and running down the steps. The beam of light was almost to the gate.

Wayne propped the big flashlight against the fence so the light would illuminate the cage.

Jack yelped and jumped and ran in circles.

"Not now, Jack. *Sit!*" He unlocked the gate. "You two, stand up."

Sherry and Taylor stood up and held onto one another. Sherry sensed something different about him. His voice sounded angry.

Wayne left the gate open and moved closer. He flicked one of Taylor's blond curls. "It's too late for Daddy to do anything to save his little Goldilocks from the big bad wolf."

He turned to Sherry, a hand over his heart. "Just think...a double funeral will get Principal Kennsington to declare a school holiday. But then you won't get to enjoy it. Don't you hate it when that happens?" He laughed in her face.

Sherry was ready to die. The words burned in her heart. Was she brave enough to say them? "I'm not gonna hate you, Wayne."

Jack lunged at the gate, growling and snarling.

"Silence!" Wayne said. He smirked, his voice imitating Sherry's. "'I'm not gonna hate you, Wayne...' Ha! Like you have a choice."

"I do," she said calmly. "I'm not gonna hate you."

"Of course you are! I've turned you into a helpless victim."

"No, you haven't."

"Then I *will!*" He lowered his head until he was nose-to-nose with Sherry.

She didn't flinch. "I'll only be a victim if I hate you. And I'm not gonna hate you."

He slapped her hard across the face. "I'm gonna kill you, smart mouth!"

Sherry closed her eyes, but stood defiantly. "Wayne, killing me is your choice. Not hating you is mine."

Wayne began shouting expletives and threats. "I can make you do anything I tell you to do! For once, *I'm* in control. It's *my* turn to call the shots! Believe me, you *will* hate me!"

Sherry could feel his breath on her face, and she just wanted it to be over with. She kept her eyes closed and prayed.

To her surprise, Wayne shoved her aside. "I didn't wait this long to do it like this!"

Sherry opened her eyes and saw him rush out of the cage, slam the gate shut, and secure the padlock. He shone the light on his watch, then in her face.

"Let's just see how long it takes you to hate me, Miss Smart Mouth. Don't expect anything to eat until I get good and ready to bring it. If I bring it at all." He yanked the plug on the space heater and looked back at Sherry with a spiteful grin. "Oops."

He laughed all the way up the stairs and slammed the door behind him.

Sherry traced the sound of his footsteps across the floor and out the front door. After a minute, only the sound of Taylor's sniffling disturbed the silence.

Sherry turned on the flashlight and was met with Taylor's desperate, questioning look. Her heart ached.

Taylor got down and crawled inside her sleeping bag. Sherry did the same, wondering just how cold it would get.

TWENTY-FIVE

Rebecca Purdy heard a car door slam. A few seconds later, the front door opened. She turned on her side and pulled the covers up around her neck.

"Rebecca…are you awake?" Velma said.

"Just dozing."

"How do you feel?"

"Yucky."

"Sorry, honey." Velma stroked Rebecca's long hair. "I thought for sure you'd feel better by now. Let me fix you some chicken noodle soup. That should help settle your stomach."

"My stomach feels gross."

"By the way, two men from the FBI came by the salon today. They're investigating the kidnapping and interviewing everyone who lost their job in the plant closing—*and* their families. They want to talk to us. I already told them to come by tonight at seven."

"Mom, I don't feel like talking to anyone."

"I know. You can stay in your room. I'll talk to them, and they can get with you another time if they want."

"What could I tell them? I was a little kid when Dad worked at the plant."

"I told them that, but they don't want to leave any stone unturned. They said it's just routine. Sounds fascinating to me."

"Will they talk to Wayne?"

"I'm sure they will. Look, honey, it's already 6:00. Let me change my clothes and get your soup."

Mary Beth curled up next to Joe on the couch. Jason and Erica were in the room, but hadn't even turned the TV on. Nothing was normal. The house was too quiet without Sherry…

"Here you go, Mrs. Kennsington." The nurse laughed. "Five pounds, fifteen ounces giving you *what for.*"

Mary Beth held out her arms and received her daughter, who was red-faced and screaming and adamantly protesting her forced entry into the cold delivery room. The moment Mary Beth's arms went around her, Sherry stopped crying. She seemed to look right into her mother's heart.

"You knew what you needed, didn't you?" she said softly, her fingers stroking the baby's fine dark hair. Mary Beth looked at every feature. "She's definitely got your coloring, Joe. And your mouth. Your nose, too, I think."

"And her mother's determination." He kissed Mary Beth on the cheek.

She smiled as Sherry's tiny hand closed around her finger. "A little woman after my own heart."

As Sherry grew older, her determination sometimes proved entertaining.

"Mary Beth, have you seen my briefcase? I've still got a stack of papers to grade…why are you smiling at me like that?"

"Come here. You've got to see this."

She led Joe to Sherry's room and stood at the door. "Look," she whispered.

Sitting at a small table was three-year-old Sherry, a stack of Joe's students' papers in front of her, a red pencil in her hand.

Joe stifled his laughter. "She didn't?"

"Oh, but she did."

Sherry had randomly chosen a letter of the alphabet and scribbled it at the top of each paper. Joe handed the papers back to his middle-school students exactly as Sherry had graded them.

"Well, what did Angela Pinkston think of her J-minus?" Mary Beth asked Joe that evening.

"She decided it meant *just right*. The whole class had a great time with it."

Sherry's questioning mind had sent them racing to the library on more than one occasion. But her spiritual questions were more difficult to satisfy.

"Mommy, where does God live?"

"God lives in heaven," she said.

"And Jesus lives with Him?"

"Yes, He does—forever."

"Where *is* heaven?"

"Not in this world, sweetie. It's a special place."

"But why did Jesus leave the special place?"

"Because He loved us so much He wanted to live in our hearts."

"Doesn't He want to live with God anymore?"

"Jesus will always live with God because He's God's Son. But He can live in our hearts at the same time."

"Oh," Sherry said, sounding as if she understood all mysteries of the universe. "Then He lives in Daddy's heart?"

"Yes."

"When he's at school?"

"Yes, sweetie, all the time. Even when he's at school."

"But Daddy said they don't allow God in school."

When Sherry was five, she slipped out of the pew and walked forward during an altar call. Mary Beth didn't even know she was gone until she saw her tiny form standing up front. She came back to the pew, satisfaction on her face and a light in her eyes, determined to live her life for Jesus…

Mary Beth reached over and plucked a Kleenex from the box. There was so much Sherry could do for God. Surely He wouldn't let her be murdered.

The grandfather clock struck 8:00 at the Logan mansion.

Marita stood across the hall and watched Juanita clear the dishes from the dining room table. The soft glow of long, tapered candles reflected on the gold rim of her favorite bone china.

Nearly full plates of beef tenderloin and fresh asparagus were on their way to the garbage disposal. She wondered what Taylor was having for dinner—if she was still alive.

Marita sighed and leaned her head back. After G. R.'s public offer of fifty thousand dollars, they'd been deluged with calls. None of the leads had amounted to anything.

All calls to the Logan residence were monitored by the FBI, but she overheard Jordan Ellis say the phones were ringing off the hook at all the law enforcement offices in town. He also said he wasn't impressed with any of the leads—or with G. R., whom he referred to as a "nincompoop."

Marita wasn't even insulted. She was too embarrassed for G. R. to feel defensive. After Helen put him in his place yesterday morning, he had kept to himself.

Tonight at dinner, he finally reacted to Mayor Kirby's address and made it clear he had no intention of turning loose of his bitterness or anything else. Regardless of his harsh manner, she knew how much he loved Taylor. Seeing him suffer brought her no satisfaction.

She walked into the library and stood looking up at the portrait of Taylor. Such a beautiful young woman with so much promise. Marita's eyes brimmed with tears. She felt someone lay hands on her shoulders.

"I thought I'd find you in here," Helen said.

"I wanted to see Taylor's face." Marita blinked away the moisture and turned around. "She reminds me so much of you, Helen. She has a way with G. R. when nothing I say makes a difference. What will happen to him if she doesn't..." Marita's voice failed.

Helen squeezed her hand. "We can't give up hope."

Ellen sat on the couch knitting a sweater, while Guy went from room to room, checking doors and windows.

She looked up when he walked into the family room. "Are you happy now?"

"I'm thinking of getting an alarm system. I'm more worried about you than you are."

"I'm concerned, but I refuse to be afraid. If he's out to get me, I doubt if anyone could stop him. But I think he's more interested in what I put in the newspaper than in hurting me."

"And on what facts do you base that assumption?"

Ellen shot him a look. "Don't use your courtroom tone with me. Have you got a better idea?"

"I'd like you to hole up here until this whole nightmare is over."

"You know I can't do that. I have a paper to run."

"Why can't you run it from here, Ellen? You've got phones, fax, e-mail, courier...what more do you need? Why risk going out?"

"Because I won't be intimidated, that's why! I refuse to be another victim in this."

"Funny, I'm worried you *might* be."

"Guy, do you honestly think I'd cave in to this guy, hiding here until heaven knows when? That's not who I am."

"It's no longer just a matter of principle, Ellen. It's dangerous."

"You think I don't know that? That's what I have the FBI for. They're not going to let him anywhere near me."

"I hate the fact that this animal is communicating with you. It's sick. He's just playing you…"

"For a fool?" Ellen lifted her eyebrows. "Is that what you think? Thanks for your vote of confidence." She got up and started to leave the room.

"Honey, wait." Guy blocked the doorway and gently took her arm. "That's not what I said. Don't put words in my mouth. He's using you to stay on center stage, and I hate it."

"Okay, let me go through this again. Maybe you'll *listen* this time. I, Ellen Madison Jones, am not being played by anybody. Is that clear? I'm making sure the news gets reported, just like I always do. He *thinks* he's manipulating me, but he's not! If it makes him feel better, fine with me. But it's one more day those girls might still be alive."

Guy inched closer. "Did I mention I love you?"

"Well, Counselor, it *is* written somewhere in our wedding vows."

Guy reached for her hands and slowly pulled her close. His arms went around her. "Well, I *do* love you, Ellen. And I'm scared. I don't want to lose you. I know you're tough, but you didn't see the look on your face when you came home Saturday night. I did."

Ellen wiggled out of his arms. "I'm already involved, whether we like it or not."

"I object!"

"Overruled!"

"Overruled? On what grounds, Your Honor?"

"Badgering the witness."

He chuckled. "Honey, you can't be the witness *and* the judge. Talk to your attorney."

"Is he still speaking to me?"

"He wishes you'd take his advice."

"Well, as part of the attorney-client relationship, he needs to put up with my idiosyncrasies."

"So noted, Mrs. Jones. Then, as part of the attorney-client *privilege,* he'd like to kiss the client."

"Seems a bit irregular."

"Well, of course it's irregular. There's nothing *regular* about his kisses. He's gifted."

"Gifted?" She felt the corners of her mouth turn up.

"Absolutely! He earned the coveted bachelor's degree in kissing science."

"A bachelor's degree? He's a married man."

"Oh, then you'd rather he call it a *master's* degree?"

"Very funny!" Ellen threw a pillow cushion at him.

Guy threw the cushion back, and within seconds, the prominent attorney and Baxter's newspaper editor were on the floor, wrestling and laughing like two kids on a rainy day.

Rebecca left her door cracked so she could hear the conversation between her mother and the two FBI agents sitting in the living room. Agent Black had asked most of the questions. It was 8:30. How much longer would they stay?

"Mrs. Purdy, you said you haven't been back to Baxter since you moved here two years ago. That seems odd for someone who raised her family and lived in Baxter for more than thirty years."

"Not really. The memories in Baxter died for me when Roger died. I don't think back much on the past. Those last years were hard. We struggled to get by. Wayne even quit high school to help."

"Didn't you resent that?"

"You bet I did. I had no respect for G. R. Logan. I don't know anyone who did. If I had a dollar for every tear I shed on account of that man, I wouldn't have had to worry about money at all. He didn't care."

"Know anyone who would want to hurt him?"

"In their dreams, probably everyone who ever worked for him. But for real? No."

"What about other family members—parents, brothers, sisters, kids, other relatives? Anyone who might want to get even with him?"

"No, not really. I don't think anyone really knew how bad we had it."

"By *we,* you mean you and Wayne and Rebecca?"

"Uh-huh."

"And Wayne is twenty-three now, living in Baxter? Is that right?"

"Yes, he lives in the house he grew up in. He works at Monty's Diner and part-time at Abernathy's. I'm sure you already know that."

"And your daughter, Rebecca. She's sixteen now, a junior at Ellison High School?"

"That's right."

"We'll need to talk with her, too, when she's feeling better."

Rebecca decided she was comfortable with the way the agents were questioning her mother. Why not get this over with? She went into the living room and stood behind the couch.

"Rebecca, are you all right?" Velma asked.

"I'm better. The soup helped."

"Come in and meet Agent Black and Agent Matthews."

"Hello," she said.

"Good evening, Rebecca. Your mother mentioned you weren't feeling well," Agent Black said.

"I feel better now."

"Well, if you're up to it, there are a few questions we'd like to ask you so we can wrap this up."

"Okay." She sat down in the rocking chair, facing the couch where the two agents were sitting.

"These questions are just routine, so there's no need to feel nervous. Just answer them the best you can."

"Okay."

"Do you remember how you felt at the time your father lost his job?"

"I felt sad."

"Did you ever talk to anyone about it?"

"Not really. Just Wayne, sometimes."

"Your brother Wayne?"

"Yes, sir."

"And how did Wayne feel?"

"The same way, I think. I was only eleven. I don't remember a lot of details. I just remember feeling sad."

"Do you know of anyone who might be holding a grudge against G. R. Logan? You knew kids whose parents lost jobs and went through hard times. Anyone come to mind?"

"Not really. Lots of people hated Mr. Logan. I remember them talking about it. My dad didn't like him either."

"So you didn't like him because he hurt your father?"

"I guess so."

"What about Wayne?"

"I don't know. I suppose he didn't like him either."

"What about your friends? Do you know anyone who threatened to get even with him? Even if they were just kidding around?"

"No."

"Okay, Rebecca, that's really all we needed to ask you. Thanks."

"That's all?"

"For now. Depending on what surfaces in the case, we may need to ask you more questions later, but for now we're done."

As her mother escorted the agents to the front door, Rebecca breathed a sigh of relief. Her voice had sounded as blah as she felt. She hoped Agents Black and Matthews would remember her as just another kid who didn't know anything.

On Tuesday night, Wayne put a package of popcorn in the microwave and left the basement door open so the girls would smell the aroma. When the timer sounded, he filled a bowl with popcorn and grabbed a Coke, then sat at the kitchen table.

He couldn't get it off his mind... What did Beck know? He

glanced at the clock. It was too risky calling her when his mother was there. No, tomorrow he'd tell Mr. Abernathy he had an errand to run. Then he'd go to the Texaco and call Beck as soon as she got home from school.

Wayne walked down the hall and into his room, and sat at the computer. His eyes scanned the newspaper clippings on the wall in front of him. He read the list of names in his high school graduating class. His eyes came to rest on his father's obituary. G. R. Logan hadn't had to flush *his* dreams down the toilet—yet.

Wayne got up and walked over to the circle of photographs by the door. Perhaps if he viewed the mouthy Sherry Kennsington as an unwelcome conscience that needed to be silenced, and Taylor Logan as nothing more than the flesh and blood of the man responsible for making his life miserable, killing them wouldn't be difficult.

But he doubted it could be more satisfying than dangling the threat.

TWENTY-SIX

Wayne turned on the Open sign at Monty's Diner, unlocked the front door, and picked up the bundle of Wednesday newspapers. He held the door for Mort Clary, who breezed by him like a man on a mission.

"What's your hurry, Mr. Clary?"

"Just needin' my caffeine. I ain't worth a hoot till I git it."

"Don't you want a newspaper?"

"Yep...almost forgot." Mort put a quarter in the jar, took a paper from Wayne, and took his place at the counter where Rosie Harris had already set his coffee.

George and Hattie Gentry walked in, Liv Spooner and Reggie Mason right behind them. Within minutes, Monty's was bustling with activity.

Wayne grabbed a newspaper from the stack, his eyes fixed on the headline "County to raise bond issue?" He spotted what he was looking for in the left-hand column.

· KIDNAPPER MAKES CONTACT

Ellen Jones, editor of the *Baxter Daily News*, received a second note from the person believed to have kidnapped local teenagers Taylor Logan and Sherry Kennsington.

The envelope, addressed to Jones and marked "Personal and Confidential," was received in the mail yesterday afternoon and contained a note and two locks of hair, confirmed to be that of the kidnapped girls.

The first note Jones received led authorities to Logan's BMW, which was recovered late Saturday night from the bottom of Heron Lake near Boat Ramp Five.

It is this newspaper's belief that a well-informed public will have sharpened senses concerning this case. Therefore, we have chosen to print the contents of the second note. Anyone who has even a long-shot lead is asked to contact the FBI at the phone number listed below.

Please do not contact the *Daily News*. Though the kidnapper made contact with our editor, the newspaper has no role in this case other than reporting developments as they happen.

Wayne felt his adrenaline pumping as he reread the note he'd sent to Ellen Jones. Why wasn't this the headline story? Was she playing games with him?

Wayne glanced up and noticed Mark looking at him. He folded the newspaper and went over to him.

"What do you think, boss man?"

"This guy must've used *I* or *my* a dozen times," Mark said. "He definitely wants the spotlight."

"Looks like he got it," Wayne said.

George whirled around on the stool. "Too bad Ellen Jones got caught in the middle of this thing."

"Bet she's scared." Reggie raised his eyebrows. "I guarantee you I'd be."

"That lady's a tough ol' bird." Mort took a bite of pancakes and kept talking. "Ain't gonna do nothin' unless she wants to."

Mark rolled his eyes. "Good grief, Mort, would you chew with your mouth closed?"

"Still no leads…" Wayne shook his head. "Too bad."

"They're gonna git him, all right," Mort said. "Probably after he kills them girls. Liable to be a lynchin' when they do. Ain't been nothin' this awful 'round here—never!"

"Well, now, stringin' him up will sure fix everything." Rosie put her hands on her hips. "What about what the mayor said? Are we going to react to this monster by acting like monsters?"

"That's a *scary* thought." Mort laughed his wheezy laugh.

"This is not the time to kid around, buster!" Rosie wagged her finger at him. "All we need is a mob mentality at a time like this. What made you even think such a thing?"

"Guess I got a nose for *noose*." Mort grinned, his teeth speckled with blueberry pancakes.

Mark groaned and turned his head. "They don't pay me enough for this."

Mary Beth sat reading the morning newspaper, the kidnapper's threatening words to Ellen staring her in the face.

How dare this maniac put them through this! What awful things were happening to Sherry? She picked up the newspaper and flung it, the pages scattering in the middle of the floor.

Why was the Lord allowing this? He promised to hear their prayers. How could He let this happen to an innocent child? Hadn't they served Him? Hadn't they been faithful to His Word? Was it all a lie?

Mary Beth dumped her coffee in the sink, not bothering to rinse the brown spatters off the white porcelain. God could do something. Why didn't He?

She sensed Joe standing behind her in the doorway. Seconds later, his arms wrapped around her.

"Honey, the Lord didn't bring Sherry into our lives to end it without a reason," Joe said. "We have to trust Him. If He doesn't deliver her, then He has a higher purpose. She belongs to Him. And wherever Sherry is, she *knows* that."

Mary Beth's throat tightened. Her lip quivered.

Joe turned her around to face him, but she couldn't bear to look into his eyes.

"Our Sherry is years ahead of her age in the knowledge of God and in her desire to serve Him," he said. "She's *not* without help."

Mary Beth burst into tears and hid her face in her husband's chest.

On Wednesday morning, Jordan Ellis sat at his desk, reviewing everything he knew so far about the case. There was a knock on his door.

"Come in."

A young agent opened the door and approached his desk. "Sir, the guy across the hall found this envelope in the men's restroom. It has your name and office number on it."

"I didn't leave it there," Jordan said. "Let me see that."

"Could be a tip from someone who doesn't want to identify himself."

"Yeah, thanks. I'll take it from here."

The young agent left and closed the door.

Jordan slipped on surgical gloves and put a Kleenex flat on his desk. He slit the envelope open and pulled out a piece of white paper. He unfolded it carefully, let two locks of hair fall on the Kleenex, and read the words:

Well, Mr. Big Shot FBI,
Admit it, I'm a clever guy.
I haven't left a single clue.
I just sit back and laugh at you.

"Boyer!" he shouted.

The young agent opened the door. "Yes, sir?"

"Seal off the building. This note's from the kidnapper."

"You're kidding?"

"Do I look like I'm kidding?" Jordan began to gather up the evidence and bag it. "Go! And get Shaffer in here."

Seconds later, Agent Shaffer stood in the doorway.

"Shaffer, get me the tape of everyone who was in the courthouse last night or this morning."

"Uh, sir, there are no surveillance cameras in this building."

"That's right. I forgot we were in *Podunk.*" Jordan sighed. "I want this creep, Shaffer. Boyer's sealed off the building. Knock on doors. Talk to everyone. He might still be here."

"Yes, sir."

Jordan's heart was racing. So much for controlling his blood pressure! He took a marker and labeled the bag, then peeled off his gloves and pushed himself up from the desk.

"So you wanna play hardball, eh? Should've checked my batting average. I'd sooner die than lose to a loser."

Twenty minutes later the phone rang in Jordan's office.

"Yeah, this is Jordan."

"McCullum here. Our perp left another calling card. We were sorting through a stack of responses to Logan's reward offer, and opened one of those notes like the one Mrs. Jones got. It's postmarked yesterday."

"Let me guess," Jordan said. "A white envelope with a clever little rhyme printed in black ink on white paper, probably with a lock of hair inside. Am I close?"

"Right on the money, sir."

"Have you put it into evidence?"

"No, it's here on the table where it was opened."

Jordan got up and started pacing. "Read it to me, Adam."

"Okay, sir." McCullum cleared his throat.

Wanna guess who I've still got?
Your daughter's life cannot be bought!
How does it feel to hurt this way,
and dread the dawn of each new day?
Taylor will die on account of you,
and everything you put us through.
Suffer, G. R., she's my pawn.
And your pain won't stop when she is gone.

There was a long pause.

"That's it, sir."

Jordan sighed. "Okay, McCullum. Get it to the lab."

"FBI lab."

"This is Special Agent Ellis. I need to speak with John Richards."

"He's in the middle of something. Can I have him call you back?"

"No. I need him now. Unless he's bound and gagged, I need you to get him on the phone."

"Hold on…"

Jordan waited for what seemed like an eternity, listening to voices in the background.

"What is it that couldn't wait?" John said, sounding out of breath. "We're all busy."

"Look, can't you find me something in all the stuff we've sent up there?"

"I'm telling you, Jordan, this guy is either really smart or really lucky. Most everything we've got is clean. No fingerprints we can match to anything. In fact, nothing solid except the black strands of hair."

Jordan sighed. "There are three more of those notes, same M.O., coming your way. John, I really need you to find something. I think the girls are still alive. If we can zoom in on something that will help us pick this guy out, there may still be time to save them. He's enjoying playing puppeteer with Logan; and as long as that entertains him, it might buy us some time. But I need *something*. See what you can do…please?"

"Excuse me, but wasn't I just talking to Jordan Ellis?"

"Yeah, I'm still here."

"Jordan Ellis never says please."

"*Pretty please,* John? Dig deeper. I need something on this one."

"All right, I'll go over the new evidence myself. If there's anything there, I'll find it."

"John?"

"Yeah?"

"Thank you."

"Please and thank you from the *grouchmeister,* all in one day? Be still my foolish heart."

Jordan smirked. "I'll be in touch."

"That's what I'm afraid of."

TWENTY-SEVEN

Wayne left Monty's Diner and pulled his jacket collar up as he walked into the wind toward his truck. When he looked up, he saw Rebecca leaning on the driver's side door, her arms crossed, her eyes fixed on him.

"Beck…uh, why aren't you in school today?"

She stared at him, her face expressionless.

"Hel-lo? Earth to Beck. Are you there?"

She didn't respond.

Wayne waved his hand in front of her face. "Come on, Beck, knock it off. Why won't you talk to me?"

"I *am*," she said. "And I'm waiting for an answer."

Her gaze felt like a hot branding iron, placed right on the hide of his conscience. "An answer to what?" he said.

"I think you know."

"No, I don't."

"The FBI came to see Mom and me."

Wayne's pulsed raced. "What for?"

"They haven't talked to you yet?"

"Why would they talk to me?"

"They wanted to know if we knew anyone who'd want to get even with G. R. Logan."

"What'd you tell them?"

"What *should* I have told them?"

"That we know lots of people who'd like to get even with G. R. Logan. Doesn't mean they would."

"Well, what do you know about the kidnapping?" she asked.

"About the kidnapping? What everyone knows. It's been in the newspaper and all over the TV. What's your point?"

"I saw your wall, Wayne."

He looked at her, his eyes probing. "What wall?"

"Your *bedroom* wall—the one with the newspaper clippings, the pictures of Taylor Logan and Sherry Kennsington, and…"

"And *what?*"

Rebecca's face turned pale. "The shoes…I saw their shoes!"

"We need to talk," he said. "Get in the truck."

"No, talk to me right here. Can you give me a reason why I shouldn't be concerned?"

"Let's go somewhere private." He pulled open the door to the truck with Beck still leaning on it. "I have to be at Abernathy's in less than an hour. You wanna talk or not?"

"All right, but I want the *truth,* Wayne."

Wayne drove his truck, bouncing and rocking, down a rutted road that led to an abandoned icehouse. He cut the motor and turned to Rebecca.

"Okay, let's talk."

"I want an answer to my question, Wayne."

"Tell me something…have I ever hurt you, or anyone else?"

She shook her head. "No."

"Then trust me on this one." He gently tilted her chin toward him; her trusting blue eyes begged to be satisfied. "Will you do that?"

"Just tell me the truth, Wayne."

"All right, I'll tell you. I borrowed Sherry Kennsington and Taylor Logan to make a point. But I'm not gonna hurt them, Beck."

"The whole world is looking for them! Where are they?"

"In a safe place. Calm down, they're fine. I just wanna make G. R. squirm a while, that's all. As long as he thinks I'm gonna hurt his daughter, he'll feel helpless. Then he'll know exactly how *we* felt."

"But it's mean, Wayne. It's not fair."

"Not fair? May I remind you it was his fault Dad died, not that he even bothered to send a card? And that it was his fault we were poor and hungry and scared? Thanks to him, I had to quit school. Didn't even faze him!"

"It's still wrong. You have to let them go."

"I will. But for once, it feels good that G. R. Logan isn't calling the shots. This is the perfect payback for what he put us through, Beck. Dad would be proud."

"Dad would never want you to do something like this—never!" She started to cry.

"What do you know about what Dad would or wouldn't want?" He sat up stiffly and stared out the windshield.

"I just know."

"There's a lot you *don't* know. You never knew how bad things really were. I made sure you had what you needed. I'm the one they laughed at because my clothes were too small and I looked like a geek. I'm the one who worked two or three jobs a day so Mom could go to cosmetology school. I gave up on what *I* wanted. And it's all G. R. Logan's fault."

"You said you did those things because you loved us."

"I did. But he made our lives miserable, and I want him to know what it feels like."

"But we're not miserable now. I'm sorry you had to work so hard to help us, but why can't you just move away and start over? You could end up in jail over this."

"Only if you betray me."

"But what about Taylor? None of this is her fault. And what was the point in kidnapping Sherry? What did she have to do with any of this?"

"Look, Beck, I couldn't get Taylor without getting Sherry. They're always together. What are you worried about? I told you I'm not gonna hurt them."

"And you think scaring them to death isn't hurting them?"

"Who says I'm scaring them to death? Don't overreact."

"I can't help it. I went to school with Sherry. I've been sick to my stomach thinking about the horrible things that could be happening to her. And all this time my own brother had her!" Rebecca wiped her tears on her sleeve. "Imagine how her parents must feel…how would you feel if someone kidnapped me just to get even with somebody else?"

Wayne let her cry. How could she possibly understand?

"Beck…you've gotta let me see this through."

"But what you're doing is awful!"

"This is a family honor thing between me and Dad and Logan. I don't expect you to understand. All I'm asking is that you keep this secret. If you tell anyone, I'll be arrested. And I promise you…I'll kill myself before I'll go to jail."

When Wayne walked into Abernathy's Hardware Store, two men in dark suits greeted him.

"Wayne Purdy?"

"Yeah?"

"I'm Special Agent Max Fulmer, and this is Special Agent Mark Billings, FBI." The men displayed the proper identification. "We're investigating the Logan-Kennsington kidnapping, and talking to former employees of G. R. Logan—and their families. Could we have a few minutes of your time?"

Wayne glanced at his watch. "I'm on the clock in five minutes."

"That's okay," Fulmer said. "We've already talked with Mr. Abernathy. Said he'd start you on the clock at three, even if we get long-winded."

Sherry shivered in the darkness. Had she ever been so cold or so hungry? How long had it been since Wayne brought them something to eat? He'd left water twice, so it must have been twenty-four hours at least.

The smell of his microwave popcorn had made the hollow aching in her stomach worse. But now, even the smell of Jack's food taunted her.

She heard Taylor's stomach growl. Her friend had been unresponsive since Wayne pulled the plug on the space heater. Sherry assumed Taylor was mad at her for provoking him. Tears stung her eyes. How could she explain anything with Jack ready to pounce?

It helped to think about her family, knowing they loved her and were praying for her safety. She also clung to the Lord, imagining that she was in His shadow.

The gnawing of Sherry's hunger was surpassed only by the loneliness she felt. With Taylor so withdrawn, Sherry was forced to rely completely on the Lord as she lay on the basement floor, wondering when and how she was going to die.

Wayne sat in the back room at Abernathy's, Agent Fulmer asking questions and Agent Billings taking notes. The conversation was being recorded. Wayne glanced at his watch—3:20. How much more did they want to know?

"So, after your father passed away, you were the primary bread-winner?"

"Yes, sir. I helped so my mom could go to cosmetology school."

"And after she graduated?"

"I continued working until she could make enough on her own."

"Did you go back to school, Wayne?"

"No, sir."

"Get a GED?"

"No, I kept meaning to, but I liked working. I'd gotten used to it."

"Had a lot of jobs?" Fulmer asked.

"I've tried just about everything." *You jerks already know this stuff. What're you after?*

"Any particular reason?"

"No, sir. I guess I haven't found my niche."

"Does it make you mad that you had to quit school?"

"Not really. At first it was hard, but I was glad I could help."

"I understand you wanted to go into electronics."

"I still might. For now, I'm enjoying my work. I like people and I like to stay busy."

"Your mother says you're living in the house you grew up in?"

"Mom inherited her aunt's house in Ellison, and found a good job. I really didn't want to leave, so she let me stay in the house here."

"You live in the house alone?"

Wayne's heart pounded so hard he wondered if his shirt was moving. "Yes, sir. My sister comes to visit on school holidays and during the summer."

"And you have a dog, let's see…a Doberman named Jack? You've had him for two years, is that correct?"

Wayne nodded. "Jack's been a lot of company. He's great."

"Any particular reason why you chose a Doberman?"

"They're really cool-looking dogs. Have you been around them much?"

"Yeah, but the ones I've been around are mean as snakes."

"Not Jack. He's great. I suppose he'd scare off an intruder, but he plays with me like a pup. Even shares a bowl of popcorn with me every night." Wayne grinned. "He likes it microwaved."

"Ever take him for training? You know, to be a guard dog?"

"A guard dog? No sir."

"So he's never been professionally trained as a guard dog?"

"No."

"What about obedience school?"

"Yeah, I took him during the first year to a place just off CR 139. I don't recall the name, but I remember it sounded kinda cutesy."

"That wouldn't be In the Dog House, would it?"

"Yeah, that's it—In the Dog House. They calmed him down and made a really good pet out of him."

Wayne glanced at his watch. It was 3:30.

"Okay, let's wrap this up." Fulmer said. "Let's see…Wayne, do you own a computer?"

"Sure. Doesn't everyone?"

"Do you own a printer, too?"

"Uh-huh."

"And, let's see…are you right-handed?"

"I am," Wayne said, wishing this guy would drop off the planet.

"Okay, thanks. Oh…one more question, just for the record. You stated that on Friday you worked at Monty's from 6:00 A.M. until 2:00, and here at Abernathy's from 3:00 until 6:00. Do you remember where you were between 2:00 and 3:00?"

"Hmm…last Friday…oh, yeah. I filled up my truck at the Texaco, and then ate lunch in the truck like I always do."

"Anyone who might remember seeing you at that time?"

"I paid Kevin Howell for the gas. He might remember. I think it was just after 2:00."

"And how did you pay for the gas?"

"Cash."

"So you don't have a receipt?"

"No, sir. I never get receipts. No need for them." *Yeah, I'm sure I keep a whole shoebox full of gas receipts.*

"And where is your truck parked when you eat lunch?"

"Different places. Sometimes I eat across the street at City Park. Depends on my mood."

"And what kind of mood were you in on Friday? Where'd you park the truck for lunch?"

"In the back of the parking lot at Miller's Market, under the trees. A real relaxing spot. I go there a lot."

"Did anyone see you?"

"I don't know. I was reading the paper and eating my sandwich."

"Isn't Miller's Market near the high school?"

"Yeah. I like the feeling in that part of town—big trees, neat old houses. Quaint, you know?"

"And what about Friday evening? Where were you?"

"At home. Surfing the net. I do that almost every night."

"Anyone who can confirm that?"

"No, sir—well, other than Jack. But he's liable to say anything if you bribe him with popcorn."

Agents Fulmer and Billings chuckled.

"Okay, Wayne, we're through," Fulmer said. "Oh, wait…I forgot to ask where you buy your computer supplies."

"At Jason's Computer Mart, unless I'm in Ellison visiting Mom and Beck. Office World has a great new store about a block from their house. I always stop there."

"Okay, Wayne, now we're through."

"That's it? I can get to work now?"

"That's it," Fulmer said, extending his hand to shake Wayne's. "Thanks for your cooperation."

Agent Billings shook hands with Wayne, and the two FBI agents got up and left Abernathy's.

Wayne took off his glasses and rubbed his eyes. Maybe he should cut out early, get back to the house, and just get it over with.

"How'd it go, Wayne?" Mr. Abernathy stood in the doorway.

"Uh, great. I was glad to help."

Mr. Abernathy patted him on the shoulder. "Come on. I need you back in lighting. Some new freight just came in and I'd like to get it out before the day gets away from us."

TWENTY-EIGHT

Jordan Ellis leaned back in his chair and glanced up at the clock. It was already 4:15 on Wednesday afternoon. *Three measly notes, John. How long can it take?* He picked up the phone and dialed the FBI lab.

"This is John Richards."

"Guess who?"

"Oh, I was just about to call you. I found something interesting in the note to you and the one to Logan."

"Speak to me."

"There were traces of popcorn—actually, the fine dust left by the kernels. More of those dark hairs, too."

"Swell. We've got a balding Edgar Allan Poe–wannabe writing sick notes during intermission."

"It may mean something."

"Okay. Thanks, John. I'll get on the computer and start sorting through the interviews and the evidence we've got. Maybe something'll click. This case is really personal."

"And when aren't they, Jordan?"

"Be good to me. It's been a long day."

"Same here. Let's call a truce. I'm not quite through with this evidence yet. Talk to you if I find anything else."

Jordan was still in his office at 5:30 when his phone rang.

"Sir, this is Agent Barnett. One of the photographers for the *Baxter Daily News* got a call from a friend who works at a photo lab in Myerson—a Jim Marcum. The guy's been on vacation and just got back. He heard about the kidnapping, but hadn't followed the story while he was thawing out in Hawaii, surrounded by beautiful women on Waiki—"

"Cut to the chase, Barnett."

"When Marcum started reading the back issues of the *Myerson Tribune* and saw the photographs of our two girls, something clicked. Says he's sure he did some processing a couple of months ago for a guy who brought in film taken of Taylor Logan and another girl."

Jordan grabbed a pencil. "Does he remember what the guy looked like?"

"What he *remembers* is Taylor Logan. Marcum thought she was a knockout, and said he never forgets a face like hers. He's absolutely sure it was Taylor on the film he developed."

"And Sherry Kennsington?"

"Can't swear to it, but he thinks so. Says her hair's shorter now."

"What can he tell us about the guy?"

"Hardly noticed him until the guy reacted to Marcum's comment that the blond in the photographs was a knockout. Suddenly, the guy seemed hurried. Marcum thought maybe he was offended, like it was his girlfriend or something. Said the guy was young, but a lot older than Taylor. He remembers the pictures were candid telephoto shots, but nothing perverted."

Jordan stood up and started to pace. "Okay, time to dig out all the customer records—paperwork, computer files, whatever it takes—and compare the names with the name of every former employee and family member on our interview lists. Maybe we'll get a match. But my guess is our perp didn't use his real name and paid cash. I wonder if the photo lab has a surveillance camera?"

"I don't know, but Agent Cassidy has a team on the way."

"Does Ellen Jones know about this?"

"No. The staff photographer came straight to us."

"Good. Persuade him to put a lid on it till we check it out."

Jordan sat at his computer, reviewing the case file. His phone rang and he picked up the receiver, his eyes still on the screen.

"Yeah, this is Jordan."

"Sir, it's Agent Fulmer. Billings and I are done with our interviews for the day. You said you wanted a rundown before we wrote it up."

"Tell me about them—impressions, irregularities…"

"We spoke with Elijah Jenkins. Lost his job in the plant closing. He's fifty-five, divorced for fifteen years, never had kids. Has a full head of curly salt-and-pepper hair. Left-handed. A pleasant sort of guy. He found employment right after the plant closed and said it turned out to be a blessing for him. He's the shipping and receiving supervisor at that big clothing warehouse between Baxter and Parker. He worked the Friday of the kidnapping from noon until 9:00 P.M. Documented. No bad vibes there.

"The second contact, Elmer Tremont, worked for *Grant* Logan for twenty years before G. R. took over. Lost his job in the plant closure. Said he never quite recovered financially. He and his wife Jill both work for some lumber company in Parker. She's the book-keeper, and he works outside. He has gray hair, not a dark strand in it. He's a lefty. He worked a twelve-hour shift, from 7:00 A.M. to 7:00 P.M. the Friday of the kidnapping, and his wife was there from 9:00 A.M. till 5:00 P.M. Employer confirmed it. These two spouted off a lot of resentment for G. R., but had nothing but nice things to say about Grant Logan.

"Let's see, we talked with Mildred Blankenship, whose husband and son both worked at the plant at the time of the closing. The husband died of cancer last year, and her son was killed in a car accident three years ago. She had no other children. Mrs. Blankenship is a sweet lady and was very cooperative. If Billings and I had stayed any longer, she would've insisted on giving us cookies and milk. Nothing suspicious there.

"We also talked with Wayne Purdy, whose father worked for Grant Logan for thirty years, then lost his job when the plant closed. His dad died of an aneurysm right after that, so the kid quit high school to put his mother through cosmetology school. His mom and sister moved to Ellison two years ago, and he stayed here.

"He's right-handed and has straight, dark hair. Works at Monty's Diner from 6:00 A.M. till 2:00—and then at Abernathy's Hardware from 3:00 to 6:00, every day except Sunday. He was at work for both shifts the day of the kidnapping.

"He's had an inordinate number of jobs in the past five years. We ran our wheels off checking them out, but his former employers all had nice things to say about him. Current ones, too. He gets along with everyone at Monty's, and Mr. Abernathy at the hardware store says he's a model employee. Never misses work."

"Any close friends?" Jordan asked.

"Just a Doberman named Jack. Seems like a real nice kid."

"Can he account for the hour between jobs?"

"Yes and no. Says he ate lunch by himself in his truck, and that's his usual routine, according to both employers. Purdy says he also filled his truck at the Texaco during that hour. Want us to dig deeper?"

"No. Just curious. Do you know if our agents have talked to his mother and sister?"

"Black and Matthews did last night. Nice folks. His mom and sister seem well adjusted. His mother's a beautician, and his sister attends high school."

"You said this kid quit high school to help his mother through cosmetology school. Do you know if he ever went back?"

"Said he didn't—not even for his GED. Says he enjoys working and has had two to three jobs a day for years."

"Okay, Fulmer. Thanks for the call. I'll take a look at your case notes when you get them in the computer."

Rebecca put a spoonful of chicken soup to her mouth and almost gagged.

"Rebecca...?"

"Huh?"

"Honey, you've hardly touched your supper," Velma said.

"I still don't feel good."

"This is starting to worry me."

"Probably just the flu or something. Lots of stuff going around."

Velma put the back of her hand on Rebecca's forehead. "You're cool as a cucumber."

"I'll be better tomorrow. I'm just a little tired. May I be excused?"

"Why don't you take a nice warm bath and get to bed early. I'll come say good night."

The phone rang. Velma went into the living room to answer it. "Hello...? Hello...? Is anybody there...? Hello...?"

She hung up the phone and walked back into the kitchen. "It was a hang-up. Look at you! You're all sweaty. Poor thing. I do hope you're over this soon."

Rebecca got up and left the kitchen, wondering how it could ever be over.

∽○∾

Wayne slammed the front door, threw his keys across the room, and hit a couch pillow with his fist.

He sat down and raked his fingers through his hair. He hadn't given the FBI anything. Maybe they'd back off.

But what about Beck? He leaned his head against the back of the couch, replaying the horrified look on Beck's face when he threatened to kill himself rather than go to jail. It was the pits having to manipulate her emotions that way, but what choice did she leave him?

Wayne's thoughts were interrupted by Jack's yelping. He went over to where his keys were lying, picked them up, and walked into the kitchen. He opened the basement door and felt a cold surge of air hit him in the face. He picked up the camping flashlight and started down the steps, wondering how many more trips he would make before it was all over.

TWENTY-NINE

Sherry lay shivering, zipped up in her sleeping bag. She listened to Jack's yelping for a couple of minutes before hearing footsteps descend the stairs. She hoped Wayne was bringing food. The familiar bright light rounded the corner, and an ominous silhouette moved toward the cage.

"Well, Jack, your winter coat is keeping you nice and toasty," Wayne said. "Are you cold, ladies? Tired of the hand you've been dealt? Looks like *Jacks* are wild. One seems to be nipping at your nose, and the other would like to be, wouldn't you, boy?"

He set the flashlight on the floor with the beam directed toward Sherry and Taylor. He unlocked the gate and entered the cage.

"Get up!" he said.

They got up quickly, standing in stocking feet on the cold basement floor.

He grabbed Sherry by the arm. "I'm not through with you, big mouth. But first I've got a score to settle with your friend here."

He sidestepped in front of Taylor, his face directly in front of hers. "Are you freezing, Miss Logan? Because I was when your father killed my father."

"M-my father never killed anyone."

Jack's vicious snarling caused both girls to step backward.

"Jack, *silence!*" Wayne looked at Taylor. "Oh, no? Your father didn't give a rip my dad had no job, or we had no food, or couldn't pay the heating bill. I remember shivering through most of the winter. How does it feel?" He pranced back and forth in front of Taylor like an army sergeant. "Well, the tables are turned now." He reached inside his jacket and took out a mirror and held it to her face. "Go on, take a look! How do you like your hair? Guess you can't afford a salon cut anymore. And what happened to your cashmere sweater? Is that a hole I see? And no fashion shoes on those cold feet? Must be hard on your ego. Oh, was that your stomach growling? Funny, I remember what hunger feels like, too. The difference is *my* dad couldn't take seeing his family suffer—so he died!"

Wayne threw the mirror against the chain-link and Sherry heard it shatter. She held perfectly still, her heart racing. *Lord, please do something!*

"I wonder how Daddy feels, knowing his little girl isn't coming home? Here, this one's for him!" Wayne slapped Taylor and she fell down.

He laughed. Taylor cried.

"You think just because you're bigger, you're more powerful?" Sherry said.

Jack began to snarl.

"*Silence!*" commanded Wayne. "Haven't you learned your lesson? I'm powerful enough to make your life miserable. Or to take it anytime I want to."

"You're just like Goliath—all mouth—lording your size and your power over us. But God is stronger."

Wayne jeered. "Oh, wait. I know that story. Isn't this where you hit me right between the eyes with a rock and I fall dead on the ground? I'm waiting…"

Sherry stood silent, aware of Taylor's sniffling.

Wayne put his face in front of Sherry's. His eyes looked wild. "Well, I *am* more powerful, and there's nothing you can do about it! You *hate* me! You *loathe* me! *Admit* it!" He pushed Sherry with short shoves until she was backed up against the cage.

"I won't let myself hate. You still don't get it, Wayne. Hate's ruined your life."

"You're crazy! G. R. Logan ruined my life. I have a right to hate him."

"Hate's done you more harm than Mr. Logan ever could."

"What are you talking about?"

"You let it go on too long, and now it won't let you go. It's become your Goliath, and it's controlling you."

"Nothing controls me!" He pinned Sherry against the cage, his hands on her shoulders.

"When's the last time you felt happy or free? You've been angry for so long it runs your life."

"I run my life. And I want revenge for what G. R. Logan stole from me!"

"But what is it he stole? He may have hurt you, I don't know. But nursing a grudge was *your* choice. That's what stole your happiness—not Mr. Logan."

Wayne's fingers dug into her shoulders. "G. R. Logan ruined my life!"

"You could've forgiven, but you didn't want to. *That's* what ruined your life."

"Well, now it's ruining *yours!*" he shouted.

Sherry felt his hands tighten around her neck.

"This is what it feels like to have someone steal your life from you!" he shouted. "To take your dreams and your dignity until you suffocate!"

Sherry didn't put up a fight. She was aware of Wayne's contorted face and heard the words spewing from his mouth. But she looked into the face of her attacker, ready to meet her Savior. *Lord, I forgive him.*

Suddenly there stood before her a grand and glorious creature, draped in white light, with massive wings and a flaming sword. The angel's penetrating eyes spoke to something deep inside her soul, and she knew he had been with her since the moment she was born.

Joy unspeakable filled her. The angel held out his hand and took hers. And then she and her lifelong guardian stepped into eternity while Wayne Purdy's hands were still clutched around her neck.

Mary Beth woke with a start.

"You all right, honey?" Joe asked.

"I didn't mean to fall asleep. I need to get dinner on the table."

"Some ladies from church brought it over."

"When?"

"An hour ago. They put it in the oven to keep it warm."

Mary Beth sighed. "I'm not hungry. You and the kids go ahead."

"Why don't you come sit with us, at least? I think it'd be easier on the kids if we keep things as normal as possible."

"Sure, let's pretend everything's just hunky-dory."

There was a long pause.

"Honey, can we pray about this—?"

"This *what?*"

"I'm worried about you."

"I'll be all right."

"Anger this strong doesn't just get up and go. I hope you're not getting too comfortable with it."

"It's about the *only* thing I'm comfortable with at the moment."

Taylor watched, paralyzed with fear, as Wayne's hands remained locked around Sherry's neck. Her eyes were fixed on him as if she didn't have a care in the world. When he finally let go and her body fell to the floor, he seemed angrier than ever.

"She should've kept her big mouth shut!" Wayne turned around and stepped over Taylor. He slammed the gate, secured the padlock, and took Jack with him up the stairs.

Taylor didn't move for several minutes. She lay curled up on the basement floor, shivering uncontrollably. Finally she crawled over to Sherry's lifeless body. She knelt beside her for a moment and began to sob. She took the cross ring off Sherry's finger and clutched it tightly in her fist, then covered Sherry up with a sleeping bag.

Taylor crawled into her own sleeping bag and pulled it up around her neck. She turned on her side, warm tears running down the side of her face and onto the nylon fabric. Why hadn't he just killed them both? At least it would be over now.

Please, God, help me through this. Sherry was the strong one, and now it's just me. I'm so scared. Please don't leave me all alone.

THIRTY

Jordan Ellis rubbed his eyes and took another sip of black coffee. He'd been at the computer, going over everything he knew about this case, piece by piece, hoping to come up with some new revelation. He was reading the kidnapper's profile for the umpteenth time.

This type of individual is male, probably working alone. Harbors a longtime grudge against someone more powerful, who took something away from him, resulting in his feeling insignificant and out of control.

His close attention to detail is part of a carefully choreographed drama, which is moving toward a day of reckoning. But first, he'll maintain possession of the thing most valuable to the target of his revenge, until his flaunting of it ceases to have the desired effect.

"All right," Jordan said out loud. "He's probably a loner. Dark, receding hair. Right-handed. Young, but a lot older than Taylor Logan. Everything he does is calculated. He owns or has access to a computer and printer. Owns or borrowed a camera with a tele-photo lens. He was somewhere around popcorn when he wrote the notes."

Jordan combed his hands through his hair, and then put them behind his head.

"This perp set the fire at the old textile plant. He left a banner on the water tower, and notes at the Kennsingtons' and the Logans', on Ellen Jones's windshield, and in the men's restroom in the courthouse. He's been all over town. Why hasn't anyone reported seeing anyone suspicious? It's like he's camouflaged."

Jordan's eyes burned as he focused on the computer screen, rereading every note left by the kidnapper. He moved closer, drawn to the word *us* in the sixth line of this morning's note to G. R.

> **Wanna guess who I've still got?**
> **Your daughter's life cannot be bought!**
> **How does it feel to hurt this way,**
> **and dread the dawn of each new day?**
> **Taylor will die on account of you,**
> **and everything you put us through.**
> **Suffer, G. R., she's my pawn.**
> **And your pain won't stop when she is gone.**

He went back up to the third and fourth lines, and then dropped down to the last line and read it again. Hurriedly he scrolled up and reread the words on the poster left at the textile plant.

> **An eye for an eye,**
> **A lamb led to slaughter,**
> **The price of revenge—**
> **Your only daughter.**

He picked up the phone and dialed Special Agent Jason Snead.

"Jason, this is Jordan. Look at today's note from our perp to G. R. Logan. I'll wait while you pull it up on your screen…"

"Okay, I've got it," Snead said.

"Read the sixth line and notice the word *us*. What if he's not talking about his coworkers?"

"Hmm…interesting thought."

"Read the third, fourth, and last lines. Do you get the feeling this guy knows from *personal* experience that the pain won't stop?"

"Puts a whole different spin on it," Snead said.

"In fact, it sounds like this guy wants Logan to feel *exactly* what he felt."

"Could mean that."

"Now, pull up February 14 and read the note left at the plant, the part about an eye for an eye."

"Okay, Jordan, I'm looking at it. I think I know where you're going with this, but spell it out so I'm sure we're on the same page."

"We've gone at this from the perspective that the kidnapping was a payback by someone who got cut in the plant closing. But let's zero in on family members and relatives and find out who blames G. R. Logan for the death of someone they loved. I'm thinking our perp is sandwiched in there somewhere."

"I'm getting jazzed," Snead said.

"I need you to access all the case interviews we've completed on the kidnapping. Let's narrow it down to young males who fit the description, have a direct connection to someone who lost their job in the plant closing, who've lost someone close to them since G. R. closed down the operation, and who live in or around Baxter. I'll be here all night, Jason. Let me know when you've got something."

"Sure, Jordan. I didn't want to go home to my beautiful bride and candlelight dinner anyway."

Jordan grimaced. "Sorry. I really need this favor."

"I know. I'll try to connect the dots. If he's in there, I'll give him a face."

The overhead light came on, and Taylor's eyes flew open. She squinted in the bright light and heard footsteps coming at a fast pace. She glanced over at Sherry's body covered with the sleeping bag and wondered if it was her turn to die. She scrambled to her feet and cowered in the back of the cage.

Wayne rushed to the gate and ordered Jack to sit. He opened the lock and flung the gate wide open.

"Stay out of my way!" he shouted. "Sit over there in the corner, and don't say a word!" He pointed a pistol at her. "You're *next*. First I've gotta get rid of Sister Sherry over here!"

It's the first time Taylor had seen Wayne in the light since the kidnapping, and she was repulsed at how ugly and evil he looked now. His dark eyes were wild and threatening.

He tucked the gun into the waistband of his jeans and stood looking down at Sherry's body. "Well, you won't be preaching at me anymore, will you?" He nudged Sherry's body with his foot.

Taylor noticed dried mud on Wayne's boots and jeans, and dried clumps of dirt on the basement floor. She didn't watch when Wayne put Sherry's body into the sleeping bag, but she whimpered when she heard him zip it up.

He slung the bag over his shoulder, walked out of the cage, and slammed the gate behind him. He secured the padlock and whistled for Jack, then walked away, hauling the body of Sherry Kennsington to her grave.

Wayne shouted back at Taylor, "By this time tomorrow night, you'll be dead and buried, just like your preachy friend here. The only thing that matters now is that your pitiful old man is miserable for the rest of his life. Your death will guarantee his misery, and there's not a thing he can do about it."

THIRTY-ONE

O n Thursday morning, Mary Beth Kennsington sat on the side of her bed, staring blankly at the golden-pink swirls on the pale blue horizon.

"Honey, I need to leave for work now," Joe said. "I'm worried about you being alone. I wish you'd go over to Rhonda's."

"What for? I can't think of anything but Sherry. And the minute I walk out the door I'll have every media maniac from here to kingdom come all over me, not to mention the FBI smothering me so I won't get smothered."

Joe gently pulled Mary Beth to her feet. "The more you give in to this, the worse you're going to feel. The kids and I can get our minds off it for brief periods at school, but I'm concerned you're not getting a break from it."

"How can I? I've almost lost hope that Sherry's coming home..."

Joe's eyes locked on to hers. "Mary Beth...Sherry is the *Lord's*."

She tried to pull away from him, but he held onto her arm.

"You think I'm not feeling it, too?" he said. "I have to confront Sherry's absence in the eyes of every student I see..." His voice cracked with emotion. "But God gave her to us, and it's up to Him to give her back or take her home. Either we believe He's sovereign, or we don't."

"I don't want to hear it, Joe!"

"Shutting Him out is the worst thing we can do. Shutting each other out is a close second."

Jordan Ellis rubbed his morning stubble. He glanced at the black-and-white clock. Eight-thirty? What was taking Snead so long? He always came up with something when he had enough data.

He got up from the computer and opened the blinds, then poured the last cup of coffee and reached for his electric razor. The phone rang.

"Yeah, it's Jordan."

"This is Agent Snead, newlywed-in-the-doghouse."

There was a long pause.

"Jordan, I'm kidding. Cheryl understood."

"That's good."

"Listen, I don't have anything solid yet, but I'm narrowing down the field. I need more time. If it's all the same to you, I'd like to stay with it today."

"Get some rest, Jason. I don't want to kill you off. I *need* you."

"If I promise not to die, can I keep working?"

Jordan smiled. "You remind me of me. Are you sure it won't cause problems at home?"

"Cheryl understands this is big. I want to crack this case as much as you do."

"All right, stay with it. I'll be planted here until the cows come home. Keep me posted."

Rebecca Purdy's eyes flew open, and she sat straight up in bed.

"Honey, are you all right? I heard you call out." Her mother rushed over to the bed. "Look at you! You're soaked with sweat again. That does it. You're going to see Dr. Martin and find out what's wrong."

"I just had a bad dream."

"More like a bad bug. I'm calling his office right now to make you an appointment. Do you want me to stay home from work and take you?"

"No, I can go by myself."

"You sure you're up to it?"

She nodded.

Her mother left to make the call.

Rebecca laid her head on the pillow. How long could she ignore what she knew just because she was afraid of getting Wayne in trouble? A wave of nausea swept over her, and she felt as if she were going to be sick.

"All right, honey, Dr. Martin will see you at 10:00. I'm riding to work with Charlotte and leaving you the car. Call me as soon as you get home. I want to know what he says."

Rebecca nodded.

Velma bent down and kissed her on the forehead. "I love you."

Rebecca wrapped her arms around her mother and held on longer than she meant to.

"Honey, what is it?"

"Nothing. I just love you."

Monty's was bustling with activity on Thursday morning, and Wayne was glad to be busy.

"Wayne, would you clean up those empty booths?" Mark Steele said. "We've got people waiting. I think everyone in the media gets hungry at the same time."

"Sure. No problem."

Wayne carried a plastic tub to the first booth and began filling it with dirty dishes, aware of his hands. He was surprised how little it bothered him that he had strangled Sherry Kennsington.

Had things not gone into high gear, he might have been irritated that Ellen Jones didn't print the contents of the note he sent to G. R. and made no mention at all of the one left for Jordan Ellis.

But what difference did it make now? He didn't need the *Baxter Daily News*. He was going to kill Taylor Logan before the day was over and make headlines around the country. He was moving on to the ultimate payback, when G. R. Logan would be brought to his knees.

"Wayne, what are you grinning about?" Mark asked.

"Huh? I don't know. Just feeling *up* today, I guess."

Mary Beth heard the phone ring and ignored it. When the answering machine clicked on, she heard Rhonda's voice.

"I'm not giving up, Mary Beth. Even if I have to call you a dozen times before you answer it. You haven't talked to me since Sunday. You don't return—"

"Hello."

"There you are," Rhonda said. "I was hoping you'd finally answer."

"Sorry. I haven't felt like talking."

"I'm coming to get you. It'll do you good to get out."

"What's the point?"

"It's called sanity. You can't keep holding it all in. *Talk* to me."

"What do you want me to say, Rhonda? That God's in control? That He knows where Sherry is? That she belongs to Him? Well, I already know all that, and I'm sick and tired of... Look, it's better if I don't talk right now."

"The very thing you need to do is talk. Be honest with God, Mary Beth. You're the one who told me He can handle our feelings, that we're the ones who have trouble with it. You believe that or you wouldn't have told me."

"I'm not sure what I believe right now."

"Your feelings are mixing you up."

"Joe and the kids seem to be handling it better."

"What's the standard for handling something *better?*" Rhonda said. "You handle it the way you handle it. Everyone's different. You need to be honest with yourself and with the Lord. If you do that, you can deal with it."

"No, I can't! I'll never be able to deal with it if Sherry is murdered." She started to cry.

"Mary Beth, please. Let me come get you and bring you to my house. There's nothing you could say to make me not love you. You need to vent, get your feelings out. Let me help. This whole thing is hurting me, too…" Her voice cracked.

There was silence.

"All right, Rhonda. It's 9:00. I'm doing exactly *nothing,* so when do you want to pick me up? You know we're stuck with FBI, don't you?"

"We'll pretend they aren't around."

"But can you deal with the media? I doubt if the president has ever had this many people camped outside the White House."

"I can deal with just about anything except your not talking to me."

"I warn you, they're like a pack of wolves waiting for some fresh kill to devour. After all the times I've watched tragedies unfolding on TV and appreciated the media coverage, I never dreamed one day the cameras would be on me. I resent the intrusion. Ironic, isn't it?"

"I'll be there in ten minutes to rescue you. Wear a scowl."

"A scowl? Why?"

"I'll bring you a two-by-four. Even the media knows better than to mess with a crabby redhead carrying a big stick."

Mary Beth smiled. "I didn't realize how much I've missed you. Hurry up, Okay?"

The white Ford Taurus rounded the last hill and descended into Baxter. Through the bare trees, Rebecca spotted the water tower and remembered the awful words her brother had hung there.

She dismissed the thought. She had to figure out where Wayne was hiding Sherry and Taylor. They deserved to know Wayne wasn't really planning to hurt them.

But even if she found them, would she be able to talk Wayne into letting them go and turning himself in? Surely the FBI would go easy on him if he explained that his feelings were mixed up over the loss of their father? At least she hoped so. Wayne was no criminal.

Rebecca counted the chimes as the clock tower struck 11:00. Why not start at the house and rummage around? Maybe she'd find some clue that would tell her where Wayne was hiding the girls.

If she found them, she'd confront him at 2:00 when he left Monty's.

The phone rang in Jordan Ellis's office.

"Yeah."

"Jordan?"

"Who else would be in here?"

"Did we get up on the wrong side of the bed?" John Richards said.

"I haven't been to bed. I didn't mean to snap, John. I want this guy, and you know how I get. Anything new for me?"

"Maybe."

"How promising is *maybe?*"

"I won't know until after lunch. I just called to dangle the carrot."

"That's really lame, John. I'm not in the mood for your humor."

"Oh, sure you are. I'll call as soon as I know if I'm right."

"Aren't you going to give me even an itty-bitty hint?"

"Well, let's just say I've got a wild hair. Talk to you later." *Click.*

Mary Beth sat in the Wilsons' kitchen, while two FBI agents stood outside the front door.

"I'm glad to see you eat something." Rhonda cleared the dishes out of Mary Beth's way.

"The quiche tasted good. Thanks. Half the time, I forget to eat."

"Mrs. Kennsington?" Jennifer stood in the doorway to the kitchen. "I'm sorry to interrupt, but I wanted you to know I'm thinking about you and your family. This must be so hard."

Mary Beth nodded. "Thanks, Jen."

"I'm going for a walk," Jennifer said. "If I don't move, I'll just take another nap or watch some dumb soap opera."

"Okay, honey. Bundle up," Rhonda said. "By the way, we're having your favorite for dinner."

"Chicken and dumplings?"

"Uh-huh. I thought it might go down pretty well."

"How'd you know I was craving that?"

Rhonda shrugged, a smile on her face.

"If I'm not back in thirty minutes send a tow truck." Jennifer turned and went out the front door.

"It's nice to have Jennifer home. I've missed her dry humor."

Mary Beth's eyes filled with tears.

"I'm sorry," Rhonda said. "That was insensitive. I—"

"Not at all. I'm happy for you. I just miss Sherry…" She began to sob, and felt Rhonda's hand on hers.

"Mary Beth, I don't pretend to understand exactly how you feel, but as a mother, I can imagine your pain. I'm so sorry you have to endure this."

"She's loved God since she was five years old. She's served Him with all her heart. Where is He now when she needs Him?"

"You're the one who taught me that God has a plan and that *everything* works together for good when you love Him and walk with Him. You told me He doesn't waste anything. Mary Beth, that's one of the reasons I became a believer."

"I'm not sure I even believe that right now."

"I think you do. You're just hurting and have a million questions. Who wouldn't? I don't understand it either, but I do believe in the God we serve. He *is* with Sherry. She can't be out of His presence."

Mary Beth sighed. "Part of me knows that. Part of me doubts it."

"Then hold on to the part you *know*," Rhonda said. "I'll hold up the other half."

Mary Beth was home by noon. She lay on the couch, her feet up, wondering if she had ever felt more exhausted or more defeated.

She remembered the envelope Rhonda had given her and reached over and took it from her purse. She opened it with her thumbnail and removed a notecard. On the outside was a picture of Jesus tenderly holding a child's face in His hands. She opened it and founded a folded piece of paper inside. She began reading the card:

Dear Mary Beth,

You've taught me so much about loving God and trusting Him. I know the truth of that hasn't left you, even though it's hard to get in touch with it when you're overwhelmed with fear and anger. But those are just feelings. They don't change what you know deep inside: God is faithful and you can trust Him, even with Sherry's life.

You gave me the enclosed words, and I'm giving them back as a reminder. I hope they reach clear down to your heart and put you in touch with the loving God you helped me to find.

I love you,
Rhonda

Mary Beth unfolded the piece of paper and recognized her own handwriting on a page from her prayer journal. She read the words:

When silence is God's only voice,
And waiting on Him my only choice,
A banner of faith I humbly raise
And offer a sacrifice of praise.
Though answers He may not impart,
Forever I can trust His heart.

Mary Beth's hands shook. She stared at the words, wondering if she would ever believe them again.

THIRTY-TWO

Rebecca Purdy pulled to the end of the gravel driveway and shut off the motor. She rested her arms on the steering wheel and sat quietly for a minute. She took the key out of her pocket and held it in her hand. Did she *really* want to do this?

She opened the car door, pulled the hood of her coat up over her head, and hurried to the front door. Feeling like a trespasser, she unlocked the door, pushed it open with her shoulder, and stepped inside.

She walked down the hall to Wayne's bedroom and stopped outside the door. She took a deep breath, then pushed open the door. *What...?* A variety of sports posters adorned the four walls! She went in for a closer look. All that remained of what she witnessed on Monday were a few tiny pinholes.

Rebecca removed two thumbtacks, her hands shaking, and looked under a Peyton Manning poster that covered the place where the knife had been stuck in the wall. The hole had been filled in and freshly painted. The color match was so close that, except for the subtle smell of paint, the repair was hardly detectable.

She went through her brother's room, looking for clues, anything that might point to where he was hiding the girls. She found nothing.

She went through every drawer and closet in the other bedrooms, but found nothing that told her what she had come to find out.

Rebecca walked to the kitchen and pulled receipts, bills, and junk mail out of the kitchen desk. She sat at the table and looked through each piece. Nothing even hinted at where Taylor and Sherry might be. She sighed. Where would she hide them if she were Wayne?

As she was putting things back in the desk, she noticed that Jack's food and water bowls were not on the floor by the basement door. There'd been no sign of him on Monday, either. Had Wayne gotten rid of him? Why hadn't he told her? She opened the kitchen door and looked out back, then turned and opened the basement door.

"Jack?" She whistled for him. "Jack, come here, boy!"

Rebecca heard him whimpering and yelping, but he didn't come to her.

"Poor doggy, did Daddy chain you down there in that spooky old basement?"

She flipped on the light and started down the stairs.

Jordan Ellis sat at his desk, holding a wadded-up piece of memo paper. He tossed it toward the waste can in the corner, and it landed on the floor with a dozen others that had missed their mark.

Why hadn't he heard anything new from Agent Snead? From John Richards? From Agent Cassidy at the photo lab? It was almost lunchtime.

He got up from his desk and placed his hands on the windowsill, his eyes looking down at City Park. *Come on, guys. I'm ready to blow this case wide open. Find me something!*

The phone rang and he grabbed it. "This is Jordan."

"Sir, it's Cassidy. Nothing in the sales records. Looks like a dead end."

"What about Marcum?"

All he remembers is the guy who picked up the pictures left in an old truck. He's not sure of the color, thought it might be black."

Jordan mused. "No license number. No make. No model. No year. Just an old truck that *might* be black?"

"He did say there was a tarp over the truck bed, held down with bungee cords. That's it."

"Okay. Put it in the case notes. I'll call Snead. I've got him on a fast-track. Maybe we're getting somewhere."

Rebecca neared the bottom of the steps. "I'm coming, Jack. Poor poochie. Are you lonesome?"

She smiled at the sound of his playful yelping.

"Help me!" cried a female voice. "Please, help! I'm over here!"

Ferocious snarling silenced the frightened voice. It sounded as though Jack were ripping someone to pieces! Rebecca stood frozen on the stairs.

"Jack, sit!" she shouted, her voice quavering. "Sit!"

Rebecca grabbed a wood-handled broom from the corner at the bottom of the stairs. She clutched it tightly, her heart beating wildly, her breathing rapid.

"Sit, Jack!" She shouted with all the authority she could muster. "Sit!"

The snarling and growling stopped.

Rebecca paused for a moment, then turned the corner of the stairwell in time to see Jack spring into the air. The sudden jolt knocked her backward, and her head hit the cement floor.

She lay staring at the ceiling, the basement turning to gray fuzz—and then nothing.

Jordan glanced up at the clock—11:55. His phone rang. He grabbed it on the first ring.

"John?"

"You're not a bit anxious, are you?"

"Come on, Richards. What've you got?"

"Remember I told you I had a wild hair?"

"Yeah...?"

"I was right. One of the strands of hair found in yesterday's notes is *canine*. Our perp may be receding, but he's been around a dog with hair that's as dark and straight as his. We're working on identifying the breed, but maybe Snead will put two and two together and figure it out even before we're sure."

"You're a genius. Thanks!"

Jordan hung up the phone and dialed.

"Jason, it's me. I need you to add something to the scenario. See what happens when you factor in a dog with short, straight hair about as dark as our perp's. John Richards found a dog hair in with the popcorn dust. Also, factor in an old truck, possibly black, with a tarp over the bed. See if that does anything. I'll be here. Go!"

Rebecca opened her eyes. Jack's wet tongue was licking her face.

"Jack, stop it...yuck." She pushed him away.

The Doberman ran in circles, yelping and barking.

She touched a sore spot on her head and noticed blood on her fingers. In an instant, Rebecca remembered everything. She got to her feet and saw something at the other end of the basement. A *cage?* Rebecca walked toward it, disgusted that the basement smelled like an outhouse. Hadn't Wayne bothered to clean up after Jack?

Suddenly she stopped, her eyes colliding with those of a girl who stood like a POW on the other side of a padlocked gate.

Rebecca's throat tightened. She could hardly utter the word. *"Taylor?"*

The girl nodded, though she scarcely resembled the beautiful daughter of G. R. Logan. Rebecca noted the hole in her sweater… the butchered blond curls…the stocking feet.

"I'm so sorry! I didn't know until yesterday my brother did this. I'm Rebecca Purdy. I'm getting you out of here."

Taylor pointed to Jack, brought a finger to her lips, and shook her head.

"Can't you talk?" Rebecca asked.

Taylor shook her head and pointed again at Jack.

"I don't understand."

Taylor backed away from the gate, her hands over her ears. "He's trained to attack if I talk."

Jack lunged at the gate with such ferocity that Rebecca squealed and stumbled backwards. "Jack, sit! *Sit!*"

The Doberman obeyed.

Rebecca leaned over, her hands on her knees. She took slow, deep breaths and then stood up. "Does he do that every time you talk?"

Taylor nodded and mouthed the words *Please help me.* Her eyes were desperate.

Rebecca examined the padlock. "Do you know where he keeps the key?"

Taylor shrugged and shook her head.

"I need something to break this. I'll be back."

At the height of the lunch rush at Monty's Diner, the phone rang. Mark Steele picked it up. He walked over to Wayne.

"It's your Mom. She sounds upset. Better take it in back."

Wayne slipped into the back room and picked up the phone. "Hello, Mom."

"Do you know where Rebecca is?"

"Isn't she in school?"

"No, she's been sick all week," Velma said. "At first I thought it was physical, but I'm beginning to think it's emotional. I should never have let her drive to Baxter and get in the middle of all that media hype. I think the kidnapping has really upset her. I made her an appointment with Dr. Martin this morning, but she never showed up. She's not at school. She's not at home. Something's wrong!"

"Whoa, Mom. Slow down, let's—"

"I don't know what to do! She's never done anything like this before. I'm really scared. I don't know if I should call the police or—"

"Mom," he said gently. "Calm down for a minute and let's think. It's way too soon to involve the police. How long has she been gone?"

"I'm not sure. I rode to work with Charlotte at 8:30 and left the car for Rebecca so she could keep her appointment. It's almost 1:00 now, so—"

"So at worst, she's been gone a few hours. Could she have gone shopping, just to get her mind on something else?"

"She's too sick. I'm totally baffled why she didn't keep her appointment with Dr. Martin. I've never seen Rebecca like this. She's a different child. I know she's not on drugs or anything like that. She was perfectly fine until she got home from Baxter on Monday. Something's horribly wrong, Wayne. This is so out of character for her!"

Wayne's heart raced faster than his mind. He looked at his watch.

"Mom, I'm sure Beck's fine. She probably started feeling better and took advantage of having the car. Don't panic and *don't* call the police. She'd have to be gone longer than a few hours before they'll do anything. Who knows, maybe she'll show up here again. If she does, I'll call you right away. She's a really responsible kid. Let's not panic, okay?"

"All right, Wayne. Maybe you're right. After what happened to those two girls in Baxter, I guess I'm a little frightened."

"Mom, the kidnapping wasn't some random act. It was planned. You don't have to worry about Beck. I'd stake my life on it."

"All right. I'll wait a while and see if she comes home."

"I'll check with you later," he said. "Try not to worry."

Wayne hung up the phone. He went over to the utility sink, splashed cold water on his face, then grabbed his bomber jacket and his keys and went out front.

"Mark, can you get by without me for the rest of my shift? I know it's busy, but something's come up and I need to help my mom. It can't wait."

"Is she all right?"

"She's really upset about something. I know how to calm her down."

"Sure, go on. I'll see you in the morning." Mark patted him on the shoulder. "Do what you need to do."

At 12:55, Jordan got a call from Special Agent Snead.

"Jordan, there's a guy here who's a match on every count."

"Now you're talking! Who?"

"His name's Wayne Purdy. On the surface, it doesn't make sense. He's lived here all his life. Never been a problem of any kind. He's hardworking, a model employee. He's high profile—works six days a week down at Monty's Diner and at Abernathy's Hardware. Everybody likes him. Our agents thought he was a real nice kid.

"But listen to this: twenty-three, dark hair starting to recede, right-handed, lives by himself, doesn't have friends to speak of, and owns a Doberman who loves popcorn—even joked about it in the interview."

Jordan was on his feet.

"It gets better. He owns a computer and printer, and drives an old truck with a tarp over the bed, *and* his old man died just a few weeks after the plant closing. The only thing not accounted for is the telephoto lens, and my guess is he's got one somewhere."

"Jason, what's his work schedule—where and when?"

"The interview file says Monty's from 6:00 A.M. until 2:00, and then Abernathy's from 3:00 to 6:00, Monday through Saturday."

"Yeah…I remember Fulmer and Billings telling me about him," Jordan said. "Didn't he have an alibi for the day of the kidnapping?"

"Showed on time for both jobs, but had lunch by himself from 2:00 to 3:00. Purdy said after leaving Monty's, he filled his truck with gas and then ate in his truck in the back lot of Miller's Market because he *likes the quaint neighborhood*. Yeah, right. It's only a couple of blocks from the high school."

"Anyone see him there?"

"Nope. A kid named Kevin Howell, who works at the Texaco near downtown, remembers Purdy stopping to fill up his truck. He wasn't sure of the exact time, but said 2:00, give or take, sounded about right."

"And the girls left the school just after 2:00? You're the *best,* Jason. Thanks!"

Jordan hung up the phone and dialed.

"This is agent Fulmer."

"Fulmer, where are you?"

"At some barbecue place on the north side of town, having lunch with Billings."

"Get over to Monty's Diner. We have a suspect, a kid you interviewed yesterday afternoon—Wayne Purdy."

"*Purdy's* a suspect?"

"He's a perfect match! Pick him up ASAP and bring him in. Don't wait for a doggy bag. Move!"

Rebecca frantically rummaged through the garage, hoping to find the hacksaw she remembered seeing her father use on a wrought-iron railing. Where did he keep that thing?

She'd already tried hitting the padlock with a hammer, but she couldn't break it. She looked through every tool hanging on the wall, piled in the tool chest, and stacked in the corners. She pulled open drawers, feeling around for anything that might work. But nothing looked like it would cut or break the heavy padlock that stood between Taylor and freedom. *God, I need help!*

Rebecca climbed the step stool and began looking on the shelves above the workbench. She discovered jars of nails and screws and bolts, but nothing helpful. She picked up an empty square box with a padlock pictured on the front and accidentally dropped it on the floor.

She climbed down, picked up the box, and pulled out the packing. She saw something on the bottom. *A key!*

With renewed determination, Rebecca ran down the basement stairs and hurried to the gate.

"Jack, *sit,*" she said. "Hang on, Taylor. This might be the extra key. And if I can get you out of here, there's still time to find Sherry before I have to confront Wayne."

Rebecca held the padlock, her hands shaking, her heart racing, her body heat trapped inside her wool coat.

"Please let this be right." She turned the key. "Taylor, it worked! It's open!"

Taylor backed into the far corner of the cage, her eyes fixed on Jack.

"Don't worry. I'll take Jack upstairs and shut him in Wayne's room. I'll call for you when the coast is clear."

Taylor nodded.

"Come on, Jack." Rebecca went up the stairs with Jack, put him in Wayne's room, and shut the door. Then she called to Taylor from the top of the stairs.

Rebecca watched Taylor climb the stairs and was surprised when she threw her arms around her.

"Thank you," Taylor whispered.

"Do you know where Wayne is hiding Sherry?" Rebecca asked.

The agony in Taylor's expression was unlike any Rebecca had ever seen. Taylor dropped to her knees and wailed without making a sound. She hugged herself and rocked back and forth.

Rebecca dropped down next to her. "Wayne promised me he wouldn't hurt you. He said his threats were just to scare your father, that he wasn't going to hurt either of you!"

Taylor looked at her, her lip quivering, her eyes full of tears.

"Did my brother hurt Sherry?"

Taylor nodded, tears trickling down her face.

"Are you sure? Did you see him?"

"Last night…he strangled her…I couldn't do anything to help her. Please get me out of here!"

They were startled by a noise outside. Rebecca ran to the picture window in the living room and saw Wayne's truck coming up the gravel drive.

"Oh, no! It's him."

Rebecca slipped off her coat and put it on Taylor. "Quick, out the back door! Let's run to the woods! After you get away, I'll go back and calm my brother down. Keep going till you get to the brick house on the other side. That's the Reynoldses' place. Run!"

Jordan's phone rang and he grabbed it.

"Yeah."

"It's Fulmer. We're at Monty's and we've got a problem. Wayne Purdy left twenty minutes ago. His boss doesn't know where he is. Says his mother called and was upset about something, and he left to help her."

"That's just great! He hasn't missed a day in six months, and he picks the *one* day we're onto him to leave early!" Jordan got up and paced. "You've got his address. Check out the house."

⌒∾⌒

Wayne dashed into the house and spotted the kitchen door wide open and the girls running toward the woods.

"Oh, no, you don't!" He grabbed his hunting rifle from the rack next to the back door and stepped outside. He fired at Taylor Logan, who fell like a young doe at the hands of a poacher. Rebecca kept running until she disappeared in the woods.

Wayne ran toward his fallen prey, feeling the rush of victory. But as he got closer, panic overtook him. He raced, out of breath, to where his trophy lay, then fell to his knees where his eyes told him what his heart had feared. "Beck!"

Wayne felt for a pulse and found none. He pulled his sister's limp body into his arms and rocked her, his hands trembling, her warm blood soaking the knees of his jeans.

Rebecca was transfixed on the most radiant creature she had ever seen. He stood as a towering giant with enormous wings and a flowing robe that glowed like the sun. His smile melted deep into her soul, and she knew he had been with her all her life. The angel held out his hand and took hers, and in the next instant, they entered eternity.

"Noooo!"

Taylor cringed when she heard a man cry out. She'd heard the shot but never looked back.

Deeper and deeper into the woods she ran, bundled in Rebecca's coat, enduring the excruciating pain of running in stocking feet across the unforgiving forest floor.

Was she awake or was it a nightmare? Taylor didn't know anymore. All she knew was she had to find the Reynoldses' brick house.

THIRTY-THREE

Wayne sobbed, his arms wrapped around Rebecca's limp body, his heart breaking. *Why didn't you listen to me? I tried to keep you out of this. Don't die, Beck. Please don't die...*

After several minutes, he gently laid her limp body on the cold, hard earth.

He was suddenly aware of the discarded things in the family's backyard: the old Frigidaire, his father's rusted-out VW bus, an old wringer washing machine, a once-loved tricycle that had survived both siblings. In this dumpy graveyard, he had to leave the most valuable thing in his life. He wept bitterly.

Wayne kissed Rebecca's cheek, then took off his bomber jacket and laid it lengthwise, covering as much of her as possible.

He got up and ran back to the house. He stood at the kitchen sink, washing the blood from his hands, and then hurried to his room to change clothes.

"Down, Jack! Sit! I can't take you with me."

He retrieved a roll of bills stashed in a cigar box and put the money in his pocket. Then he grabbed his pistol and some ammunition and fled the house.

Taylor ran up to the brick house and banged on the front door.

"Help! Please, somebody help me! Mr. and Mrs. Reynolds, are you there? Help!" She pounded again on the door.

"Can't ya give a body time to git there?" hollered a woman.

"Mrs. Reynolds! Mrs. Reynolds, help! Rebecca Purdy told me to come here. I don't know where else to go…please, Mrs. Reynolds!"

A white-haired woman opened the door. "Heavens, child," she said softly. "What happened to ya?"

The woman led Taylor into the house and sat her on the couch. She took an oblong doily out from under a centerpiece on the coffee table, doubled it over, and placed it under Taylor's feet. For the first time, Taylor realized she was bleeding.

"I'm Lucy Reynolds. Sit here while I git some warm water."

Taylor heard footsteps coming down a creaky staircase.

"Lucy, I heard ya callin'," said a man's voice. "But where'd ya go and disappear to?"

"I'm in the kitchen, Edgar. Gittin' somethin' ta soak the feet of some wounded child sittin' in our livin' room."

"What happened?"

"Not sure. Rebecca Purdy sent her over here. She's in some kinda trouble. Or met with somethin' more awful than she cares ta talk about."

Taylor heard the words, but it was as if they were talking about someone else.

Edgar walked into the living room. He glanced at her torn and bloody socks, then sat in a chair across from her. He tried not to look shocked, but Taylor could tell he was.

"I'm Edgar Reynolds. Lucy out there's my wife." He nodded

toward the kitchen. "She's gittin' somethin' ta help ya. I think it'd be a good idea to call the police."

Taylor shook her head. "Please, I want to go home. Just let me go home. If I call my dad, he'll come get me."

"We can do that, too," he said gently. "But the police will keep ya safe so that whoever hurt ya can't do it no more. We've got a real fine police chief. How 'bout if we give him a call so he can let yer dad know yer safe and git him over here, or take ya to him?"

Lucy walked back into the living room, carrying a large plastic tub. "Child, who done this to ya?"

"Please, I want to go home," she said, starting to cry.

Lucy set the water on the floor, then sat next to Taylor and patted her hand. "Now, darlin', we'll see to it ya git home. But we need to know yer name."

"My name's Taylor Logan."

"Lord have mercy, girl, we've been prayin' fer ya, and here ya are—*alive*. Is yer friend out there runnin' through them woods, too?"

Taylor shook her head slowly from side to side, the words she couldn't speak forming a lump in her throat.

"Lucy," Edgar said, "I'm gonna call Chief Cameron and tell him Taylor is safe. Her folks are gonna be the happiest folks in Baxter tonight."

Taylor closed her eyes and let the warm tears roll down her cheeks. Sherry's parents would be the saddest.

Velma Purdy saw Agents Henry Black and Carl Matthews enter the beauty salon. She left her station and rushed over to them.

"Rebecca! Has something happened to Rebecca?"

The two agents looked puzzled.

"Uh, ma'am, we're not here about Rebecca. We'd like to ask you a few questions about Wayne," Agent Black said.

"Then Rebecca's all right?"

"Like I said, ma'am, we're not here about Rebecca."

Velma saw heads turn in her direction. "Let's go in the back and talk." She led the agents into the back room, then turned and said, "What did you want to ask me about Wayne?"

"He received a call from you today at Monty's, and his boss gave him permission to leave early to help you with something. Is that accurate?"

"Well, yes, I did call him. I was worried about Rebecca. Wayne never said anything about helping me, but maybe he went looking for her. But that doesn't make sense…how would he know where to start? Even I don't know. That's why I'm worried."

"Worried, ma'am?"

"Ever since Rebecca got sick, she seems sad and depressed, totally different. I made an appointment for her to see the doctor this morning, but she never showed up. She's not at home or at school, and she's got my car. It's completely out of character for her."

The two agents looked at each other knowingly.

"What?" Velma said. "Should I call the police? Wayne thinks I'm overreacting, so I decided to wait. But I still haven't heard from her."

"Any idea where we can find Wayne?"

"Not really."

"Could Rebecca have met Wayne for some reason?"

"Why would she go back to Baxter? She was just there to see him on Monday."

"Ma'am, what kind of relationship does your daughter have with her brother?"

"They're incredibly close. Wayne's been big brother and father ever since my husband died. But they've always been close."

"So Wayne might confide in Rebecca, and she might confide in him? Is that a fair assessment?"

"I suppose so. Why are you asking me these questions?"

"We're following up on the kidnapping. We just want to ask Wayne a few more questions."

"More questions? What kinds of questions?"

"Ma'am, we're not at liberty to discuss the details of the case, but if you see or hear from your son, have him get in touch with us right away. Sorry to bother you at work. This couldn't wait."

"Well, what should I do about Rebecca? How long should I wait before involving the authorities?"

THIRTY-FOUR

Jordan paced in front of the window in his office. The phone rang, and he grabbed it.

"This is Jordan."

"It's Fulmer. Billings and I are at Wayne Purdy's home. Looks like he's our man."

"Have you got him?"

"His truck's here, but he's not on the premises. We found the front and back doors of the house wide open, and his *pet* Doberman chewing its way out of a bedroom. We checked outside and found a dead girl, shot in the back with a 270 Winchester. Blood all over the place. It isn't pretty."

Jordan sighed and sat in his chair. "Which girl, Fulmer?"

"This kid's blond and blue-eyed, about the same age and height as the Logan girl, but doesn't look a thing like her."

"What makes you so sure it's not Taylor Logan? Who knows what she's been through? She might look different."

"Sir, this Jane Doe's no beauty queen, trauma or no trauma. Plus, her long hair hasn't been chopped on, and it's squeaky clean. Her nails were recently polished—in blue, no less. She's wearing costume jewelry and heavy eye makeup. Looks like half the high schoolers we see, but doesn't fit what we know of Logan's daughter. Her face isn't even close."

Jordan leaned back in his chair and raked his hand through his hair. Just what he needed—a dead body he couldn't identify. "Where'd you find her?"

"At the edge of the woods behind the house. Must've just happened. Looks like she might've been running away, and it's not hard to see why."

"Fill me in."

"We found a cage of some kind in the basement—floor-to-ceiling chain-link with a gate—furnished with only a sleeping bag and a flashlight. There was a camping toilet, but the sanitary conditions were awful. Let's just say he's a lousy custodian. Heck of a way to treat a houseguest."

"Anything else?" Jordan asked.

"We found dog dishes outside the cage and an open padlock on the floor."

"You think Purdy's in the woods?"

"Maybe. There're some shoeprints out back, but the ground is hard. I don't know if they'll tell us much."

"This doesn't fit his profile." Jordan said. "This guy's no serial killer."

"An ID on the girl might dot a few i's."

"You're reading my mind. Did you call for backup?"

"Should be here any minute."

"Okay. Go after Purdy. I'm on the way. And Fulmer, hear me…if you get him, do everything by the book. If he's our man, I don't want anything thrown out because we didn't do our job right. I want the pleasure of taking him down lower than a snake."

"Yes, sir. It'll be a pleasure."

The second Jordan hung up the phone it rang again. "This is Jordan."

"It's Chief Cameron. Are you sitting down?"

"No, the case has blown wide open. I'm on my way—"

"So Edgar Reynolds called you, too?"

"Who's Edgar Reynolds?" Jordan said.

"The man who called to say Taylor Logan's alive."

"Alive? Are you sure?"

"She's sitting in his living room."

Taylor couldn't stop crying. She didn't want to talk to the police. She didn't want to wait for the FBI. Why couldn't she just go home?

Edgar Reynolds brought two women into the living room.

"Taylor, I'm Amanda, and this is Jessica. We're FBI agents. We're here to make sure you get home to your parents safely."

"Is he still out there?" Taylor asked.

"Wayne Purdy?"

She nodded.

"Is he the man who kidnapped you and Sherry Kennsington?"

She nodded again.

Amanda sat beside her. "Don't worry, sweetie, we're here to protect you. Every law enforcement officer in the state is looking for him. We won't let him near you."

"Rebecca said after I got away, she'd go back and calm him down. I heard a shot, and I heard a man yell...but I just kept running like she told me until I got to the brick house. I kept banging on the door until Mrs. Reynolds let me in."

"Who is Rebecca?"

"Wayne's sister. She's the one who took Jack away and found the key to the lock, and then helped me escape."

"Who is *Jack?*"

"Wayne's Doberman."

"Taylor, where is Sherry Kennsington?" Amanda asked.

Taylor looked down, her hands shaking, her fingers locked together.

"Take your time, sweetie."

"Wayne, uh…strangled her."

"When?"

"Last night, I think. The basement was dark, and we were never sure if it was day or night. But Wayne always came down after work to see Jack. And to scare us." Taylor put her hand to her mouth and whimpered.

"You don't have to talk about this right now if you don't want to," Amanda said. "But anything you can tell us will—"

"He just left her there on the floor…like she was nothing. I covered her up." Taylor started to sob. "He came back later and kept screaming at me…told me I was next. I couldn't watch when he put Sherry in the sleeping bag…" Her voice cracked. "Then he took her away."

Amanda put a fresh Kleenex in Taylor's hand. "So when did Rebecca come to set you free?"

"A little while ago. But Wayne came home before I could get away, so Rebecca said to run here."

There was a gentle knock on the door, and Edgar Reynolds poked his head into the living room. "Excuse me, another FBI fella is at the front door."

The two lady agents excused themselves and followed Edgar to the front door. They lowered their voices, but Taylor strained to hear.

"Purdy's truck is at the house, but he's on the loose. And I heard we have one dead girl on the premises. Shot in the back. Must've just happened because there's fresh blood on the ground."

"The dead girl…where was she found?"

"At the edge of Purdy's property. Must be Sherry Kennsington, though Billings swears it isn't. Keeps referring to her as a Jane Doe."

"Taylor just told us that Purdy strangled Sherry last night, put her body in a sleeping bag, and took her away. Good grief, you don't suppose…"

"Suppose what?"

"This gets creepier by the minute. I'm thinking our perp killed his own sister."

Marita Logan sat between G. R. and Randy in the second seat of the FBI van, trying to grasp the fact that Taylor was alive.

Agent McCullum's eyes appeared in the rearview mirror. "I need to prepare you for what you'll see when we get to the hospital."

"What do you mean? What did he do to her?" G. R.'s hands turned into fists.

"She's not been sexually assaulted, so if that's what—"

"Oh, thank God!" Marita said. "I've had nightmares."

"But be prepared to see startling changes," McCullum said. "Sometimes the family expects to see the child as she was. Taylor's been through a harrowing experience. If she seems like a stranger, don't be alarmed. She needs you to be there for her right now."

"We will. Anything else?" G. R. asked.

"Realize your daughter's been without running water, so she's not going to be fresh as a daisy. She's lost weight. Her hair's been chopped on. Her feet are bruised and cut and swollen pretty badly."

"How serious is it?" Marita asked.

"Until your family physician examines her, we won't know for sure. But her *physical* injuries don't appear to be serious."

"Our doctor's meeting us there," G. R. said. "I don't want anyone else touching her."

"You made that very clear," McCullum said.

Marita leaned toward Randy. "There's the hospital. We're really going to see her. I still can't believe it."

"One more thing," McCullum said. "It's important to respect her feelings. It's better if you don't resort to patronizing phrases like, 'I know it was awful, but it's all over now.' Because truthfully, folks, no one knows what all she's been through. And it *isn't* over yet. She'll probably feel guilty because she survived and the Kennsington girl didn't. She might even be angry with you, Mr. Logan, over the revenge issue. Each victim responds differently, and sometimes the responses aren't rational, but they have to be dealt with."

"Will the counselors help us with that?" Marita asked.

"I'm sure they will, ma'am."

"I don't need a counselor to understand my own daughter," G. R. said.

"Like I said, Mr. Logan, expect her to be different for a while."

Joe Kennsington knocked softly and opened the bedroom door. Mary Beth lay on her side, facing the window.

He sat on the side of the bed, his hand rubbing her back.

"How'd the kids handle it?" she asked.

"They're shaken and terribly disappointed. But they're strong. It's going to take time."

"Where are they?"

"In the living room. I think they could use a hug from their mother about now."

"I'll go talk to them..." Mary Beth's voice trailed off. She started to sob. "Why didn't God do something to save her? He could have! Instead, He just sat up there on His throne and let it happen. I keep seeing that animal's hands around her throat..."

Mary Beth clenched her fists and hit her pillow over and over.

Joe waited a few moments; then he held her arms until he had her attention. "Honey, we have to pull together and get through this. We have two kids who need us."

"What about the one who needed us last night, Joe? Who was there for her?"

~∞~

Taylor sat on a couch in a private sitting area at Baxter Memorial Hospital, her eyes focused on her hands.

"Nervous?" Amanda asked.

Taylor nodded. "A little. I don't want to talk about it. Especially about Sherry."

"Sweetie, your parents are on the way. No one expects you to talk until you feel like it."

Taylor looked up at Amanda's kind face and wondered if she would ever feel like it.

"Do your feet hurt?"

"Some. They told me my dad doesn't want anyone to examine me but our family doctor."

Taylor looked up and saw her father standing at the door, his eyes filled with tears.

"Dad!"

He rushed to the couch, took her in his arms, and wept. "It's really you! I didn't think we would ever see you again."

"Wayne left us the newspapers…the horrible words on the water tower…" Taylor's voice failed. She collapsed in her father's arms.

In the next instant, Marita and Randy were on the couch and the four were linked in an embrace.

"Honey, I love you so much," said her mother. "I didn't think I would ever get to tell you that again…"

Taylor recognized Randy's affectionate tap on her head without even seeing him. She closed her eyes and held on to the moment, afraid she might wake up and find herself back in the thick darkness.

On Thursday evening, Jordan Ellis sat with Sheriff Hal Barker in the Kennsingtons' living room.

"I know this is devastating," Jordan said. "We share your grief. We'll get Purdy and bring him to justice."

"That won't bring back my daughter," Mary Beth said.

Jordan swallowed hard. "No, it won't. And I can't fully experience your grief, but I share your anger."

"Well, we can thank G. R. Logan for *all* of this!" she said. "Wayne Purdy is a horrible monster, and I hope he gets everything he deserves. But this is still G. R.'s fault!"

"Mary Beth..." Joe said softly.

"Well, it's true. G. R. doesn't care who he steps on. Anyone who gets in his way gets flattened. Well, the revenge was supposed to be against *him,* for the way he's treated people. Why did our Sherry have to pay the price?"

"Wayne Purdy did the murdering," Jordan said. "He's the one responsible."

"See it however you want, but I'll never forgive G. R. Logan for this! And isn't it just wonderful that he gets *his* sweet daughter back, while I'll never see mine again? Show me the justice in that!"

"Mom, can I get you some water or something?" Jason asked, his hand on her arm.

"No. I'm fine."

"Mrs. Wilson sent over a spaghetti casserole," Erica said. "Maybe it'd be good if you ate something."

"I said *no*. I'm fine."

"Gentlemen..." Joe said, his voice shaking. "Uh, do you have any idea...where to look for Sherry's body?"

Jordan nodded at Hal to answer.

"Something Taylor said leads us to believe Sherry's body may have been buried. Teams are combing the woods near the Purdy house. FBI, police, and sheriff's department are giving it everything we've got to find Sherry and to get Wayne Purdy."

"You were too late to stop him, though, weren't you?" Mary Beth said.

Hal leaned forward, his Stetson in his hands. "Mary Beth, we tried. We really did. Lots of us stayed up nights trying to put the puzzle together. Who would've ever suspected Wayne was capable of this? If it hadn't been for Rebecca…" Hal paused, his face quivering with emotion. "Taylor wouldn't have made it either."

Mary Beth stared at the floor, her lips forming a straight line.

"If there are no more questions, I need to get back to the investigation," Jordan said.

"Thanks for your hard work," Joe said. "This has to be difficult for you, too."

"I'll call you as soon as we find her," Jordan said.

When he stepped down from the porch, Jordan felt the stabbing pain of defeat and wanted a place to bleed in private. He hurried to his car and drove away, wondering for the umpteenth time in his career what motivated him to stick with it.

Through a crack in the living room drapes, Velma Purdy watched the media gathered outside her home. How did she end up the mother of both the villain and the heroine in this horrible kidnapping?

She sat on the couch, her head in her hands. *Is this how God feels when His children do the unthinkable?*

How could Wayne have done such a thing to Taylor and Sherry? How could he have killed Rebecca? She leaned her head on the back of the couch and moved it from side to side. How?

She got up and paced, glancing at the door to Rebecca's empty room. This couldn't be happening.

She heard cheering outside and peeked through the crack in the drapes. In the middle of her front lawn, someone had planted a wanted poster with Wayne's picture.

Velma put her hands to her mouth and began to sob.

THIRTY-FIVE

Monty's Diner was buzzing with conversation on Friday morning. Mark Steele stood off to the side, his arms folded, his eyes staring at the floor.

"You okay, Mark?" George Gentry got up and put his hand on his shoulder.

"I still can't believe it," Mark said. "I let Wayne leave early, the one and only time he ever asked, and he kills his sister. I worked with him six days a week. How could I not notice *something*? Man, I had no clue. None. He seemed like a nice guy, a great employee. I feel like a real dupe."

"Don't be so hard on yourself," Rosie Harris said. "None of us saw it coming. If Wayne had all that bottled-up anger, I don't know how he kept a lid on it."

Hattie Gentry nodded. "I don't remember him saying anything hateful about G. R. Logan."

"Six mornings a week for six months..." George shook his head. "And he's never been anything but nice. Are they *sure* they've fingered the right guy?"

"When you stop to think about it," Reggie Mason said, "he had nothing goin' for him. No ambition. He was a second-generation throwback from the Logan era. It all makes sense."

"*Sense?* What planet do you come from, buddy?" said a stranger in booth two. "Nothing about sick rhymes, kidnapping, or murdering young girls makes sense!"

Reggie looked over his shoulder. "I just meant it adds up, that's all."

"Yeah, adds up to *sick.*"

Rosie poured Reggie a refill. "The one I feel the most sorry for is his mother. Can you imagine what's going through that poor woman's mind?"

Hattie shook her head. "Has to be devastated."

"I would never have thought him capable of this," Rosie said. "I saw how he was with Beck. He was crazy about her. How could he just shoot her in the back?" Rosie's voice cracked.

Liv Spooner touched her hand. "Can you imagine how Sheriff Barker felt when he identified her? I heard his face turned sheet-white, and all six-foot-four of him nearly keeled over. Poor man. He'd known that girl all her life."

"The sheriff was sitting with Beck on Monday," Mark said. "Right there at the end of the counter. I just can't believe she's dead, *or* that Wayne killed her."

"Hel-lo?" said the stranger in booth two. "The guy strangled Sherry Kennsington! You people better face it: He's a cold-blooded killer. Taylor Logan was an eyewitness."

Mark put his hands in his pockets and hung his head.

"I wonder if they'll find Sherry's body," Jim Hawkins said. "The paper says the search is underway."

Mort whirled around on the stool. "Wanna know what I think?"

Mark sighed. "Not really."

"I'll betcha Wayne buried her in his backyard, like one o' them serial killers. You just never know who ya been rubbin' elbows with, do ya?"

"Mort, you read too much Stephen King." George dismissed him with a wave of his hand.

"Where do you suppose Wayne is?" Reggie asked.

"I'll tell you one thing," said the stranger. "If I was in charge of this case, I'd make darn sure Taylor Logan was locked up tighter than a tick. As long as Purdy's still out there, it ain't over."

Taylor lay in her hospital bed, memorizing the sunrise, which cast a pink glow across the white walls. Never again would she take light for granted. She heard activity in the hallway and was vaguely aware of a shift change in progress.

She closed her eyes and imagined Sherry's clear, sweet voice…

> *Blessed assurance, Jesus is mine!*
> *O what a foretaste of glory divine!*
> *Heir of salvation, purchase of God.*
> *Born of His Spirit, washed in His blood.*
> *This is my story, this is my song,*
> *Praising my Savior all the day long.*
> *This is my story, this is my—*

"Good morning," said a female voice. "How are you feeling today?"

"Ready to go home."

"I'm sure the doctor will talk to you about that when he makes his rounds. Now, young lady, I need to check your vitals. I hope you're hungry. I saw the breakfast cart headed this way. Is your mother still here?"

"She stayed last night, but I talked her into going home for a while. It's sort of nice not having to talk."

"At least she doesn't have to worry with the FBI outside your door."

Taylor let the woman take her blood pressure and her pulse, and was glad when she left and the room was quiet again.

She couldn't stop thinking about Sherry or the spiritual experiences they had shared in that dark, awful place. Why did God let Wayne kill her? It didn't make sense. It wasn't fair.

There was a loud crash in the hallway. Taylor jumped, her heart pounding, forgetting for a split second that she was safe from Wayne's clutches.

She closed her eyes again. She imagined the sound of Sherry's singing, and God's presence seemed as real to her as it had then.

On Friday morning, the phone rang at the Kennsingtons'. Jason picked it up before the answering machine clicked on.

"Hello, Kennsington residence… Yes, ma'am, would you hold on for a minute, please?" Jason turned to his parents, his hand over the receiver. "It's Taylor's mom. She wants to speak with one of you."

Mary Beth shook her head.

Joe took the receiver from Jason and cleared his throat. "Hello, Marita."

"Joe, we're so sorry about Sherry…" She sounded mournful, struggling for composure. "It's hard to know what to say."

"I know. We would've called you, but it's been crazy around here. They're still—uh—searching for Sherry…everyone's taking it pretty hard…" Emotion stole his voice.

"Joe, I'd give anything if we could turn the clock back a week."

"Me, too, Marita."

"How's Mary Beth?"

"Not good. It's going to take some time." He noticed Mary Beth's angry glance and figured she knew they were talking about her.

"I want you and Mary Beth to know how very sorry we are."

"Thank you, Marita."

"Please tell Mary Beth I called."

"I will. And when you see Taylor…" He paused, coughing to cover his emotion. "Tell her we're all grateful she's…that she's safe."

"You're so kind…thank you."

Joe hung up the phone and turned to Mary Beth. "I guess you heard? That took courage."

"Courage? *This* is courage, Joe: sitting here waiting for our daughter's body to be found. What Marita just did is a *cakewalk!*"

Ellen Jones pored over the front page of Friday's edition. Every grim detail Taylor Logan had reported to the authorities was now officially part of the community's history, a matter of public record. Hate and murder had reared its ugly head here, the one place that had always seemed eternally innocent.

As Ellen's eyes moved over the headlines, she pictured each of the four young people caught in such a sinister web.

Sherry Kennsington Murdered—Taylor Logan Escapes
Kidnapper Wayne Purdy at Large;
Rebecca Purdy Dies During Rescue

Ellen blinked to clear her eyes. How could Wayne plot his evil scheme without anyone knowing what was in his heart?

She read the front-page story for a third time, picturing the squalor of the girls' fenced-in prison. She imagined Sherry's strangulation…Taylor's terrifying escape…Rebecca being shot in the back.

What if Wayne's vendetta made the hunt for Taylor Logan more important to him than whether or not he escaped? After all, he'd shot his own sister in the back. How could anyone feel safe with Wayne still out there?

More than anything, her heart was heavy for the Kennsingtons. Sherry had lost her life—and for what? No vengeance was exacted on G. R. Logan. His life would eventually return to normal.

In time, Ellen knew she would find the words for a feature story that would help the community to heal. But right now, it seemed as though a mountain had exploded and spewed its angry, molten contents upon everyone and everything in Baxter; and when it cooled, they would find it had reshaped their community forever.

At the Kennsingtons' the vigil continued. While friends and family were gathered in the kitchen, Mary Beth sat in the dining room by herself.

"There you are," Rhonda said.

"I don't feel like being around anyone."

"Mary Beth, if I could, I'd take your sorrow and carry it myself."

"Well, you *can't,* Rhonda. This is one battle I have to fight alone."

"The Lord can help you."

"He can but He hasn't! I'm having a little trouble with the 'trust' thing. We prayed with all our hearts, and He turned a deaf ear. So much for two or three gathered in His name…" Mary Beth was startled at the coldness of her own words.

"I promise not to preach at you," Rhonda said, "but please don't shut me out. Seeing you hurt causes me to hurt. I'm grieving for Sherry, too. All of us who love your family are."

Mary Beth got up and stood facing the pictures on the mantel.

"You want to know how I feel? I'm furious with God! And I loathe G. R. Logan. I'll probably hate Wayne Purdy for the rest of my life, but it was G. R. who turned him into a murderer."

Mary Beth glanced over at Rhonda and saw tears streaming down her face. She wished she'd kept her feelings to herself.

❧

Shortly after 9:00 A.M., the phone rang. Joe got up to answer it. Every eye was on him, every ear attentive.

"Where…? When…?" He looked at Mary Beth, his eyes glistening with tears. "Uh…should I come alone…? No, I'll tell them…I know you are, Jordan. I'm sorry, too." Joe hung up the phone, his chin quivering.

"No!" shouted Mary Beth. "I can't listen to this!" She ran from the room and up the stairs. Joe heard their bedroom door slam.

He blinked several times, trying to focus on the faces of those who surely must have surmised what he was about to tell them: Sherry's body had been found. The wait was over.

THIRTY-SIX

J oe Kennsington pulled into the driveway just after 2:00, vaguely aware that he and Mary Beth hadn't said a word since they got back in the car. They had chosen Sherry's casket and headstone and arranged for her burial at Oak Hills Cemetery. But after their first stop, everything else had been a blur...

"The search team found her in a shallow grave in the woods," Jordan had said. "Bruises on her neck are consistent with strangulation."

Joe took Mary Beth's hand and followed Jordan into a room where they stood looking down at a stainless steel table covered with a white sheet. A man in a lab coat pulled back the sheet. Joe nodded and began to weep, his hand clutching Mary Beth's, the image of his daughter's lifeless face frozen in his memory...

"Mr. Kennsington?"

Joe looked up. FBI agents opened the car door and escorted him and Mary Beth to the front door. He was aware of cameras flashing and people calling out, but he felt removed from it.

Once inside, Joe's gaze met Erica's and Jason's, the look in their eyes heavy and questioning. He opened his arms and they rushed to him, yielding to his comfort. Mary Beth walked past them and up the stairs. A few minutes later, the kids retreated to their rooms.

Joe got on the phone and called his parents and his in-laws. Then he hung up the phone and sat with his head in his hands. The sound of Jed Wilson's voice startled him.

"Joe? Why don't you go upstairs and crash," Jed said. "I'll make the rest of the phone calls."

"You wouldn't mind?"

"Not at all. I know everyone on your list. I can tell them what they need to know."

Late Friday afternoon, Joe and Mary Beth sat with Pastor Thomas, making arrangements for Sherry's funeral service.

"I'm expecting a huge show of support," Pastor Thomas said after they had settled on a date and time. "We don't have to decide today, but we'll have to consider whether or not to let the media cover the service."

"As overwhelming as their presence is, there's an upside," Joe said. "I wonder how many people have been praying for us—people we don't even know?"

"Hard to say," the pastor said. "Probably thousands. Maybe tens of thousands."

"I'm grateful for every single prayer." Joe's face quivered. "I couldn't do this without the Lord." He glanced at Mary Beth and wished he hadn't.

"Only God can give peace that passes understanding," the pastor said. "There's nothing else like it, but you already know that. Let's ask the Lord to lift us above the sorrow and let us rest in the knowledge that Sherry's in His presence right now, even as we're grieving…" He choked back the emotion. "I'm going to miss her, too."

Pastor Thomas prayed with them and then stood up. "Take some time to be alone with your thoughts. I'll talk to you tomorrow."

As they walked to the front door, Joe could tell by Mary Beth's steely silence that the pastor's words hadn't made a dent in her armor of anger.

Joe hung up the phone. He sat quietly for a few moments, and then headed up the stairs. He opened the bedroom door and closed it behind him.

"Honey, that was Taylor on the phone." He paused to let the words sink in. "She's still in the hospital, and her parents have gone home for the evening. She has something to tell us and asked if we would go over there."

"There's no way I can do that."

"Why not?"

"Seeing Taylor would…well, I just can't, that's all."

"She sounded eager to tell us something, Mary Beth."

"Jordan already told us everything, and seeing Taylor right now might throw me over the edge."

He looked into her eyes and saw only a wall. "I think it might help."

"Joe, I'm *not* going. Besides, there's no way I can hide my disdain for G. R., and Taylor's already paid enough for his mistakes."

"So what do you want me to tell her?"

"That I just can't see her yet. She'll understand."

Joe sighed. He kissed his wife on the forehead, then went downstairs and told his children about the phone call.

"I'll be back in a little while. Are you two sure you'll be all right?"

"We'll be okay," Erica said. "I wish Mom would go with you, though. I'm worried about her. Why do you think Taylor wants to talk to you?"

"I don't know, but I have a good feeling about it."

"Dad," Jason said, "will you tell her I'm glad she made it?"

"Me, too," Erica said, her arms wrapped around her father's neck.

"Of course." He swallowed the lump in his throat. "I shouldn't be late. You're sure you'll be all right if I leave?"

"Dad, go," Erica said. "We'll be fine."

Joe arrived at the hospital at 8:45. After being cleared by FBI agents, he knocked gently on Taylor's door.

"Come in," she said.

Joe slowly opened the door and saw Taylor sitting up in bed. His eyes filled with tears as he struggled for the right words.

Taylor burst into tears. "Mr. Kennsington, I'm so sorry about Sherry!"

Joe went over to her bedside and pulled up a chair. He took her hand in his. "Me, too, Taylor…but I'm glad you're alive." Joe held her hand to his cheek, letting tears fill a long moment of silence. "Mary Beth said you'd understand if she couldn't see you yet. After they found Sherry's body this morning…" He swallowed the emotion. "It's been pretty tough."

"I kept something for you." She slid a ring off her pinkie finger.

Joe recognized Sherry's cross ring. He took it from Taylor as if it were a priceless jewel and held it in his palm, his face quivering and his heart racing. He blinked away the moisture. "She's worn this since she was five years old. How did you…?"

"I knew Sherry would want you to have it," Taylor said, sounding surprisingly calm, her eyes filled with empathy beyond her years.

"I can't thank you enough."

"Mr. Kennsington, some things happened when Sherry and I were kidnapped that I can't explain. I thought maybe you could help me understand."

"What kinds of things?"

"Well, they may have been supernatural…" Taylor seemed tentative, as if she were sizing up his reaction.

"Tell me about them," he said.

"Do you know about the cage, and how Wayne left Jack in the basement so we couldn't talk?"

He nodded.

"Well, that was horrible enough. But when Wayne brought us the newspaper, and we read that I was going to be 'a lamb led to slaughter,' I just gave up. I curled up inside my sleeping bag and cried. I couldn't stop crying, but Sherry couldn't stop praying."

"Born determined." Joe almost smiled.

"I could tell Sherry was praying, but neither of us moved for hours. Then all of a sudden, I heard this lovely voice singing 'Blessed Assurance.' But the words had *feeling*—so much feeling—like the most beautiful words I ever heard. The weird thing is Jack didn't hear them! He didn't get vicious or react at all.

"I turned on the flashlight and saw Sherry kneeling on top of her sleeping bag, singing the words with all her heart. Something inside me felt so wonderful that I started singing, too. And guess what, Mr. Kennsington? The basement wasn't dark anymore, even though there wasn't a light on or anything. I can't really explain it.

"I looked at Sherry, and I could see her face! She smiled at me, and we kept singing for the longest time, and it was the most wonderful experience. It was like—well, almost like *God* was right there in the room with us."

Joe studied Taylor's face, his heart overflowing.

"But that's not all," she said. "It happened again. Only the second time I didn't know the song. Let me sing it for you, Mr. Kennsington. I want you to hear the melody." Taylor's voice was sweet and clear. "'On my bed I remember You; I think of You through the watches of the night. Because You are my help, I sing in the shadow of Your wings.'"

She sang it again, and Joe memorized the words and the melody.

"The words were so comforting," Taylor said. "It was like God had given them to Sherry, knowing they were exactly what I needed to hear. I felt like God had His arms around me. They gave me hope!"

Joe dabbed the tears from the corners of his eyes.

"The room stayed light for a while and we got to talk without Jack scaring us. Sherry asked me if I had ever been to the foot of the cross. She said something about God not saving the whole youth group as a package deal, that I had to choose Him as my Savior. We got so involved in conversation we didn't notice the light fading. Pretty soon Jack started attacking the fence. We never got to talk again after that."

There was a long pause. Joe squeezed her hand, and his eyes filled with tears, his heart overflowing.

"What an amazing and wonderful experience," he said. "God *was* with you. I knew He would be. But this is more than I ever prayed for."

"Mr. Kennsington, I've had time to think about this, and I want to give my heart to Jesus. If being saved is what made Sherry the way she was, I want to be like that. You know why Wayne strangled her? It was because Sherry…" The words caught in her throat. "I'm sorry…I thought I could talk about it."

He put his arms around her. "It's okay. Maybe someday you'll be able to talk about it. Maybe not. But you've blessed me more than you know. You started this conversation wondering if I could explain these experiences to you, but I think you already know why the Lord allowed them to happen. Not only did they sustain both of you girls through that horrible time, but they also brought *you* to the place where you want Jesus in your life. That's the most important decision any person could ever make. Plus, I now have these wonderful images in my mind of Sherry's faithfulness until the minute God took her home…" He choked back the tears. "Thank you. I'll treasure this forever."

There was a period of comfortable silence.

"Taylor, are you ready to accept Jesus tonight?"

"Yes. I've been thinking about it all day."

"Tell me what you understand about Him."

"Well, I know He's the Son of God, and He died for me because I'm a sinner and do things that are wrong. I need Him in my heart so He can change me and make me more like Him. That's what I saw in Sherry. She told me it was a whole new way of life that begins and ends with Jesus, that you kind of learn as you go."

"That's right. Inviting Jesus into your heart begins a lifetime of transformation. You might say that if God is your Father, there should be a family resemblance."

"I sort of know about that because I saw it in Sherry, but I've never heard it put that way before. I believe *all* that, Mr. Kennsington. And I'm ready to invite Jesus into my heart."

"Taylor, let's give the angels in heaven something else to rejoice about. You know they do that, don't you—rejoice every time a sinner repents and accepts the saving power of Jesus?"

"Really?"

Joe nodded and reached for her hand. Then, filled with the strangest mixture of grief and joy, he knelt beside Taylor's hospital bed, where his daughter's best friend gave her heart to Jesus. Taylor thanked God for Sherry's example, and Joe thanked Him for His immeasurable grace.

Then Joe took Sherry's cross ring out of his pocket and slipped it on Taylor's finger.

THIRTY-SEVEN

Wayne was behind the wheel of a blue Ford pickup he had stolen, and which bore license plates he had switched with an SUV parked at a bottling plant in Nashville. He thought it was funny the poor sap probably wouldn't notice until it was time to renew the plates.

Wayne kept glancing in his mirrors. He wasn't about to spend the rest of his life in some sorry jail cell. He had shaved his head and bought a black leather jacket and a clip-on earring at a Goodwill Store in Atlanta. He bought a phony tattoo and applied it to his left cheek.

A car full of teenage girls passed him; and a girl with long, blond hair looked over and smiled. He pounded the steering wheel with his palms. How could he have messed up and shot Rebecca? He worried about his mother being alone with her grief.

Blinded by the headlights of a tailgater, Wayne picked up his speed.

The headlights reappeared in his rearview mirror. Wayne sped forward for quite some distance to escape the glare. But seconds later, the tailgater resumed his position, the headlights too close to be visible.

Wayne reached over and put his right hand on his gun. What difference did it make now?

Everyone was asleep when Joe Kennsington arrived back home. How could he adequately convey what had just happened? Certainly he could tell the story, but the glow on Taylor's face...the sound of her singing the precious words that had flowed miraculously through Sherry...and the vivid picture painted in his mind and heart of Sherry's faithfulness, even to her death...how could he give *that* to Mary Beth?

Joe experienced a dichotomy of grief and gratitude, of sorrow and satisfaction, of love and longing. He was amazed and proud and grateful for the person Sherry had become, and sorry he wouldn't get to tell her until they met again in eternity.

He was full, and yet so empty. He didn't try to sort out the deep emotions that converged on him all at once; he just buried his head in his hands and quietly wept.

Wayne cursed the first time the tailgater tapped his bumper, wondering what his problem was. But when the vehicle accelerated and bumped him a second time, Wayne made an obscene gesture.

The vehicle pulled alongside him, and Wayne noticed it was a red truck with custom designing. When the passenger rolled down the window, there were two guys about his age looking over at him.

"Hey, freak! Pull over. Make my day!" said the man in the passenger seat.

Wayne repeated the obscene gesture, and then sped forward. The red truck accelerated and stayed on his left.

The passenger shouted out the window. "This Bud's for you!" He threw a can of beer at Wayne, hitting him on the side of the face.

Wayne grabbed his pistol and pointed it at the man. "What's your problem?"

"Whoa, take it easy! Can't a fella offer you a beer?"

"Maybe I should blow your head off!" said Wayne, all too aware he couldn't afford the publicity. He stepped on the gas, but soon realized he couldn't see well enough to drive that fast on the curved highway, so he dropped back.

The red truck stayed on his left.

Wayne saw a set of headlights approaching and figured these guys would pull into his lane. They didn't. The headlights were getting dangerously close, and Wayne fell back. The red truck backed off until it was again side by side with his. Wayne glanced over. The two men were laughing. The oncoming headlights were closing in.

Wayne swerved sharply onto the shoulder, lost control, and crashed through a guardrail. The truck rolled over and over down a steep, rocky embankment.

THIRTY-EIGHT

Jordan Ellis was awakened by the sound of his cell phone ringing. He fumbled around in the dark until he finally pushed the right button.

"Yeah…"

"It's Agent Fulmer."

"What's up?"

"The Tennessee Highway Patrol found a John Doe at the bottom of an embankment last night. Had to use the Jaws of Life to free his body from a stolen truck, and—"

"It's four o'clock, Fulmer, get to the point."

"There was a name written inside his boots: *W. Purdy.*"

"Purdy?" Jordan sat up and rubbed his eyes.

"They can't be sure until his DNA comes back. But the prints on the stolen truck match his. Personally, I'd like to throw the first shovelful of dirt over him. I'd have preferred to do it while he was still *alive,* but hey…"

"Watch it, Fulmer, you're starting to sound as cynical as I am. So how'd Purdy end up dead at the bottom of an embankment?"

"A woman called 911 last night, and said she was almost hit head-on when two vehicles approached her, side by side on a two-lane, just outside Nashville. One of the vehicles pulled off the road and went through a guardrail. The other pulled over in the right lane and kept going. The lady was scared to stop. Called 911 on her way out of there."

"Okay, Fulmer. File the report."

Ellen Jones sat at her desk, letting the news soak in. Wayne's unseen presence had been both ominous and terrifying. Was it really over? Her thoughts were interrupted when the phone rang.

"Hello, this is Ellen."

"Did you hear?" exclaimed Guy.

"Agent Barnett just told me. What a relief!"

"Honey, I'm taking you out to breakfast. I'm ready for things to be back to normal… What's wrong? Why so quiet?"

"I'm not sure I remember what normal is like," she said. "Maybe it's impossible for things to be the way they were."

"Don't say that."

"I'm sure things will start to settle down now. But surely it's changed us, Guy. I'd hate to think we can put something this horrible behind us without some reflection."

"I didn't mean to be insensitive, honey. I'm just so relieved."

"I know. I am, too. But I've been holding everything in. I need to get it down on paper. A human interest story seemed inappropriate and invasive while the girls were missing. But now that it's over, people will need to deal with everything that's happened… Who am I kidding? *I* need to deal with it."

"We all do."

Ellen sighed. "Would you mind terribly if I stayed here and put my thoughts together? I'm not sure I'd be very good company."

"Not at all. How about dinner at the Lakeside Inn? I'll make reservations for a nice corner table by the window. Just the two of us."

"That sounds better. Thanks for understanding."

"See you when you're ready to come home. I love you."

"Love you, too."

Ellen walked to the window and leaned her head against the cold glass. Saturday's sky was gray and sorrowful. Charlie's words still bothered her. *Was* she part of the problem? Why hadn't she mustered the courage to call her father? Why couldn't she forgive him?

Her challenge paled in comparison to the one the Kennsingtons faced. She wondered how they would ever get through this.

Joe Kennsington went into the bedroom and shut the door behind him. He didn't want too much time to pass before he talked to Mary Beth about his conversation with Taylor. But every time he brought it up, she found a way to change the subject.

"Mary Beth, I'd like to tell you what happened at the hospital last—"

"What do you think they'll do with Wayne?" she asked.

He sighed. "I don't know. I suppose his mother will make his burial arrangements... Mary Beth, did you hear what I said?"

"About what?"

"About wanting to discuss what Taylor talked to me about."

"I guess not. I can't seem to focus on anything right now."

"All right," he said softly. "We'll talk later."

"I'm glad they found Wayne."

Joe nodded. "I'm relieved he's no longer a threat to anyone, but it's impossible to feel satisfaction when someone unsaved dies. Wayne's eternal fate is much worse than life in prison."

There was a long, unexpected pause.

Mary Beth's eyes filled with tears, and she clutched his arm. "I know I should feel sad that he's lost, but I don't. All I feel is anger that I'll never get to confront my daughter's killer! What's happening to me, Joe? I've never been so cold before. I'm scared. I'm really scared…"

Mary Beth fell into his arms and began to sob.

Marita Logan put the china cup to her lips and took a sip of hot tea. She heard a whistle in the distance, indicating that the ten o'clock train from Parker was running on time. She smiled, grateful for some semblance of normalcy.

"Taylor, are you sure you don't want to try this?" Marita asked. "Juanita made her special blend."

Taylor nodded.

Marita could hardly take her eyes off her daughter. "It's hard to believe you're really home."

"I'm glad that lowlife is out of the way," G. R. said.

"When Jordan called us, I felt as if we'd *all* been set free." Marita warmed her hands with the teacup.

"Taylor, how come you're so quiet?" G. R. said.

She shrugged. "I was just thinking about the last time I saw Wayne… It's hard to explain how I feel."

G. R. sat back in his chair. "Be glad he's dead."

Taylor rested her head on the back of the chair and turned her face toward the fire.

"Is there something you want to talk about, honey?" Marita said.

"A lot's happened, Mom. Some of it's hard to explain."

G. R. raised his eyebrows. "I thought you talked to the doctor from psych."

"Some things are private."

"Like what?"

"Like what Wayne did to Sherry…and Rebecca."

"You can't change what happened to them, so why dwell on it?"

"I'm not *dwelling* on it, Dad. I haven't had a chance to sort through everything yet, that's all."

"What's there to sort through? Wayne Purdy's dead. You can get back to your life now."

Marita jumped up. "Taylor, come sit with me in the sunroom for a while. We can crack the windows. Fresh air and sunshine will do you good."

"Okay, Mom. I'll get my sweater."

"Here, let me help with your crutches," Marita said.

When Taylor left the room, Marita walked over and stood in front of G. R., who was reading the newspaper.

"That girl isn't just going to go back to 'life as usual,' G. R. She's been through a horrible trauma. She's been terrorized. She's seen her best friend strangled to death. And Rebecca Purdy's death was a blow, too."

"What?" he said from behind the newspaper. "Why would Taylor care about *her?*"

Marita stood with her arms folded. "Why do you think?"

"You're both making too much out of that. Purdy's sister was no heroine. The girl didn't want her brother to get caught, that's all. I doubt if she cared one bit about Taylor. And you see how much her brother appreciated it."

"G. R., look at me! You don't know the first thing about what's going on inside your daughter's heart. If you pass this off, you're going to hurt your relationship with Taylor."

"Impossible. The girl adores me. And she knows I'd do *anything* for her."

"Except stop the madness?"

"What are you talking about?"

"Taylor is going to figure out, if she hasn't already, that the revenge against you didn't start for no reason. I'm not excusing Wayne Purdy's despicable actions, but when are you going to stop excusing *yours?* You stepped on a lot of people on your way to the bottom line. We both know that's what caused this."

"You're not laying that on me, Marita. I'm a businessman. I do what I have to do to make a profit. Closing the plant was the right move, I don't care what you or anyone else thinks about that."

"That's my point, G. R.! You don't care! If you *cared,* you might have shown a little sensitivity when you made choices that were difficult and life changing for other people. Why can't you see that? For a man as smart as you are, you seem awfully dense. You almost lost your daughter, and *why?* Because bitterness was planted in a young man's heart. Oh sure, he grew it. He watered it. He let it get out of control. But your attitude threw him the seeds!"

G. R. lowered the newspaper. His face and neck were red.

"It was your indifferent attitude," Marita said, "far more than your decision to close the plant, that caused that family so much grief. I saw it then, and I see it now. Do you have any idea the power you possess to hurt or to heal? You're a powerful man, G. R. God's going to hold you accountable for the way you use that power. All I'm say—"

G. R. stood up. "Don't start preaching to me about God! What does He have to do with anything?"

"Everything, G. R.! He has *everything* to do with *everything!*"

"Well, He's not running my business, *I* am. When I want God's help, I'll ask for it!"

"How can you be so arrogant? We're so blessed to have Taylor back. Has it even occurred to you that maybe God's been trying to get your attention with the kidnapping?"

"Get *my* attention? Good grief, He got the whole world's attention! But I got Taylor back without His help. I told you from day one that I wasn't going to ask Him for anything. Just look at the Kennsingtons! They begged Him all week, and you see how God answered *their* pr—" He stopped talking, and the color drained from his face.

Marita saw that he was looking past her. She turned around in time to see the horrified look on Taylor's face before she turned on her crutches and hobbled away, tears streaming down her face.

∽∾

Velma Purdy arrived home after a taxing day and collapsed on the couch. Plans were in place for Tuesday morning's graveside service at Good Shepherd Memorial Gardens. Burying her children would wipe out everything she had saved and everything she could borrow.

Charlotte brought her a cup of hot chocolate and sat next to her.

"Thanks for going with me," Velma said. "I don't know what I would've done without you."

"What did Pastor Mills from your church have to say? You said he stopped by earlier."

"He's sorry about Rebecca, confused about Wayne. It was awkward."

Charlotte patted her hand. "*I'm* confused about Wayne. But that doesn't change how I feel about you and Rebecca."

There was a long pause.

Velma's voice cracked with emotion. "It's so weird, Charlotte. Wayne's the one person who comforted me through the dark weeks and months after Roger's death. And now he has inflicted an even greater grief."

"Honey, don't do this to yourself. Try to get your mind on something else."

"You're right." Velma set the hot chocolate on the coffee table and picked up Saturday's mail. She sorted through the stack, and took out the envelope on the bottom. Her hands shook as she grabbed the letter opener, tears rolling down her cheeks.

"What is it?" Charlotte asked.

"It's his handwriting!" Velma said. "It's from Wayne!"

Velma quickly slit the envelope and pulled out a sales receipt from a Goodwill Store in Atlanta. She wiped the tears from her eyes and tried to focus on the words scribbled on the back:

Dear Mom,

No matter what anyone tells you, I didn't mean to shoot Beck. I thought I was aiming for Taylor Logan to get even with G. R. for everything he did to us, but she had on Beck's red coat, and I shot the wrong one. I'm sorry I failed. I never meant to hurt you. I'll always love you.

Wayne

Velma began to sob, and then to sob hysterically.

"Velma, what is it?" Charlotte said. "What did it say?"

"Why?" Velma cried. "Didn't I raise them both the same? Didn't I love them both the same? Didn't I teach them the very same values? How did my son's thinking get so twisted? *How?*"

Her tears fell for Wayne. Her daughter was in heaven, but her son...where would he spend eternity? The answer was almost more than she could bear.

THIRTY-NINE

Taylor Logan stood at her bedroom window, letting the light soak into every fiber of her being. Never again would she take for granted things that had always been hers. Having experienced the deprivation of light and fresh air, of comfort and cleanliness, of communication, freedom, and dignity, she would never forget to be grateful for them. She heard a gentle knock at the door.

"Miss Taylor, I bring lunch," Juanita said.

"Thanks. I'm really hungry."

Juanita set the tray on top of the dresser. When she turned around, her eyes brimmed with tears. "I so happy Taylor come home. You happy, yes?"

Taylor got up and hugged her. "Yes!"

"You come out today? Eat downstairs?"

Taylor sat on the side of the bed. "It's quiet up here. I need space to think."

"Maybe you come out soon? Meester Logan look sad."

"We'll see."

Juanita turned and left the room.

Taylor lay down on the bed, her hands behind her head. She wasn't blind to her father's gruff nature, but until yesterday she had never been wounded by it. How could she ever tell him about the songs and the light? Or that she had given her heart to God?

Taylor got up and sat in the window seat, marveling at how ice had transformed the trees into giant crystal figurines. She beheld the dazzling view of the Logan estate, stretching as far as her eyes could see, and wondered what heaven was like, and what Sherry was seeing at that very moment.

Taylor was relieved the icy streets would prevent them from going to the funeral home tonight. She wasn't ready to leave the solitude of her room.

She rose and leaned her crutches against the wall, and then sat down at the vanity table. She combed her fingers through her short hair and wrinkled her nose. Her face looked thin and pale. But the blue eyes staring back at her had a sparkle that hadn't been there before. She looked at the cross ring and smiled. *I hope Sherry knows.*

Joe Kennsington had arranged for a private family viewing of Sherry's body, after which the casket was closed. The Kennsingtons held hands and prayed until their emotions were in check, and then Erica took Jason outside for some fresh air.

"The kids handled seeing her better than I thought they would," Joe said. He sat down beside Mary Beth and wiped the tears from her face.

Mary Beth glanced up at the casket, and then down at the floor. She seemed to be miles away. "I know Sherry isn't in there, but the *body* I loved is. I remember kissing those fingers and that button nose. I can still feel the softness of her hair and the way she felt in my arms. I can smell her hair, see her smile, hear her laugh. But I can never touch her again." Mary Beth took a Kleenex and wiped her eyes. "I know her spirit's with the Lord, but that doesn't help the *missing...*"

Joe put his arm around her, her pain his own. The sound of Erica clearing her throat caused him to look up.

"Dad, what time did you say people were coming?"

Joe glanced at his watch. "Visitation started ten minutes ago."

Jason went over and picked up Sherry's picture. "Nobody's coming in this weather."

An outside door opened, and the sound of footsteps echoed in the hallway.

"Looks like the Joneses made it." Joe squeezed Mary Beth's hand, and then got up to greet them.

Jed, Rhonda, and Jennifer Wilson were behind Ellen and Guy, and a steady stream of others filed in over the next half hour until people stood elbow-to-elbow.

Joe was glad to put his tears on hold and draw comfort from others who shared his sorrow. He glanced across the room at Mary Beth, pleased to see her surrounded by comforters.

Joe spotted Rusty Rawlings standing alone at the casket. Rusty pressed his lips to a corsage of red roses and laid it in front of Sherry's picture. Joe was jolted by the sudden impact of past and present, and everything else was a blur until he felt Mary Beth's hand in his.

None of the comforters said much. But there was a lot of hugging and holding. And at 9:00, those gathered prayed together before leaving to brave the ice.

When they were safely back home, Mary Beth sat with Erica and Jason in front of a crackling fire, while Joe told them what Taylor had said to him.

Mary Beth listened to every detail, and the words Rhonda had brought back to her echoed in her head: *Though answers He may not impart, forever I can trust His heart.* How could she not have trusted

God? Even though her faith had failed, His faithfulness had not.

When Joe was finished, she stood up.

"I've been selfish and so angry..." Mary Beth choked on the words. "All I kept thinking about was my pain and my loss, and how Wayne stole Sherry from *me*. But God had a plan for her life, and He accomplished it in spite of everything. We're going to hurt for a long time because we miss her, but we can be so very proud of the person she was..." Her voice cracked. "And grateful for the time God allowed her to be ours."

FORTY

warming trend hung a brilliant sun in Monday's bluebird sky, and by noon, most of the ice had melted.

Cornerstone Bible Church opened its doors early, and a somber crowd started to gather inside the historic stone building for Sherry Kennsington's funeral service.

The sanctuary had been lavished with flowers, wreaths, and plants. A blooming tree with a white ribbon around its trunk signifying Sherry's eternal homecoming sat next to the pulpit.

Behind the pulpit, a cross-shaped stained glass window rose to the ceiling, its colorful inlays depicting the life of Jesus from His birth to His resurrection.

The media presence was evident but not intrusive, and crews operated as much as possible from the back choir loft. Only KJNX had been invited to do a live broadcast.

The church parking lot filled up early, and some had to park blocks away and walk through a flood of reporters and cameras to get to the churchyard. But local police, assisted by the county sheriff's department, allowed no unauthorized media past the wrought-iron

fence and giant oak trees that framed the grounds around Cornerstone Bible Church.

Mary Beth Kennsington looked out the tinted windows of the
white limousine.

Joe squeezed her hand. "You all right?"

"Better."

"I noticed you weren't in bed a good part of the night. Couldn't
you sleep?"

"Not really. I needed to pray. I can't believe how awful I've
been."

"Honey, you've been through your worst nightmare."

"That's no excuse, Joe. I know better than to hold on to anger. I
wish I'd gone with you to the hospital... The Lord provided an
amazing opportunity, and I missed the blessing because I was too
busy being mad." Her lower lip quivered.

Joe tilted her chin toward him. "What's done is done, Mary
Beth. There's a lot you can do from this point on."

"I've asked the Lord's forgiveness, and I'm doing my best to forgive G. R.," she said. "Not that he has a clue I was mad. I don't feel
like greeting him with open arms yet, but at least the animosity's
gone."

"Good. The healing will come."

The driver turned into the church parking lot and pulled up to
the side entrance behind two other limousines.

"Grandma and Grandpa are here," Jason said from the back
seat. "Their limo beat ours."

"And there's Taylor and her parents," Erica said.

"Wow, she looks different." Jason moved his face closer to the
glass.

Erica jabbed him with her elbow. "Her hair'll grow back. Stop
staring."

"Okay," Joe said. "Are we ready?" He took Mary Beth's hand and pressed it to his lips. "Sherry's in the presence of God. This is her day. We *can* celebrate that."

The congregation rose. Velma Purdy started to cry when the pall-bearers carried Sherry's casket down the center aisle.

Charlotte put the TV on mute. "Are you sure you want to watch this?"

"I can't just ignore what's happening," Velma said. "It's because of my son the Kennsingtons are burying their daughter."

"Yes, but it's because of your daughter the Logans *aren't* burying theirs."

"I want to watch," Velma said.

Charlotte turned the sound back on.

When the clock tower on the town square struck 1:00, a male soloist rose and began to sing "It Is Well."

Velma sat somberly, listening to the words and observing the outpouring of sympathy for the Kennsingtons. Who would even care when she buried Wayne and Rebecca?

Taylor sat between her parents in the front row of the church, sensing the stares of those who must wonder what it felt like to be her. She glanced up at Sherry's casket and blinked away the image that ran through her mind.

The soloist finished singing, and a somber hush lasted for several uncomfortable seconds. Then Pastor Thomas lifted his eyes and began to speak.

"Joe...Mary Beth...Erica...Jason...Taylor...families and dear friends... Is there anyone who doesn't feel the grief of this tragedy? We have all been impacted by something so evil that we are compelled to seek comfort, encouragement, and answers.

"I've struggled with this. Sleeplessness has plagued me since I learned of Sherry's death. This kind of tragedy happens to someone else, to some other family, in some other community…but this time, it happened here. I cannot think of a less likely place for such a heinous crime, and yet we are gathered here to mourn its victim.

"Sherry was a lovely, spirited, thought-provoking teenager, who lived her life with zeal and a heart for Jesus Christ. As to why she fell prey to the malicious act of one confused young man, I have no answer. But I know that in Christ she is more than conqueror and that death has no sting…"

He paused to gather his composure. "I received a phone call yesterday afternoon from Taylor Logan, the other young lady who was kidnapped. She felt compelled to speak today."

Taylor didn't hear any more of what Pastor Thomas said. She dabbed the perspiration from her lip and rose to her feet, her heart pounding. She looked into the eyes of her parents and gave a slight nod, then hobbled toward the pulpit on crutches, trusting that what was in her heart would find its way to her mouth.

She felt the eyes of every person in the church with every labored step she took. When she reached the pulpit, Pastor Thomas lowered the microphone and moved aside.

Taylor took a piece of paper out of her pocket, unfolded it, her hands shaking, and laid it on the podium. She looked out over the congregation.

"My best friend, Sherry Kennsington, should not only be remembered but also honored, because the way she died has changed the way I'm going to live. There's something I haven't been able to say until now. By sharing it with you, maybe my pain and the pain of this community can start to heal.

"I *hated* Wayne Purdy. From the moment I realized he was going to kill us, I was filled with dread and just gave up. Sherry didn't. I think she knew if she gave in to the hate, the strength she needed wouldn't be there. She told him, 'I'll only be a victim if I hate you. And I'm not gonna hate you.' Even when he terrorized us, turned off the heat, and stopped bringing us food, Sherry refused to hate him.

"Do you know how hard that was? For me, it was impossible. But Sherry had something I didn't that gave her strength to do something I couldn't. God was her Rock, and it was so obvious that's where her strength was coming from. It was amazing to watch. Wayne could control her circumstances, but he couldn't control her choices..." Taylor's voiced failed.

"On that last night, Wayne was angrier than I'd ever seen him, and he began taking it out on me. I thought he was going to kill me. Sherry stood up for me and said that just because he was bigger didn't make him more powerful—that he was like Goliath, all mouth, lording his size and power over us, but God was stronger.

"Wayne laughed and told Sherry he was more powerful. 'And there's nothing you can do about it!' he said. 'You hate me! *Admit* it!' But she wouldn't. Sherry told him she wouldn't let herself hate, that hate is what had ruined *his* life.

"Wayne said he had a right to hate, that...G. R. Logan had ruined his life and he wanted revenge for what G. R. had stolen from him."

Taylor heard murmuring and avoided eye contact with her dad.

"Sherry said, 'But what is it he stole? He may have hurt you, but nursing a grudge was *your* choice. You could've forgiven, but you didn't want to. *That's* what ruined your life.'

"Wayne lost it. He didn't want to hear the truth, so he tried to silence it by strangling her." Taylor paused, her lip quivering. "But even while it was happening, Sherry never wavered in her conviction, and peace was all over her face." Taylor looked into the eyes of Joe and Mary Beth Kennsington. "I *saw* it. Wayne's anger was powerless against her."

Taylor's throat tightened. She swallowed the emotion.

"I'm ashamed to admit I was mad at her. I couldn't figure out why Sherry didn't say whatever Wayne wanted so he wouldn't hurt us. It took me until yesterday to figure it out: The real enemy wasn't Wayne; it was hate. Sherry wasn't the victim; she was the conqueror! The real enemy couldn't touch her because she refused to let it in.

"I want everyone who's listening to understand: If you're living with bitterness, a giant is growing inside you. If you don't slay it, it can get big enough to kill your joy, your purpose, your hopes, your dreams…and maybe even someone you love.

"Which brings me to Rebecca Purdy. Wayne's sister stood up for what was right, too, and she lost her life saving mine. She deserves to be recognized for what she did.

"Tomorrow morning, when Rebecca is laid to rest next to her brother, I'm going to be there out of gratitude for her and as a support to her mother. With God's help and Sherry's example, I won't let my feelings for Wayne become a stumbling block in my life, either.

"It still hurts… It's going to take some time to work through the bad feelings. I chose to forgive, but that doesn't mean that what happened didn't matter or that the pain is gone yet. But it does mean I'm going to get past it. You can, too. Maybe if more of us refuse to get bitter, this world will be a better place.

"Sherry, I'll never forget your faith, your courage, or your example. And because, in the darkest of circumstances, I saw the Jesus you love shining through you, I've invited Him into my heart. Because of Him, you had the power to do what I couldn't. And because of you, I want to be more like Him. I can't think of a greater thing to be remembered for."

When she finished speaking, Taylor began to cry. She was aware of Pastor Thomas's arms around her and the congregation's clapping. But high above all the accolades, she thought she heard Sherry singing "Blessed Assurance."

❦

On a rolling hillside in Oak Hills Cemetery, in the midst of a protective fortress of giant hardwood trees, Taylor stood silent as the spirit of Sherrill Elizabeth Kennsington was ceremonially given back to the God who had breathed life into her sixteen years ago.

There was no doubt in Taylor's mind that Sherry was in the presence of God. As Pastor Thomas prayed, she fought to erase the awful images of Sherry's death by picturing her walking down streets of gold with the angels applauding her arrival.

Taylor felt the corners of her mouth turn up slightly. The angels had applauded for *her*, too.

FORTY-ONE

Jennifer Wilson sat at the kitchen table rereading Taylor's words in Tuesday morning's newspaper: "Sherry had something I didn't that gave her strength to do something I couldn't…"

"Jen, you're up early." Jed poured himself a cup of coffee. "Are you feeling all right?"

"I can't stop thinking about Taylor and Sherry and what happened to them. Taylor's words at the funeral blew me away. This should be tragic. I mean, it *is*, but isn't."

Jed sat down at the table beside her. "It helped that God allowed the Kennsingtons to know how He used it for good. For someone losing a child, it'd take a whole lot of faith to believe God had a plan."

Jennifer turned away, her chin quivering.

"Jen, something's been bothering you. You need to get it—"

"You never wanted *me,* did you, Dad?"

Her father's face was flooded with red. There was a long pause.

"Not at eighteen, honey. Not with your mother being pregnant out of wedlock. That was the ultimate disgrace in those days.

People weren't very forgiving. I went through the motions of taking responsibility and marrying your mother, but I felt guilty and angry and couldn't seem to get past it. It got worse over time until I felt trapped in it."

"I always knew something was wrong," she said. "All these years, I thought it was *my* fault."

"I'm sorry, Jen. I was a lousy father. A lousy husband, too. I spent all our married life nursing a grudge. Made all of you miserable. I didn't get over it until I *chose* to get over it."

"When you became a Christian?" Jennifer asked.

"Actually, it had more to do with *why* I became a Christian. The bitterness between your mom and me had gotten to the point where it controlled my life. I guess Taylor would say it was my Goliath. I didn't want to fight it anymore, so I gave my life to Christ. I figured He'd help me."

"Did He?"

"He sure did. But I also had a ton of baggage to sort through. Joe and Mary Beth helped me realize something that changed the way I look at things. Even though *I* made a mistake, *you* were never a mistake. God knew you were coming, and He already had a plan for your life. I wish I'd understood and been able to forgive myself years ago instead of taking it out on all of you. Anyway, all that's history now. It's never too late to do what's right. God had a plan all along."

Jennifer looked into his eyes, her hands on her tummy. "So you really believe *this* child is no accident and that God has a plan? Even though Dennis and I aren't getting married, and my baby isn't coming into the world the way it should?"

"Jen, God isn't caught off guard by anything, and His plan can't be messed up. Just look at what He did with Sherry and Taylor. It may not be the happily-ever-after we all hoped and prayed for, but what they did will reach more people than we could've imagined. Even when we don't see His plan, it's there. I think someday all believers will see the big picture when we're together in heaven."

Jennifer sighed. "I still haven't decided whether or not to raise this child as a single parent. It's overwhelming."

"I know, honey. But your mother and I and many others are praying that you'll reach a decision and come to peace with it. But no matter which choice you make, God still has a plan."

"I'm not sure I want to love anyone that much. It's kind of scary. I saw yesterday what losing a child does to people."

"Yes, but did you see what loving a child does to people? I'm sure the Kennsingtons wouldn't erase one day they had with Sherry… You know, Jen, I'd give anything to go back to when you were born, and recapture what I lost out on—"

"Good morning, you two," Rhonda said. She poured herself a cup of coffee. "I've made a decision."

"What's that?" Jed asked.

"I'm going to Ellison with the Kennsingtons. I talked to Mary Beth last night before I came to bed. They've decided to go to the graveside service for Rebecca and Wayne. Isn't that something?"

"Are you serious?" Jennifer said. "Do you think they're doing it just because Taylor is?"

"No, it's much more personal than that, especially for Mary Beth. Anyway, I've had some pretty hateful feelings toward Wayne for everything he's put them through. I need to let go of a few things myself."

Jed looked up at the clock. "It's only 6:45. If I call in, Al will let me take another day off. How about if I go with you?"

"Jed, that's so sweet. But you don't have to go. I'll be all right."

"Truthfully, babe, I'm hung up on my feelings about Wayne, too. He's on the bottom of my list of people to care about. My attitude needs to change."

"Plus, I keep thinking how Velma must feel," Rhonda said. "After all she's been through, can you even imagine what it would be like having to bury her children alone?"

"Do you mind if I tag along?" Jennifer asked. "I'm not sure I understand. But if you and the Kennsingtons are brave enough to support Mrs. Purdy, maybe I should be there to support *you*."

Jed smiled and winked at Rhonda. "I'll make that call."

Taylor stood in front of the full-length mirror, straightened her collar, and brushed off a few of Oliver's white hairs that had found their way onto her black dress. She felt a twinge of anger and dismissed the temptation to renege on her promise to attend today's graveside service.

"Taylor, you about ready?" Her mother's voice rose from the bottom of the staircase.

"I'll be just a minute."

Taylor closed her eyes and whispered a prayer, then hobbled out to the hallway and slowly worked her way down the staircase on her crutches. She felt sure this was the right thing to do. Why were the butterflies in her stomach fluttering in disagreement?

"Come on, honey," Marita said. "We need to allow plenty of time. It's going to be hard for you to get across the grass with those crutches. Are you sure you want to do this?"

"I need to do this. I want to show my gratitude for what Rebecca did. I wouldn't be alive if it weren't for her."

"And Sherry *would* be alive if it weren't for her brother," Marita said.

"I know that, but I've let it go, remember? Did you hear anything on the morning news about the graveside service?"

"Only a mention. I'm not looking for a great deal of sympathy for the Purdys."

"Well, are you ladies ready?" G. R. stood in the foyer, dressed in a dark suit and tie, the keys to the family Mercedes dangling from his index finger.

"*Dad?*"

"If you can do this after all you've been through, so can I. Besides, you and your mother are going to need help."

He held out one hand for Marita and laid the other on Taylor's shoulder. "Let's go, before I talk myself out of it."

At 9:45, the Logans' white Mercedes turned into the east drive of Good Shepherd Memorial Gardens.

"We'll probably stand out like a sore thumb," Marita said. "I can't imagine many people will be here. The media ought to have a real heyday. Are you both bracing yourselves for this?"

"Mom, it'll be fine. Think about Mrs. Purdy. This must be horrible for her. She'll probably be grateful for anyone who shows up."

"Shocked is more like it," G. R. said. "I have a feeling I'm the last person she's expecting to see."

"There must be another burial this morning," Marita said. "Look at all the cars."

"There...that must be it at the top of the hill," Taylor said. "I see two caskets. And there's a lady standing by herself. Is that Mrs. Purdy?"

Marita turned and looked. "Yes, that's her. But I'm not going up there until right before the service starts. What am I going to say to her?"

"Mom, relax. Just our being here says a lot."

"Easy for you to say." G. R.'s eyes met Taylor's in the rearview mirror. "You're not the enemy."

"Dad, the only enemy is hate, remember?"

During the next ten minutes, a handful of adults, a small group of teenagers, and a pastor joined Velma.

G. R. looked at his watch. "Okay, let's go."

He got out of the car and walked around to the passenger side. He helped Taylor out of the backseat, then turned to Marita and offered his arm, and the three began walking up the hill, Taylor hobbling on crutches. An entourage of cameramen and reporters pursued them.

As they neared the gravesite, Taylor spotted two simple caskets, each draped with greenery and a single white lily.

Velma Purdy looked up, then lowered her eyes, dreading the awkward apology she felt compelled to summon. She hadn't expected to see G. R. and Marita! What could she possibly say? The sound of voices interrupted her panic, and she looked up again.

Who were all these people making their way up the hill? Scores of people…faces from the past…others she didn't recognize…all moving toward her? Velma's eyes darted from person to person until she spotted the Kennsingtons. She turned away, overcome with emotion. Pastor Mills squeezed her hand.

FORTY-TWO

B y Sunday, life in Baxter had quieted down. The intrusive media had finally departed, allowing this close-knit community the space to deal with its grief.

Joe Kennsington sat with his elbows on the kitchen table, his chin resting on his hands. He lingered over the words of the editorial Ellen had written in today's newspaper. Could anyone have predicted such a positive outcome to Sherry's kidnapping and murder?

His eyes moved quickly down the page, and then rested on the last few paragraphs. He savored them another time.

It will be a while before the unwanted feelings are completely purged from our midst, but the choices made on that hillside in Ellison will undoubtedly reap a harvest of forgiveness in due season.

I cannot imagine anyone not being inspired by the courage of these young girls who relied on the God of their faith to light the way. Though I possess no such faith, I will never again deny its power, or the unseen Sovereign from which it radiates. If, indeed, there is a God calling us out of darkness, I want to hear His voice.

It seems fitting to end with the words Pastor Bart Thomas prayed at Sherry's graveside. These have become my hope.

"Father of lights, God of all comfort, use the example set by this faithful child so that those who remain in darkness will be brought into relationship with You and carry the torch passed to Taylor Logan from Sherry Kennsington from Your beloved Son, who gave His life that all who believe might have this light to overcome the darkness.

"For once that holy fire is lit within them, Your eternal flame will burn forever, and bitterness can be thrown into an infinite furnace of forgiveness. For You, O God, are a consuming fire."

Joe shook his head and blinked the moisture from his eyes. *Ellen Jones, avowed agnostic, wrote this?*

He got up and stood at the window, his head leaning against the glass, his eyes waiting for the sunrise. The horizon's pale blue canvas had been streaked in orangy-pink and purple, a glowing golden rim separating earth and sky. The first ray of morning broke through, and then another, and another, until a handful of white rays fanned out across the expanse of eastern sky.

Somewhere beyond it, Sherry was smiling. He just knew it.

The publisher and author would love to hear your comments about this book. *Please contact us at:* www.multnomah.net/baxterseries

Dear Reader,

Few of us will ever encounter someone like Wayne Purdy; but I hope you will never forget him. He is the embodiment of unresolved anger at its most destructive. Every day on the news, we see examples of angry, bitter people lashing out, taking others down with them when the giant gets too big to handle.

Most of us don't resort to violence. So what happens to our unresolved anger? Many times it results in depression, illness, or anxiety—at the very least, a bitter attitude. It zaps our energy, steals our joy, and distorts our perspective. Even worse, it puts a wedge between God and us, and between us and everyone else.

Mary Beth took us to the honest depths of a believer's anger at God. Most would agree that she had just cause to be angry. But anger acts as both symptom and catalyst. As long as Mary Beth refused to let her anger serve as a catalyst to spiritual growth, she was a victim of her own rage.

My hope is that we recognize how insidiously the enemy of our souls uses anger to destroy us. Make no mistake about it: Unresolved anger is a killer. How much we allow it to destroy depends entirely on how we choose to deal with it.

True forgiveness is not found in our carnal nature, and involves both a trade and a transformation: By surrendering our anger to God, we give Him room to fill our hearts with forgiveness. Often it's a process that takes time. But He's the only One who can cause us to forgive the undeserving. After all, He's had all of us to practice on!

I'd love to hear your comments about this book. Write me at www.multnomah.net/baxterseries.

I invite you to come back to The Baxter Series in book three, *Vital Signs,* where you'll meet up with many of the same characters. It promises to be another nail-biter—might want to hold off on the manicure!

In His love,

Kathy Herman

Dead Men Tell No Tales. *Or Do They?*

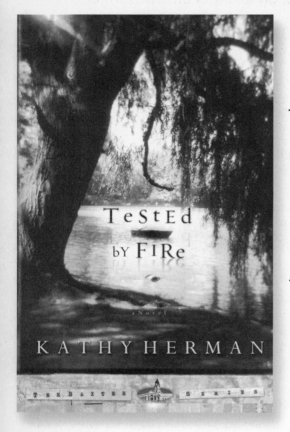

"A suspenseful story of touching characters that is richly seasoned with God's love."

—Bill Myers,
author of *Eli* and the
Fire of Heaven trilogy

When a bizarre houseboat explosion rocks the close-knit community of Baxter, firefighters and friends stand by powerless as the blazing hull of their neighbor's home sinks to the bottom of Heron Lake. Have all five McConnells perished in the flames? No one wants the truth more than Jed Wilson, Mike McConnell's best friend. When rescuers recover the remains of all but one family member, suspicion spreads like wildfire. Was it an accident—or murder? Jed finds himself in a race with the FBI to track down the only suspect, and is thrust into a dynamic, life-changing encounter with his own past. Baxter's mystery and Jed's dilemma are ones only God can solve in this suspenseful, surprising story of redemption amidst despair in small-town America.

ISBN 1-57673-956-2

Nothing happens by chance...

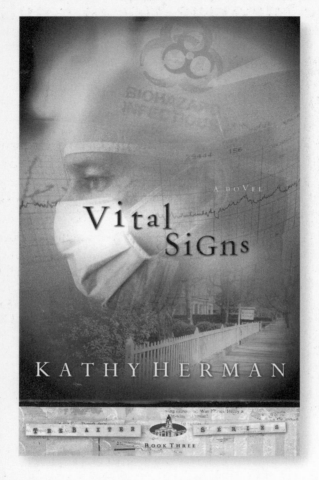

Furious that his girlfriend chose to bring twin babies to term, Dennis walks out of Jennifer's life. And now the Centers for Disease Control have quarantined Jennifer, along with 200 others who attended the reception for a missionary couple bearing a deadly virus. Is Jennifer at risk? Does Dennis even care what will happen to the twins, separated from their mother at birth? Fear takes hold in the town as violence erupts, and Baxter experiences an outbreak deadlier than any virus. Still, woven through the tale of violence and victims is another story: one of divine love and purpose.

ISBN 1-59052-040-8

On the Surviving Side of Gunfire

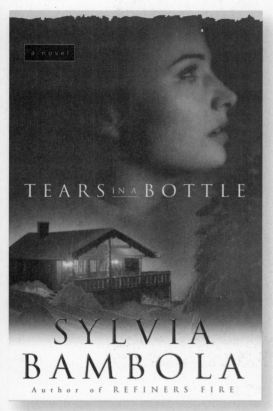

"*Tears in a Bottle* is a gripping story of betrayal, hurt, and triumph that accurately portrays the real truth behind the political correctness of 'a woman's right to choose.'"

—**Vicki Thorn**,
executive director, National
Office of Post-Abortion
Reconciliation and Healing

Becky Taylor, a young woman burdened by great expectations, is lying on a cold recovery table in an abortion clinic when she hears a man's voice, then gunshots. She holds her breath and lies perfectly still behind the curtain. When the gunman is finished, Becky is the only one left alive in the clinic. This act brings together two strangers who both seek answers to one of life's most wrenching questions: Are God's love and mercy big enough for every sin? The answer transforms multiple lives.

ISBN 1-57673-802-7

"Henderson is an expert in romance."

— The Belles and Beaux of Romance

"Dee Henderson is an extraordinary author whose writing connects with your heart and soul."

— The Belles and Beaux of Romance

Book #3 in the bestselling O'Malley Series

Women are turning up dead. And Lisa O'Malley digging into a crime means trouble is soon to follow. She's a forensic pathologist and mysteries are her domain. Book three in the O'Malley series brings back Lisa O'Malley and U.S. Marshal Quinn Diamond from *The Guardian* in a tense investigative thriller. She's not a believer, and her journey toward faith is a fascinating look at how a forensic pathologist views the Resurrection. Quinn has found loving her is easier than keeping her safe. Lisa O'Malley's found the killer, and now she's missing too...**ISBN 1-57673-753-5**

Mystery, Suspense, and Domestic Violence in a Tiny Coastal Town

Linda Hall's thrilling fiction, which confronts the toll domestic violence takes within American homes and explores how the church might address it, melds contemporary characters with a powerful story's punch. *Sadie's Song* opens with the disappearance of nine-year-old Ally Buckley, which bears too much resemblance to recent and chilling events. As fear spreads throughout the New England fishing village of Coffins Reach and the local church that Sadie and her family attend, she discovers odd evidence that danger may be closer to home than she'd ever known.

ISBN 1-57673-659-8

Let's Talk fiction

www.letstalkfiction.com

Let's Talk Fiction is a free, four-color mini-magazine created to give readers a "behind the scenes" look at Multnomah Publishers' favorite fiction authors. *Let's Talk Fiction* allows our authors to share a bit about themselves, giving readers an inside peek into their latest releases. Published in the fall, spring, and summer seasons, *Let's Talk Fiction* is filled with interactive contests, author contact information, and fun! To receive your free copy, get on-line at www.letstalkfiction.com. We'd love to hear from you!

Multnomah® Publishers   *Keeping Your Trust...One Book at a Time*®